"We shouldn't be seen together any more than necessary," Natalie said.

"Why not? We've shared a breathing apparatus, a fishing boat and a taxi."

"Still. If there's a chance of me being taken rather than one of the other girls, I'd rather it was me."

Duff touched her cheek. "Again, they might not take you. Since we returned to the cave and those thugs fired at us, I'd say there is a strong possibility they'd shoot you rather than take you as a hostage."

"How else am I supposed to find where they hid my sister? I can almost bet they won't tell us if we ask."

"Then we have to find a way to follow them to where they are hiding your sister and the other girls."

"The longer she's missing—"

"We'll find her." Duff tipped her chin upward and lowered his lips to hers. "I promise."

NAVY SEAL SURVIVAL

—

New York Times Bestselling Author

ELLE JAMES

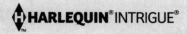

This book is dedicated to all those men and women who serve in the armed forces protecting our country and our way of life. Thank you for your dedication and service.

ISBN-13: 978-0-373-69890-5

Navy SEAL Survival

Copyright © 2016 by Mary Jernigan

The publisher acknowledges the copyright holder of the additional work:

What Happens on the Ranch
Copyright © 2016 by Delores Fossen

Recycling programs for this product may not exist in your area.

This edition published by arrangement with Harlequin Books S.A.

For questions and comments about the quality of this book, please contact us at CustomerService@Harlequin.com.

® and TM are trademarks of Harlequin Enterprises Limited or its corporate affiliates. Trademarks indicated with ® are registered in the United States Patent and Trademark Office, the Canadian Intellectual Property Office and in other countries.

Printed in U.S.A.

HARLEQUIN®
www.Harlequin.com

CONTENTS

Elle James, a *New York Times* bestselling author, started writing when her sister challenged her to write a romance novel. She has managed a full-time job and raised three wonderful children, and she and her husband even tried ranching exotic birds (ostriches, emus and rheas). Ask her, and she'll tell you what it's like to go toe-to-toe with an angry 350-pound bird! Elle loves to hear from fans at ellejames@earthlink.net or ellejames.com.

Books by Elle James

Harlequin Intrigue

SEAL of My Own

Navy SEAL Survival

Covert Cowboys, Inc.

Triggered
Taking Aim
Bodyguard Under Fire
Cowboy Resurrected
Navy SEAL Justice
Navy SEAL Newlywed
High Country Hideout
Clandestine Christmas

Thunder Horse

Hostage to Thunder Horse
Thunder Horse Heritage
Thunder Horse Redemption
Christmas at Thunder Horse Ranch

Visit the Author Profile page at Harlequin.com for more titles.

NAVY SEAL SURVIVAL

ELLE JAMES

CAST OF CHARACTERS

Dutton "Duff" Calloway—Highly trained, skilled demolitions expert and navy SEAL from SEAL Boat Team 22 on vacation in Cancun. Comes from a large family in Port Aransas, Texas.

Natalie Layne—Former Stealth Operations Specialist with special sniper skills who gave up her secret agent life to be with her sister when their parents were killed in a car wreck.

Sawyer Houston—Highly trained, skilled gunner and navy SEAL from SEAL Boat Team 22 on vacation in Cancun.

Benjamin "Montana" Raines—Expert sniper and navy SEAL from SEAL Boat Team 22 on vacation in Cancun.

Quentin Lovett—Highly trained, expertly skilled weapons specialist and navy SEAL from SEAL Boat Team 22 on vacation in Cancun. Considered the charmer of the team. Never without a female companion.

Royce Fontaine—Head of the Stealth Operations Specialists, a secret government organization that comes to the rescue when no one else can get the job done.

Lance Johnson—Stealth Operations Specialists agent with highly evolved computer and technical skills useful in field operations.

Melody Layne—Natalie Layne's sister, a college student on vacation in Cancun with her friends. Natalie's only living relative.

Rolf Schwimmer—Handsome man who befriends Natalie and Melody's college friends.

Frank "Sly" Jones—Former army Special Forces soldier, now a handyman in Alexandria, Virginia.

Cassandra Tierney—Real estate agent from Washington, DC, on vacation in Cancun alone.

Chapter One

"This is the life." Dutton "Duff" Calloway stretched out on the lounge chair beside the pool and closed his eyes.

Sawyer handed Duff a chilled and fruity Pain Killer drink before easing into the chair beside him. "I'm surprised all four of us were granted leave at the same time." He pulled the colorful miniature umbrella out of a chunk of pineapple and dropped it on the end table between them.

Duff downed a third of the drink. Normally he preferred an ice-cold beer. But the combination of orange juice, pineapple and whatever else went into the icy concoction was refreshing and helped add to the sense of relaxation he'd hoped to find in Cancun, Mexico. "I didn't look that gift horse in the mouth. I took the leave and ran."

"Flew," Sawyer corrected. "Yeah, I wasn't questioning our luck, either."

Duff shaded his eyes and stared past the palm trees to the beach beyond. "Where do you suppose Quentin and Montana got off to?"

"They said something about reserving a diving excursion for tomorrow. I told them to sign us up while they were at it."

Duff closed his eyes and soaked in the warm rays of sunshine. "Sounds good. After our last mission to clean up that terrorist training camp in Honduras, I'm satisfied to just be a bum and let the hotel staff and excursion coordinators do all the work."

Sawyer crossed his hands behind his head and leaned back, grinning. "Yeah. This is the life."

Duff's grin matched Sawyer's. "No boss, no guns, no terrorists. Just me, my friends and this..." He lifted the Pain Killer. "Now all we need is a good beer."

"And women," Sawyer added.

Silently, Duff agreed. How many months had it been since he'd been with one? He sighed. Too many to count.

A giggle sounded at the opposite end of the pool and the tittering of female voices drifted through the balmy air.

Sawyer leaned his head up. "Speak of the devils."

Life couldn't get more perfect. Duff swallowed more of the fruity drink.

The gaggle of young ladies appeared to be college-aged, all wearing bikinis and makeup, and carrying beach bags filled with towels and sunscreen.

Duff sighed. "Too young."

"Hey. We're not old men, yet." Sawyer sat up and studied the women as they strolled past their lounge chairs, headed for the beach. "Oh, wait. You are an old man at the ripe old age of thirty."

"That's right. And twenty-year-old, vapor-headed women don't do it for me. I like mine more mature."

"Here you go." Sawyer chuckled. "Mature women, three o'clock."

Two women who couldn't be a day under fifty strolled by.

Duff nodded. "I bet they know a lot more about passion than the girls headed for the beach."

"What about her?" Sawyer tipped his head toward the woman who'd just stepped out of the resort building. She wore a one-piece black swimsuit, the front cut in a sharp V down past her navel, her blond hair loose around her shoulders. Pausing for a moment at the door, she slipped sunglasses onto her nose. Then she strode across the concrete, her bare feet tipped in bright red polish.

His pulse quickening, Duff couldn't take his gaze off her. Now, this was a woman. She couldn't be much older than the college girls, but she carried herself like a model, placing one foot in front of the other, emphasizing the sway of well-rounded hips. As she passed in front of Duff and Sawyer, Duff's jaw dropped.

A low whistle from the lounge at his side said it all.

The woman's one-piece dipped low in the back and wasn't much more than a G-string, exposing a lush bottom with tight glutes.

Another chuckle sounded beside him. "I'll take that as a yes. And if you don't go after that one, I will," Sawyer said.

"Who said anything about going after her?"

"Not interested?" Sawyer swung his legs over the side of the lounge and stood. "You might want to lie in the sun all day, drinking Pain Killers..." He raised his hands. "And there's nothing wrong with that. But I want to feel a woman beneath me, calling out my name in the night. And I believe she's the one." Sawyer touched two fingers to his temple in mock salute. "See ya later."

"Good luck." Duff leaned back and closed his eyes. Yes, she was gorgeous and made his blood hum through his veins. He wouldn't mind seducing her into his bed. If he wasn't so darned tired, he'd follow her out to the beach with Sawyer and give the poor boy a little competition.

A yawn crept over him and he set his cool drink on the table beside him. *Later.*

Besides, he was on vacation and had no intention of working too hard. Women tended to be high-maintenance and time-intensive. After he got a satisfying nap, he might consider striking up a conversation with the sexy blonde. Until then...

He yawned and stretched. The sun warmed his skin and soothed his soul. Duff fully appreciated this nice place free of gunfire and explosions.

Yeah, this was the life.

As soon as he settled his body against the lounge chair, something bounced off his head.

Duff jackknifed to a sitting position and faced a small child, her big brown eyes round and frightened. "I'm sorry, mister." Her gaze darted to the beach ball rolling beneath his chair.

Duff reached down and extracted the ball, handing it to the child.

"Thank you." She smiled and ran back to the pool where what appeared to be her sister and two brothers stood near the edge, all under the age of ten.

"Last one in is a rotten egg," the tallest brother called out. The girls squealed and all four children launched themselves into the water, splashing Duff.

They came up talking and squealing.

So much for peace and quiet. Duff couldn't blame the kids. They were having a great time. He would have done the same.

Instead of grousing over a missed nap, he rose and followed Sawyer out to the beach. If he had to be awake, he might as well enjoy the scenery on the beach. Sawyer was sure to strike out with the blonde, and Duff would ask her if she'd like to have drinks later.

The worst she could do was say no.

NATALIE LAYNE STEPPED onto the Cancun beach, her toes curling into the warm, white sand. She'd followed her sister's footsteps as closely as possible without having her sister there to guide her. A week ago Melody had come to the resort with her Kappa Delta sorority sisters. Six young women with nothing but fun in the sun on their minds.

As Melody's only living relative, Natalie had asked her younger sister to report in each day. Melody had happily complied, texting each evening, letting Natalie know she was okay and having a great time. Until the fourth day.

Natalie's chest tightened. She hadn't received the call until late that night when a heavily accented voice came over the line announcing, "We are most sorry to report that your sister, Melody Layne, disappeared on a dive this afternoon at approximately three o'clock."

Having lost their parents two years before to a ten-car pileup on Interstate 10, Natalie hadn't been able to grasp what the man was saying.

Her sister? Disappeared? "What do you mean *disappeared*?"

"She was diving with a boat operated by Scuba Cancun. When she didn't come up with the others, the dive boat operator searched but could not find her."

A hundred questions had raced through her head as

she'd held the phone to her ear. "What else has been done to find my sister?" she'd asked, her voice sounding as if it came from someone else down a long tunnel.

Her sister. Gone.

Natalie had given up the highly volatile and extremely rewarding career she loved as a special agent to return to New Orleans to see her sister through high school graduation and the start of college. Someone had to be there for her after their parents died.

Now this.

No way.

Natalie had taken the information from the Cancun police officer and hung up. Stunned and numb, she'd turned to her computer. She'd been leery of her sister traveling to Mexico. The endless reports of corruption in the Mexican government and law enforcement had been enough to convince Natalie it had been a bad idea.

Melody had insisted Cancun was insulated from the corruption and had its own security to protect the thriving tourist industry.

At the time Melody was making arrangements to go, Natalie should have put her foot down. Not that it would have done any good.

Melody had a mind of her own and the money their parents had left. She had reached the age of majority and could make reservations without her sister's consent. And she had.

That gut feeling had proved right.

Within minutes of receiving the call, Natalie had hit the number for her former employer, Royce Fontaine, and asked for help.

As the head of the Stealth Operations Specialists, he could help her as no one else could.

"Natalie, are you ready to come back to work for us?" He'd chuckled. "Travel journalism too tame?"

"Royce, I need your help."

The laughter ceased. "Name it. We're here for you."

She'd explained the situation and paused for him to digest the information.

"I'll run a scan on the area to see if there are any other occurrences of missing women," Royce told her. "You're right to be suspicious."

"Let me know what you find. In the meantime, I'm headed to Cancun."

"Will do," Royce said. "I'll send Lance Johnson out on the private jet with the equipment you'll need to keep you wired so that we can find you if you run into difficulty."

"Thanks, Royce. I knew I could count on you."

"Anytime. I had Lance lined up to take on another mission tomorrow, but I can take it myself."

"I hate to pull you from other important assignments—"

"Nat, we're talking about your sister. Family comes first. That's why I'm sending Lance. Technically he's as good as Geek and a better shot if you need backup."

"Good." Natalie's mind had already been five steps ahead, working through everything she had to accomplish before leaving for Mexico. "I don't expect any cooperation from the Mexican government or police."

"Look, why don't you fly in the corporate jet with Lance? It'll save you time and money."

"I don't know. I'm thinking I need to perform this mission undercover. I might get more answers that way."

"Fair enough. But you'll get there faster on the SOS plane than flying commercial. I can have Lance dropped at a different airport. He'll meet up with you later. That way you arrive separately."

"Agreed. As long as I'm in Cancun by tomorrow."

"You will be."

While Natalie packed for Cancun, she went through her text messages and photos from Melody, searching for clues. Her mind played through many scenarios for what might have happened to her sister, each one worse than the last.

When her cell phone rang she was so deep into her thoughts, she jumped.

"It's not good, I'm afraid," Royce said without a greeting.

Natalie's heart plummeted into her belly. "What did you find?"

"In the past two days three young women under the age of twenty-five have disappeared from the Cancun resort area and Riviera Cancun."

"Why hasn't it been in the news?"

"All three were from different countries—Sweden, Australia and now the U.S. To each country, it was a solitary incident. The Mexican government isn't advertising this as a serial event. Contacts in Cancun say they're treating two of them as individual unfortunate incidents."

Rage shot through Natalie. "Bull! Three women? Did they all disappear diving?"

"Two diving. The third? They claim the young woman wandered off and probably fell into an abandoned underground tunnel associated with the Mayan ruins located at Chichén Itzá, a little over an hour outside Cancun."

Natalie couldn't believe in this day and age any country would give up that soon. But then Mexico had its share of internal issues. The police force could be run by the local drug cartel. They might not have an interest in finding the women. "Did the authorities even *try* to find the women?"

"My contact said they gave it a perfunctory look and abandoned the search when it grew dark. If you go—"

"There's no *if*," Natalie said. "I'm going."

"Of course." Royce continued. "You have your extra passports, yes?"

"I do."

"Pick one that's foreign, but not Australia or Sweden. And stay blonde. The three women thus far were all blonde."

"Nice to know."

"I had Geek run a background check on their families. They were from rather small families who have little money to pay ransom, much less to pursue lengthy litigation or to hire private investigators to search for their daughters."

Natalie's jaw hardened. The women were targeted for their blond hair, youth and their family's lack of financial backing.

"So what you're telling me is that you don't think they were snatched for ransom."

"No." Royce's single word in that flat tone said it all.

If the women had been kidnapped, their captors weren't going to bargain to give them back. They would be sold or drugged and forced into the sex trade.

Forcing the emotion out of her heart, Natalie said, "The sooner we find them the better off they'll be."

"Right." Royce gave her the details about meeting Lance at the New Orleans airport the following morning.

Once she ended the call, she sat back, tapping her bare toe, while she sifted through her passports. Part of her old life as an agent, the passports were vital to getting around the world without raising suspicion. Though she'd given up her job as an agent, Natalie had been hesitant to destroy the passports. Now she was glad she hadn't.

Picking the United Kingdom passport, she stared at the image inside. The likeness was still valid: blond hair, blue eyes. And the woman in the photo looked like her with shorter hair. Hell, it was her, three years ago when she'd been active as an agent, sent all over the U.S. and other countries to do what the CIA, FBI or Interpol either couldn't do or hadn't successfully managed to accomplish.

The passport would serve its purpose to get her past authorities and establish her as a young, single woman of limited assets and family connections on vacation in Cancun.

With the backing of her old team, she made hotel reservations for the same resort where Melody and her friends had stayed, using her UK alias, Natalia Scranton, age twenty-three.

Sleep had been impossible, but she'd tried anyway, keeping her cell phone on the pillow beside her in case, by some miracle, Melody was able to text her.

The next day she'd met Lance at the airport and climbed aboard the SOS private plane. Once the plane took off, Lance came at her with a loaded syringe.

Natalie held up her hand. "Stop."

"You need to be tagged with a tracking device. Should whoever took the other girls manage to snag you, we'll need to follow you to wherever they've taken you and the others."

"Yeah, but why the syringe? Can't I keep a tag in my pocket?"

"That would be fine if you were wearing clothing with pockets at all times. I suspect, since we'll be at a resort, you will be wearing a bathing suit."

"I could sew the device into the suit."

"Will you sew one into every item of clothing you could possibly wear?"

Natalie frowned. "Maybe. I've just never liked the idea of being tracked all the time, by anybody."

"In this case, it's for your protection."

"Okay, but put it somewhere I can dig it out if I decide I don't like it anymore."

"Sure. Where would you like it?"

"Between my toes." She lifted the hem of her sundress and held out her leg.

Lance injected the tracking microchip and sat back in his seat with a hand-held device. He hit the on switch and waited. "There." He pointed to the dot on the screen. "There you are. Now, if you're swimming, scuba diving or taking a shower naked, we'll be able to find you."

Natalie snorted. "Nice to know I'll have company in the shower."

Lance grinned and opened an aluminum suitcase. From it, he selected what appeared to be a tiny hearing aid and handed it to her. "You remember how these work?"

"Yeah, yeah. Let's get to the good stuff." She leaned toward the suitcase and plucked out an H&K .40-caliber pistol and several boxes of rounds. "I prefer the stopping power of a .45 caliber or 9 mm, but the smaller weapon will be easier to hide."

"Exactly." He handed her a set of throwing knives similar to the ones she had locked in her safe at home in New Orleans.

Natalie ran her hand over the handles, wishing she had time to practice throwing. These, too, she had given up when she'd decided to retire from SOS operations. How would she explain to Melody the need to have her own set of knives, especially when she was terrible in the kitchen?

Melody had no idea what Natalie had done before she'd returned home to New Orleans to be there for her after their parents died. Her sister thought she had given up the boring desk job in D.C., the first job she'd taken when she'd finished college.

That seemed such a long time ago.

Loaded with all the equipment and weaponry she could easily hide in her suitcases, in the room or on her person, Natalie arrived at the hotel, smiling like a young single woman on vacation, ready to soak up the sun and play in the sand.

She greeted the desk clerk in an English accent she'd perfected when Royce had assigned her to a case in Oxford, England. Despite staying there, she was so busy working the case, she didn't have time to play tourist and get to know the area. She asked for a room on the same floor as the one her sister had shared with her three girlfriends from college. Hopefully she'd find out more by hanging out with them at the bar, if they hadn't already gone home, frightened by the loss of their roommate.

As soon as she unpacked her suitcase and stowed her weapons in the room's lockbox, she stripped out of her sundress and pulled on the sexy swimsuit her sister had insisted she buy. She had, against her better judgment. Whatever made Melody happy made Natalie happy.

In what little there was of the black suit, Natalie had to agree with Lance and the subcutaneous injection of the tracking device. Anything other than her body beneath the suit would have stood out.

Dressed for the beach and hanging out with young people, Natalie grabbed a beach towel and sunglasses and headed down to the lobby. She passed through the lobby and out to the pool area, checking out all of the people she passed, wondering if one of them was behind her sister's disappearance. None of the young women looked anything like those in Melody's selfies.

Once out on the beach, she noted someone changing the yellow flag to red, indicating it was dangerous to swim.

Mothers herded children out of the shallows and teens frowned and complained as they slogged through the water to shore. A group of young women in colorful bikinis stood in water up to their waists, taking pictures of each other. The man hoisting the red flag, waved for them to return to shore, yelling something about riptides.

Natalie glanced farther down the shoreline, thankful for her sunglasses. The white sand was bright behind her lenses, but without the glasses the beach would be blinding.

Sand crunched beside her and a shadow crossed over her face.

Natalie tensed.

"Looking for someone?" a deep male voice asked.

She turned toward the man wearing nothing but black swim trunks and a smile. And, good Lord, he didn't need anything else. Suntanned and tattooed, his body was magnificent, his white teeth shining in his tanned cheeks. Dark hair, dark eyes and a friendly face topped him off.

"Not particularly," she answered, remembering to use the proper British accent before promptly turning the other way.

"Name's Sawyer," he said. "Me and my buddies just got here today."

"That's lovely." As handsome and well-muscled as the man was, he wasn't in Natalie's plan. She was there for her sister, not to flirt with muscle-bound men in sexy black swim trunks.

"Bug off, Sawyer," another voice said from behind Natalie and she spun to face an even taller man with jet-black hair and a jaw that looked hard enough to crack walnuts.

She tipped her sunglasses down, curious about the true color of his eyes. Her heart fluttered as the deep green orbs stared down into hers and took her breath away.

No. She didn't have time for the sudden tug of attraction. If she knew for certain where her sister was and that she was all right, Natalie might consider flirting with this incredibly handsome man with the tribal tattoos on his shoulders.

"Excuse us," he said. "It's been a while since we've been around a beautiful woman."

"No need to explain." *Just leave.*

A shout rose up, drawing those startlingly green eyes

away from Natalie and to a couple of splashing figures farther out than was safe. Both figures appeared to be women, one closer in than the other. The woman furthest out seemed to be moving out to sea despite her attempt to swim ashore.

Mr. Green Eyes left her and jogged toward the water, the one called Sawyer on his heels.

Natalie hurried after the two.

"Looks like the current is dragging them out," Sawyer said.

The man with the green eyes didn't respond; he raced toward the water without slowing. He charged in up to his knees and dived into the surf.

His friend dived in after him. Soon both men cleaved through the water.

No matter how strong they could swim, the current had a way of doing its own thing.

Sawyer stopped at the first woman, while Mr. Green Eyes continued out to the other.

A teen stood at the water's edge, watching the event unfold, a surfboard clutched under one arm. Natalie altered her direction and ran toward him. "Mind if I borrow this?"

He passed it to her without question.

Natalie ran toward the water.

By the time she slid onto the board, Sawyer was on his way back to shore with the first girl. Green Eyes had reached the other.

The poor woman was so frightened she clung to him, climbing up his body to get farther out of the water.

They were so far out, Natalie wasn't certain she'd get there before the two went under, but she had to try. The lifeguard wasn't far behind her. Between the three of them, they should be able to help the woman.

As she neared, Green Eyes was attempting to untangle the woman's arms from around his neck. The more he tried, the more desperate the woman became.

Then Green Eyes went under.

The woman clinging to him went down with him, but immediately let go and struggled to the surface.

Natalie paddled faster, searching the water for the man who'd disappeared. *Come up Green Eyes*, she prayed. Come up!

Chapter Two

Duff should have stayed at the pool with the kids. Now he was in over his head in the ocean, with a dangerous riptide and a panicked woman climbing all over him.

So much for relaxing.

When he'd had his fill of water up the nose, he dived down. The woman who'd clung to him despite all his reassurances that she'd be all right, let go and fought her way to the surface.

Duff stayed down long enough to circle the woman and come up beneath her. She slapped at the water, her strength waning.

Grabbing the woman by the ankles, Duff yanked her down, climbed up her back and secured an arm over her shoulder and diagonally down to her waist. Then he surfaced, leaning her back so that she faced the sky, her arms and legs batting at the water like a puppy learning to swim.

"Damn it, woman. Stop struggling," Duff bellowed.

"Way to make a frightened victim less scared," a female voice said from behind him.

He glanced over his shoulder into the blue eyes of the woman in the black swimsuit he and Sawyer had been talking to before they'd gone for a swim. "What are you doing out here?" Duff demanded. "Didn't you see the red flag?"

"I did. But I thought you might need something more than your muscles to get the woman to shore. The current is too strong to get her back on your own."

Duff treaded water with his one arm, his other clamped tightly around the woman, holding her head above water.

"What's your name?" the woman on the surfboard asked the one in the water.

"Lisa," she responded weakly.

"I'll bet you're tired."

The woman in Duff's arms nodded.

"My name is Natalia," the blonde said. "And this is...?" She raised her brows, giving Duff a pointed look.

"Duff," he said.

"And the lifeguard is here, as well," Natalia said.

Duff glanced behind Natalia at a young man barely out of his teens paddling toward them on a surfboard.

"Lisa, do you want to go back with me, or the lifeguard?"

Lisa gulped and answered, "You."

Natalia nodded. "Good. I think Duff can help you climb up on this board. Would you like that?"

Lisa nodded though her hands tightened on Duff's arm.

Natalia held out a hand and smiled encouragingly. "Take my hand, Lisa. The man behind you will help you onto the board and stay right beside you all the way back to shore. Won't you?" Natalia prompted Duff.

"I will." Between them, they hoisted the woman onto the board.

Duff took a moment to breathe normally before starting back to shore.

Natalia had Lisa lie on her stomach and then she did the same, lying over the woman's back. She started paddling. "Paddle, Lisa. The more you paddle, the faster we get to shore."

Lisa paddled, weakly flailing her arms, her face turned toward the shore.

Duff circled behind them and pushed the surfboard. With all three of them working it and cutting at an angle, they eventually made it to the beach, the lifeguard following. A group of young women met them, helped Lisa out of the water and enveloped her in a half dozen hugs.

Duff stood beside Natalia, propping the surfboard in the sand. "Thanks."

She responded in her pretty English accent without looking up. "You're quite welcome."

Duff held out a hand. "Name's Duff."

Natalia glanced at his hand and hesitated. Finally she shook it. "I'm Natalia. Lisa was lucky you were on the beach today."

He shrugged. "I'm glad I could help. Look, we didn't get much of a start back there. Would you like to have dinner with me tonight?"

She didn't even bat an eyelash before responding. "No, thank you."

"Duff!" Sawyer approached, his arm around a woman wrapped in a beach towel. "Glad you made it back to shore. Wouldn't be the same diving without you tomorrow."

Duff snorted. "Nice to know you missed me."

Lisa broke free of her group of friends and wrapped

her arms around Duff's neck. "Thank you so much for saving my life. I hate to think what would have happened if you hadn't gotten to me when you did."

"I'm sure someone else would have helped."

Lisa turned to Natalia and hugged her, too. "You two are my heroes. After the horrible past two days, I needed you."

Natalia hugged the woman. "Horrible? Did you get caught in the current yesterday?"

Lisa shook her head, her eyes tearing. "No, I lost one of my sisters." The rest of the young women gathered around her, all hugging each other.

"What do you mean?" Natalia asked.

Lisa sniffed. "We were on a diving excursion. She was my dive buddy. I turned away for a moment to see a moray eel in the coral. When I turned back, she was gone."

Natalia's face paled.

"Are you telling me she wasn't found?" Duff asked.

Lisa and her friends all shook their heads as one.

Natalia reached for Lisa's hands, her own shaking slightly. "What a horrible experience."

"If we could have a do-over, we never would have gone diving." Lisa dashed away a tear. "Melody was one of the nicest people I know."

"Didn't the dive master look for her?" Natalia asked.

A brunette in a pale pink bikini nodded. "He spent the next two hours searching."

A sandy-blonde added, "They radioed to shore and the shore patrol came out and helped in the search."

"Nothing." Lisa sniffed again. "I don't know why we came out to the beach today. I don't think I'll ever go in the water again."

The young lady wrapped in the towel, standing in the circle of Sawyer's arm, stepped away from him and slipped an arm around Lisa. "We can't leave Cancun until our scheduled flights. Lisa and I thought we'd look around in the water, even though Melody disappeared a long way from here. We kind of hoped the current would have carried her back this way. That's why we were out so far."

"It was stupid," Lisa said.

"At least you two are okay," Duff said.

Natalia nodded. "You should go back to your rooms and rest."

Lisa and her friends thanked them again and left the beach to return to the resort hotel.

"Wow, what rotten luck," Sawyer said. "To lose your friend and almost lose your life all in the space of two days. Not my idea of a great vacation."

"If you'll excuse me, I think I'll go lie down, as well," Natalia said.

"If you won't have dinner with me," Duff persisted, "will you let me buy you a drink later?"

She gave him a half smile. "We'll see."

He watched as the gorgeous blonde left, walking up the beach in her sexy black swimsuit, her long hair drying in soft curls around her shoulders. Beautiful and strong. What other woman would have jumped in to help in such a dangerous situation?

Sawyer made a diving motion with his hand followed by the sound of an explosion. "Turned you down, did she?"

Duff nodded, his gaze on the sway of Natalia's hips. "The battle's not over."

His friend clapped his hand onto Duff's shoulder.

"That's my man. We're on vacation here. What's a vacation without a beautiful woman to keep you company?"

Indeed. And Natalia had captured his interest in more ways than one.

He headed back to the hotel, Sawyer walking alongside him. "Didn't you say Quentin and Montana were looking into a diving excursion?"

Sawyer nodded. "I hope it wasn't with the crew who lost the girl yesterday."

Duff almost hoped they went with the same crew and to the same spot where the girl disappeared. Something wasn't right about losing a diver and not finding anything to indicate what had happened.

NATALIE HURRIED BACK to the hotel, grateful she and the two muscular men had been there to help save Lisa and her friend from the strong current. Not only was she glad the girls were still alive, she was also happy it had served as an introduction to hang out with them without arousing suspicion. She'd make it a point to find them at dinner or at the bar that evening. Perhaps someone had seen something they didn't realize might be a clue to what had happened to Melody.

Deep inside, Natalie believed her sister was alive. Finding her would be the challenge.

She stopped at the excursion planner's desk and asked about dive trips for the next day. She let the planner, Maria Sanchez, go through the different options and dive companies. When Maria didn't mention Scuba Cancun, Natalie made it a point to ask.

"Friends of mine came last month and went on a dive with Scuba Cancun. They said if I came to Cancun, I had to book with them. Do you book trips with them?"

Natalie blinked her eyes, trying for young, sweet and innocent, when all she wanted to do was to jerk the binder out of the lovely Maria's hands and make her own arrangements.

"Yes, we do book Scuba Cancun, but the last time I looked, they were full for tomorrow. Let me check and see if they've had any cancellations." She clicked her keyboard and stared at the screen, her brows puckered. Then they smoothed and she smiled up at Natalie. "You're in luck. They have one space available for tomorrow morning. Would you like me to book it?"

Natalie let go of the breath she'd been holding and nodded. "Yes, please."

If she thought it would do any good, she'd run around asking questions and demanding answers. But if there was a chance Melody had been kidnapped in some elaborate scheme to smuggle women into the sex trade, the people she wanted answers from would be highly unlikely to talk about anything to do with the missing college coed.

No, she'd have to keep her connection with Melody under wraps. Perhaps her blond hair and English accent would help set her up as the next target. The quickest way to find the kidnap victims might be to become one herself.

On her way through the lobby to the elevator, she made it a point to say hello to the front desk clerk, the bellboys and the concierge. If any one of them was involved in whatever might be going on, she wanted them to consider her as their next target.

On the way up to her room she noted the camera in the top corner of the elevator car. As she stepped out of the elevator onto her floor, she spotted one of the girls from the beach sliding her card into the door lock and hurried toward her. "I'm so very glad I caught you. I'm Natalia, from the beach." She held out her hand.

"Oh, yes. Thank you for saving my friends." She took Natalie's hand. "I'm Kylie."

"Are Lisa and her friend doing all right?" Natalie asked.

The pretty blonde smiled and nodded. "Lisa and Jodie are sleeping. Their parents were able to book them on a flight back to the States tomorrow morning. I wish the rest of us could have gotten on board, but the flight was full."

"I hope they have a safe flight back. Are you all going to dinner later? My roommate was supposed to come with me on this holiday, but her aunt died and she had to cancel at the last minute. I would love to have someone to eat with."

Kylie's brows rose. "You mean you're not with the hunky guys?"

Natalie smiled. "I only wish. They are kind of dreamy, don't you think?"

"Oh, yeah." The younger woman sighed. "They're just what I imagined finding here. If only things had worked out differently. Since Melody disappeared, none of us can think of anything else. The vacation is ruined and we're all ready to be home with our families."

"I can imagine. Nothing's worse than losing someone you're that close to." Natalie bit down on her tongue to keep from adding "Especially when she's your only living relative whom you love dearly."

"As for dinner...we will probably go down around eight. Since it's Lisa and Jodie's last night here, we'll end up at the bar for one last round before the group disperses. You're welcome to join us. I'm sure the others will agree."

"Thank you. I'm glad I won't have to sit awkwardly by myself." Natalie waved her hand. "See you around eight, then." She turned and walked toward the door next to Kylie's and let herself into her room.

First thing, she checked the disposable cell phone she'd purchased at the airport for any messages from Lance. She'd texted him as soon as she'd pulled it from the plastic packaging so he'd have her number.

Since her eventful walk on the beach, he'd had time to arrive and text her with his bungalow number.

With a couple hours to spare, Natalie figured she might as well check in with the agent.

Slipping a long, flowing skirt over her swimsuit, she plunked a floppy hat onto her head and left her room. Rather than take the elevator, she opted for the stairs, checking the locations of all the security cameras. She wondered if Lance could get into the security system and review footage from the night before last to see if it showed them potential suspects that could have been stalking the young women.

Lance had rented a bungalow on the resort property, giving him a little more privacy than a hotel room. He could set up his equipment and not worry too much about being bothered.

Natalie took a roundabout route, looking for security cameras strategically placed. Outside the hotel, the cameras were directed toward common areas and the hotel itself. The bungalows seemed to be more private.

Strolling along a pebbled concrete path as if she hadn't a care in the world, Natalie eventually arrived at the correct bungalow with its Do Not Disturb sign hanging on the door handle. A quick glance around assured her she was alone. She knocked softly.

A moment later Lance opened the door. "I was wondering when you'd stop by. I see you've already been in the water based on where the tracker located you." He jerked his head and stepped to the side. "Come in."

Natalie slipped inside. "Have you hacked into the police data files?"

"I'd love to say yes but, one, I just set up my system. And two, the local authorities' system isn't that sophisticated. I'm not even certain they keep data on computers."

"What about the hotel security system?" Natalie asked.

Lance crossed to the small desk located against one wall. "Working on that now." He sat in the chair and opened his laptop. On the screen was a map of Cancun, the resort pinpointed by a bold green dot.

"I see you're keeping up with me." Natalie was at once reassured and disturbed by being followed so closely. If it weren't for the nature of the case, she would never have let anyone inject a tracking device beneath her skin. Though she had confidence in her ability to defend herself, she knew her limits. Being drugged or outnumbered could reduce her abilities to nil. In that case, she'd be happy to have Lance track her and provide backup if or when she went missing.

"When you get into the hotel security camera files, check the bar, lobby and restaurants where Melody was to see if there are any suspicious characters paying a little too much attention to her. Royce gave you the picture of Melody, didn't he?"

"Got it. I'll let you know if I find anything."

"I'll be in the restaurant and bar tonight if you can get into the security system by then."

"I should be able to pull up the online system. I can keep an eye on you, if you'd like."

"Whatever." Natalie shrugged, staring at the green dot on the screen. "You already have me on the tracking system."

"True."

"Do one more favor for me, will you?" Natalie asked.

"Shoot."

"I met a couple of guys on the beach today. Both had tattoos and were well built. Check them out. I'd almost bet they're military, based on their bearing. They said they only got in today, but that could have been a line. Both hit on me."

Lance grinned. "If the rest of that swimsuit is as revealing as the top, I don't blame them."

Natalie frowned. "Find out who they are and when they arrived. They were certainly big enough to carry off a female with one hand tied behind their backs."

"Will do."

"Thanks. I'd better get back so I can be ready in time for dinner. If you find anything, I want to know ASAP."

Lance saluted. "Yes, ma'am."

With an hour to get ready, Natalie hurried back to her hotel room and hit the shower. Something didn't feel right about getting dressed up for dinner when her sister could be in some kind of hell, praying for someone to rescue her.

Rinsed and scrubbed free of the sticky salt water, Natalie toweled dry and then ran a blow dryer over hair, pulling the curl out. Applying the flat iron, she erased all the curl and left her hair hanging long down to her waist, the way college girls wore it. Normally, Natalie would have worn her hair pulled back in a ponytail. Her hair was long, but only because she was too lazy to go to the hairdresser on a regular basis.

Once she finished her hair, she applied makeup, another ritual she'd avoided over the past two years. With the intention of being the next blonde to be nabbed, she gave herself smoky eyes with a combination of blue and charcoal eye shadow topped with a thin stroke of black eyeliner and mascara.

Satisfied with the result, Natalie dressed in a short, soft blue dress with narrow spaghetti straps. The dress was another one of Melody's choices. Natalie hadn't worn it out of sheer modesty. The hem barely covered her bottom, revealing every inch of her long legs. The thin straps and form-fit of the garment meant thong panties and no bra.

Feeling as close to naked as one could be in a dress, Natalie slipped her feet into strappy silver stilettoes. Grabbing the matching silver clutch, she slipped money, her passport and one of the knives inside. At the last minute she flipped the switch on the earbud and stuck it in her left ear.

"Hey, Lance."

"I'm here, sweetheart."

"Don't call me sweetheart."

"You got it, babe."

Not in the mood to argue, she let his teasing slide. "Anything?"

"Your guys are two of the four who arrived today. I traced them all the way back to the plane they flew in on. Dutton Calloway, Sawyer Houston, Benjamin

Raines and Quentin Lovett. Their plane originated from New Orleans. Probably legit."

"Thanks."

"Do you want me to dig deeper?"

"Yeah, just in case they're buyers for the kidnapped women."

"Got it.

"And...Lance?"

"Yes, babe?"

"Remind me to punch you later."

A chuckle sounded in her ear.

"Will do."

"In the meantime don't talk to me unless I talk to you first or you find something major. I can barely think in my own head without a man in it, too."

She stepped into the corridor at the same time as Melody's friends.

"Oh, good." Lisa met her at the elevator. "We were just about to knock on your door."

"Thank you for letting me tag along." Natalie entered the elevator, followed by Melody's friends.

Natalie wasn't worried she might look too much like Melody that the girls would recognize her. The only picture her sister always carried with her was one of the two of them with their parents six years ago. Natalie had sported a short bob back then, her hair several shades lighter than now. And she was six inches taller than her younger sister's five feet, two inches.

"Have you heard anything from the police about your friend?" Natalie asked.

"No, but the Cancun police stopped by again to ask more questions." Lisa shook her head. "It's not like I had anything new to say. Melody was there. Then she wasn't."

Natalie's heart contracted and her eyes stung. The only way she could keep tears from falling was to remind herself that Melody was alive, waiting for her big sister to find her.

Dinner was a somber affair. Melody's friends spoke to one another in subdued tones, each quietly introspective after the past two days' trauma.

"Are you ready to go back to our rooms?" Lisa asked.

"No. We can't leave without drinking a toast to Melody," Kylie said. "Come on. One last drink before Lisa and Jodie take off in the morning. It'll be the last legal drink for them until next year when they turn twenty-one."

"Y'all go on without me. I don't feel much like partying," Jodie said.

"You have to come. We're going to drink to Melody. It wouldn't be the same without you." Lisa and Kylie each grabbed one of the girl's arms and marched her out to the cabana where reggae music was in full swing and a few couples moved to the beat on the dance floor.

Natalie followed the girls to the bar beneath a thatched-roofed cabana strung with twinkle lights.

They all ordered strawberry margaritas and stood around a table, no one making a move to take a seat.

"Melody's favorite," Lisa said, her voice cracking as she lifted her glass rimmed with sugar. "To Melody. I hope she's found safe and returned home."

Kylie's eyes filled with tears as she lifted her glass with the others.

Fighting her own tears, Natalie raised her glass. "To Melody," she whispered. *I will find you and bring you home.*

Chapter Three

Duff spotted her as soon as she stepped out of the hotel into the cabana bar.

She tagged along behind the group of young women they'd met on the beach following the rescue. They ordered sugar-laced strawberry margaritas, each with a colorful umbrella perched on the rims of their glasses. As one, they lifted their drinks in a toast.

Natalia sipped the sugary concoction and winced.

Duff almost laughed. A gut feeling told him she wasn't into fruity mixed drinks.

She set the drink on the table and glanced around the outdoor bar as though looking for something or someone. Maybe a rescue from the drink.

Duff strode to the bar and ordered two long-neck beers. Once served, he slipped up behind Natalia. "Looking for someone?"

She turned, the corners of her lips rising. "Not really."

Duff nodded in greeting to the other women at the table before turning his attention to Natalia.

She stared down at his hands, her brows cocked. "Are you a two-fisted drinker?"

"No, I kind of hoped you would prefer beer to whatever that is you're drinking."

Natalie crossed her arms over her chest. "Do I look like a beer drinker?" Her lips quirked again.

Duff chuckled. "Not really but, like I said, I hope you are."

She relaxed and held out her hand. "Actually, I don't really like sweet, fruity drinks."

"Thank goodness." He handed her one of the ice-cold bottles. "I was afraid I'd end up drinking both. Alone."

"Glad to help my fellow rescuer out." She tipped the bottle back and drank a long swallow before glancing up into Duff's eyes. "You don't take no for an answer often, do you?"

"I'm persistent. When I want something, I go after it and stay after it until I get it."

She snorted softly. "A prize to be won?"

"No, a challenge to be met." He lifted his bottle and tapped it against hers. "Anything worth having is worth fighting for."

"Like?"

"Freedom. The lives of your friends and family..." His voice deepened. "The love of a woman..."

She blinked, her smile spreading. "Wow, are you always this smooth with the ladies?"

Duff grinned. "Heard that on a movie. That's the first opportunity I've had to use it." He set his bottle on the table and took hers from her hand and placed it beside his. "Come on. Let's dance." He slipped his arm around her waist.

She hesitated. "And if I don't want to?"

"You do," he said. The fact she hadn't told him to bug off already gave him hope.

"Cocky much?" she asked.

"Only when I'm sure of myself."

"Which is often, I take it."

Despite his arrogance—or maybe because of it—she allowed him to lead her onto the dance floor. An up-beat reggae tune had some couples leaving and others stepping up the pace.

Once on the dance floor Natalie tilted her head to the side. "Sorry, but I don't know how to dance to this music. I tend to be all left feet."

"Then you haven't had the right partner." He swung her away from him and then pulled her into the curve of his arms, her back against his chest, his lips beside her ear. "Just relax. I'll do all the work."

The warmth of Natalia's hand in his and the way she wore that incredibly sexy blue dress, made Duff's insides curl and his body heat.

He twirled her beneath his arm and back to face him, his hips moving to the rhythm, his feet keeping the beat, urging her to follow.

The more he moved with her, his hand resting on the small of her back, the more her body relaxed. By the end of the song, she could anticipate his moves as if they'd danced together for years and she fit perfectly against him. Her long legs and lithe, athletic body felt right in his arms.

When the music switched to a slow, sensuous rhythm, Duff pulled her against him.

For a brief moment her body stiffened and then melted against him, her hand resting against his chest. He liked how warm and firm it felt there. Yeah, he could get used to this woman.

"So, what brings you to Cancun?" he asked, his lips

so close to her ear he wanted to nibble the pretty earlobe. In her heels, she still wasn't as tall as he was, but she was close.

His arms around her tightened and Duff leaned his cheek against her hair. "I'm sorry. Was my question too personal?"

She glanced up at him as if realizing for the first time that she was dancing with him. Her brow furrowed. "What was it you asked?"

Her question hit him in the ego. He'd have to make a better impression to keep her attention. "What brings you to Cancun?"

"I'm on holiday," she said with a smile.

"Alone?" he asked.

"I wasn't supposed to be, but that is the way of it. My friend's aunt died and she had to cancel at the last minute to attend the funeral."

"I'm sorry for her loss." He pulled Natalia close to his body and swayed to the music, his hips rubbing against hers, causing an instantaneous reaction. His trousers tightened and he wished they were somewhere more private—like his bedroom.

Natalia leaned into him, her fingers curling into his shirt, her nails scraping his chest.

Duff swallowed a groan rising up from his lungs. She was doing crazy things to him without even trying.

Natalia smiled up into his face. "What about you? Why did you come to Cancun?"

"Same. Vacation. Long overdue."

"Tough job?" she asked.

He snorted. "At times." He didn't talk much about his work, except to his Special Boat Team 22 teammates. Most SEAL assignments required top-secret clearance. Information about those operations was only shared with people cleared for that particular mission. He found himself wanting to tell Natalia all about it. But he couldn't.

The music ended and she stepped away. "Thank you for the dance." She turned to walk away.

Not wanting the night to end yet, Duff caught her hand. "Will you dance with me again?"

She lifted one shoulder. "Maybe, but for now, I'm going to visit with my new friends."

And that was it. Natalia walked away, leaving Duff standing in the middle of the dance floor.

She returned to the group of young women and took up a position on the periphery, her gaze scanning the room again and again.

Duff frowned. What was she looking for?

A hand containing a chilled bottle touched his arm. "You look like you could use this."

Sawyer handed him the cold beer and took a drink of his. "So, what's the story?"

"What story?" Duff tipped his bottle and drank a long swig of the cool liquid.

"You came, you danced and she walked away. Now she's dancing with another guy." Sawyer jerked his head toward Natalia, who was walking toward the dance floor with a different man.

Duff's jaw tightened. So it wasn't her new friends she wanted to hang out with. Natalia wanted to dance with another man.

"Did you say something to make her mad?" Sawyer persisted.

"I don't think so."

His friend shook his head. "This is a first. I haven't

known a single female to turn down the Duff's incredible charm."

"Shut up, Sawyer."

Sawyer gave him an innocent grin. "Just saying."

So, Natalia wasn't interested. He should move on and find another willing female to spend time with. Unfortunately none of them appealed to him like Natalia.

She danced with a couple of different guys before Duff had had enough. He pushed away from the bar and announced to his friends, "I'm hitting the rack."

"Me, too." Montana stood, stretched and draped an arm over Duff's shoulders. "We're on for scuba at zero-eight-hundred."

"Should be fun," Quentin added.

"What's fun about scuba without blowing something up?" Sawyer asked.

Duff shook his head. "See you guys in the morning."

Sawyer leaned toward Quentin and Montana and said loud enough for Duff to hear, "He's just sore about being shot down by the pretty blonde."

Montana laughed. "Is that it? Duff's giving up?"

Quentin shook his head. "Never thought I'd see the day."

Duff left the cabana without waiting for his friends. As he entered the hotel, he glanced back at Natalia, dancing with yet another man.

He shrugged and turned away.

Who needed a female complication, anyway?

Focus on Melody.

Natalie smiled and laughed at each of her dance partners' jokes and acted as if she cared. If someone was after young blonde women, she needed to be seen and considered. Dancing with several men put her out in the middle of view as a single white female. She had to take advantage of it, even though she'd rather be dancing with Duff. For some reason the tough-looking man with a smattering of tattoos across his shoulders and back made her feel more feminine than any other man she'd ever been around.

When she'd been with the SOS, she'd felt as if she'd had to prove herself equal if not better than her male counterparts. Most of the men and the women who worked for Royce Fontaine were prior military, secret service or FBI. Natalie had been working as a boring desk jockey with a natural ability to shoot straight and true every time.

Her love of shooting had come about when she'd moved to Washington, D.C., and realized just how dangerous the city could be for a single woman.

She'd gone to the range to learn how to fire the .40-caliber pistol she'd purchased to protect herself. After firing a few times she discovered she was good and had tried other weapons the range had in stock. Soon she was an expert shot with every weapon the range had to offer, and salesmen were asking her to test and demonstrate their new releases. When she wasn't working, she was at the range.

Natalie had landed the SOS job when she'd run into Fontaine at the range. He'd been there at the request of the salesman. Royce had watched her fire several of the new weapons the salesman had brought along that day. When she'd finished firing, she'd given her feedback and turned to find the SOS boss staring at her with a smile.

That had been the beginning of the job she'd grown

to love, utilizing her skill with guns and her love of adventure. She'd become a Stealth Operations Specialist, one of the only agents who'd never served in combat or law enforcement.

Royce had set her up to go through a special three-month training program similar to infantry basic training only with mercenary soldiers. They'd cut her no slack and expected her to play rough, despite being a female. She'd come through, scoring the highest on weapons qualification, even on the live-fire courses and urban terrain exercises. She had a sixth sense for when to shoot and when not to shoot.

She'd been an operative for two full years before her parents were killed in an automobile crash, right before her younger sister's high school graduation.

Natalie'd had no other choice. Family came first, and you didn't give up on them.

As she danced she watched the bar. Several men stood out to her. Of course Duff and his friends, who'd arrived the same day as she, because of their obvious physical fitness and laid-back charm. Natalie sensed no threat from them. The bartender was a compact man with dark hair and darker eyes. He served drinks quickly, without talking, and the wait staff seemed a little intimidated by him.

Then there were the two Hispanic men who'd sat at a table in the corner, drinking Coronas and watching Melody's friends and her as she danced with a sandy-blond-haired playboy from New Jersey.

To Natalie every man in the place was under suspicion until she proved his innocence. And all bore watching.

When Duff and his friends left, Natalie felt her energy leave with them. Melody's friends didn't have the heart to stay and party when two of them would leave the next day and Melody remained missing.

"We're calling it a night," Lisa said. "I hope you have a better vacation here than we did." She hugged Natalie. "Please be careful."

"Thank you." Natalie hugged the other woman, as if by so doing, she was a little closer to her sister.

They rode up the elevator together and parted ways in the hallway of their floor.

A soon as Natalie entered her room, she tapped her earbud. "Anything?" she asked Lance.

"Got into the security videos. I've spent the past three hours going through all the footage."

"And?"

"I ruled out the hallway. The lobby had several characters I found lurking in the outdoor cabana. Could you slip away for a few minutes to check out the faces, or do you want me to try to send snapshots to your cell phone?"

"I don't want any hackers to intercept the messages. I'll be there in five minutes."

"Wear the earbud in case you run into any trouble on the grounds."

"Will do." She slipped out of the blue dress and stilettoes and into a long casual dress and flat sandals. If someone asked her where she was going, her answer would be for a walk on the beach. She took the stairs down to ground level and walked out the back door of the hotel. The pool was lit and glowed a soft ocean-blue, the water rippled by the salty breeze.

Natalie schooled her pace to take it slow, like a person on vacation enjoying the night air, not like a woman on a mission to save her sister. When the path curved toward the bungalows, she veered in the opposite direction and took a more direct route to the beach. If someone followed her, she didn't want him or her to discover her repeated visits to the bungalow where Lance worked.

By the time she reached the bungalow ten minutes had passed and the wind had picked up, whipping her long hair around her shoulders and across her eyes.

Lance opened the door as soon as Natalie knocked.

She slipped inside and crossed to the computer screen. The video had been paused on two dark-haired men sitting in the corner of the cabana. "I saw these two tonight. Same table, same corner of the cabana."

"Happen to get their names?"

Natalie shook her head. "No. They stayed at the table the entire time."

Lance fast-forwarded the video, stopping on an image of Melody and a man dancing.

Her heart came to a hard stop in her chest and Natalie sucked in her breath. Her gaze caught on Melody, laughing, dancing and flirting. She was so happy and carefree.

When her heart started pumping again, it raced, anger pushing blood through it faster and faster.

Natalie leaned toward the screen, trying to see the man with her, only getting the back of his head. "Can you see his face anywhere in the video?"

Lance shook his head. "No matter how many times I replay, I can't get a clear shot of his facial features."

"Melody is five feet two inches tall and, based on what she's wearing, she's probably got on at least three-inch heels, making her five feet five. He's at least another five to six inches taller than her. That would put

him right around six feet tall. And he has dark hair."
She straightened. "Anything else?"

"Several men in the lobby of the hotel. Some of them
with women who appeared to be girlfriends or wives.
Others were alone." He clicked on the touch pad and another view popped up on the screen. "This is the lobby."

Lance took her through several minutes of video
he'd tagged as potential. When they were done, Natalie
didn't feel any closer to finding her sister than before.
"Tomorrow morning, I'm scheduled to go on the dive
boat Melody and her friends sailed with."

Lance's brows dipped. "Stay with your dive buddy
in case you run into trouble."

She snorted. "What are the chances the people who
took Melody will hit the same dive boat two times in
a single week?"

"Slim to none. If these creeps are smart enough to
kidnap three women without raising a red flag with
the local authorities, they won't go after someone on
that dive boat."

Natalie sighed. "I know it's a reach, but maybe I'll
get some information out of the crew. Perhaps one of
them is in cahoots with the operation."

Lance clicked another button on the computer and a
GPS tracker screen appeared. "Either way, I've got you
covered. Get some sleep tonight and be careful down
there tomorrow."

"I don't hold out hope on sleep." Natalie crossed to
the door. "I can only imagine what Melody is going
through."

"Yeah, it's gotta be tough when it's your sister. She's
not my sister, and I can hardly wait to catch the bastards."

Natalie smiled. "Thanks for your help, Lance. It's nice to know SOS is backing me."

"We miss having you around. Nobody quite equals our best sharpshooter."

Warmth stole through her. They might not be blood relatives, but the members of the SOS team had been like family.

She opened the door and checked to make certain the coast was clear. A light breeze stirred the air. The moon shone bright through the gently undulating palm fronds, stirring shadows. But nothing else moved.

Natalie left the bungalow and headed toward the beach.

She passed another bungalow and was about to cut across to the more direct path leading through some bougainvillea bushes when the snap of a twig sounded behind her.

She spun, ready to face an attacker. Again, nothing moved in the shadows except the shadows themselves.

A shiver rippled across her skin in the balmy night air. Rather than cut through the thick bushes, she continued on the pebbled concrete path toward the beach. Once on the sand, she'd be in the open. Unless whoever was following her had a gun and planned to shoot her, she'd have half a chance at defending herself.

Natalie picked up the pace, stretching her long legs, trying to put distance between her and whoever or whatever was following her. By now she heard footsteps behind her.

Whenever she turned, she saw nothing. Trained to survive in hand-to-hand combat, she knew her limitations. She was better with a gun. A large man could subdue her, if he knew what he was doing.

Once out in the open, she could face her adversary head-on. No more hiding in the shadows. By the time she burst out of the palm tree shadows onto the beach, she'd gone past powerwalking, skipped jogging and was running all-out.

She turned to look over her shoulder and ran into a solid wall. Arms wrapped around her, holding her so tightly she couldn't move.

She tried to scream but a hand clamped over her mouth.

Chapter Four

Duff wasn't ready to call it a night. Though tired from traveling, his thoughts spun, going over and over the dance with the beautiful Natalia. She'd been in a hurry to end their time together but then made time to dance with other men. Not that Duff had any right to tell her who she could or couldn't dance with. Heck, he'd only just met the woman. Okay, so they'd survived a riptide together, but that didn't mean they were a couple.

Too wound up to lie down in his cabin, Duff had headed for the beach. The sound of the ocean washing up on the sand soothing him like nothing else.

He'd walked a mile along the beach and back, finally ready to call it a night when a woman burst out of the shadows. Still hurtling forward, she'd spun to look behind her, unaware of Duff on the sand. When she hit him in the chest, he reached an arm around her middle and clamped the other one over her mouth, sure she'd scream at being caught.

Not in the mood to fend off questions by anyone wandering past, Duff held on.

Her elbow jabbed backward, slamming into his ribs.

Duff grunted but maintained his hold. "I'm not going to hurt you."

She squirmed against him, her body slim and curvy beneath his hands.

"I'll let go of you if you promise not to scream," he said. "Do you?"

She stopped moving and nodded.

Duff released her and stepped backward.

The woman flung herself out of his reach and spun to face him.

Her wild-eyed stare registered with Duff. "Natalia?"

"Yes, it's me." She shot a glance toward the path leading to the resort. "Are you by yourself?"

"Yes." His gaze followed hers. "Why?"

"You weren't expecting anyone, were you?"

"No." He stepped up beside her.

Natalia was breathing hard, her fists clenched, her knees bent, ready for fight or flight.

"What's wrong?" Duff asked.

She stared into the shadows for a long moment before her body relaxed. "Nothing."

"Are you sure?"

When she stepped closer and stared back the way she'd come, Duff could tell she'd been frightened by something.

He eased an arm around her waist and pulled her against him, still staring at the path leading toward the resort. A strong desire to protect this woman washed over him and he found his free hand curling into a tight knot. "Did someone try to hurt you?"

"No." She leaned into him for a moment. "I think I got spooked by the shadows."

The warmth of her body next to his reminded him of why he was out walking along the beach. Natalia stirred him as no woman had in a while. Back-to-back missions left little time to develop relationships. Not that he had any intention of starting anything lasting. He was on vacation. A lighthearted fling might be the only thing he could engage in. Then she'd go back to her life and he'd go back to his. If she was even willing to consider a fling.

Natalia pushed away from his side and stood in front of him. "I'd better get back to my room."

As she turned to walk away Duff realized he didn't want her to go. He reached for her hand and snagged it. "Don't go."

She paused, her brows pulling together. "It's late."

He tipped his head toward the sky. "Going in now would waste all those stars."

She lifted her chin, her hair cascading down her back. "They are beautiful."

"Gorgeous," he agreed, although he wasn't looking at the sky. He was staring at the woman in front of him. "Walk with me."

She hesitated for a moment, her gaze slipping to the path from which she'd emerged. Natalia sighed. "Okay."

As they fell in step Duff maintained his grip on her hand. Before they'd gone too far, Natalia slipped out of her sandals and looped them over her fingers. Her toes dug into the sand. "Never could wear shoes in the sand."

"Me neither." He lifted a foot, exposing his own bare feet. "I feel more at home by the sea than anywhere else. What about you? Where's home for you?"

She hesitated and then answered, "Oxford."

"I had the opportunity to visit Oxford two years ago." Natalia stiffened beside him. "Did you?"

"I had a three-day layover while the plane we were

traveling on was being repaired. I managed to get a little R & R in. I spent an entire day in Oxford."

"That's great." Her fingers tightened in his.

"What's your favorite place in Oxford?"

She stepped toward the water until the waves gently caressed her toes. "I don't know. They're all pretty great."

Her vague answer set off a sharp nudge of suspicion. He changed tactics and fed her a lie to see if she'd fall for it. "I loved visiting the Angels Church and the Old Fort Museum."

"Yeah. The Angels Church is pretty," Natalia said.

Duff stood beside her, his feet sinking into the wet sand. She'd just fallen for his lie. He'd bet she'd never been to Oxford and that she wasn't even English. Too many times she'd slipped up and lost the English accent. Why would she put up a front with him?

That she was hiding something didn't make him want to ditch her. Instead it intrigued him even more. He played her game, letting her think he fell for her line of bull. If it was an act of self-preservation, she might open up to him if she learned to trust him.

With the urge to smile tugging at his lips, he went along with her charade. "My favorite is the Bridge of Sighs. There's something hopelessly romantic about the name and the beauty of the bridge itself." The bridge in Oxford was one of the most beautiful bridges he'd seen in all of his travels.

Natalia tilted her head to stare up at Duff, her lips twitching on the corners. "I would never have taken you for a romantic."

He puffed out his chest. "I can be as romantic as the next guy." Even though he killed terrorists as part of his job. Perhaps that was what kept him grounded. He noticed the beauty all around him, even in the worst places he'd been.

And the woman in front of him was truly beautiful with her blond hair and perfect figure. So what if she was lying? What did it matter? He wasn't planning on marrying her. As long as he kept a close eye on his wallet and made sure she wasn't hiding a knife beneath her skirt, he would be all right.

"I really should get back to the hotel," she said. When she tried to step away, the sand and sea kept her feet anchored. She lifted one foot, took a single step and the other foot refused to break the suction of the sand. Natalia—if that was her real name—teetered to one side and almost fell.

Duff swooped in and caught her in his arms, crushing her to his chest. "Are you all right?"

"Of course. I'm perfectly fine." She laid her hands on his chest but she didn't push against him. Her fingers curled into his shirt, her gaze focusing on the material bunched in her fist.

Duff might have been all right if Natalia had been old and ugly. But her beautiful body pressed against his length, her hips brushing his, was almost his undoing.

Her breathing grew shallow and rapid. "I really should go," she whispered with less conviction.

"You really should stay. The weatherman said there'd be a meteor shower in—" he glanced down at his watch "—twenty minutes."

"No, that wouldn't be advisable. I have a lot to do tomorrow. I need sleep." She didn't make a move to leave.

Raising his hand, Duff touched her cheek. "Stars weren't meant to be viewed alone."

"You have your buddies."

He chuckled. "Wouldn't be the same." Duff lowered his head. "There's something about a beautiful woman, a starlit night and the sound of the waves lapping the shore..."

"There's that poet again..." As Duff closed in on her lips, Natalia lifted her chin.

Their mouths joined, sending a spark of electricity shooting through Duff, the charge spreading throughout his body, culminating in his groin.

He deepened the kiss, sliding his tongue along the seam of her lips until they parted, opening to him.

Duff slid his hand down her neck, over her shoulder and around to the small of her back. At the same time his tongue slipped between her teeth and caressed hers in a long, slow glide.

The slender fingers lying against his chest climbed up around his neck and threaded through his hair. A soft moan rose up her throat, the breath it escaped on filling his mouth, warm and sexy.

When at last he lifted his head, he stared down into Natalia's eyes. "You bewitch me." He brushed a loose strand of hair behind her ears. "When can I see you again?"

She blinked, her glazed eyes seeming to focus at last. "I... I'm sorry...this shouldn't have happened. I have to go."

Though he wanted to take the kiss to the next level, he figured he would be pushing her too fast. If she didn't trust him enough to let him know who she really was, she certainly wouldn't trust him enough to make love to him.

He would make love to her before he left Cancun and she'd want to as badly as he wanted to.

She stepped away, but not before he captured her hand in his. "At least let me walk you back to the resort."

Her gaze darted toward the path she'd emerged on. "Okay."

With her hand in his, Duff walked her to the main hotel. Once they reached the entrance, she stopped. "You don't have to take me farther. I can manage on my own."

He tugged on her hand, pulling her up against him. "Will I see you tomorrow?"

Natalia shook her head. "I don't know."

"I'll find you."

"Really, I… We…shouldn't."

"You're probably right." He smiled and touched her cheek with the backs of his knuckles. "But I can't seem to resist." Duff bent and stole a kiss, intending a swift brushing of his lips. As soon as his mouth touched hers, he couldn't hold back. He circled his arms around her and crushed her to him, taking her mouth and her tongue in a soul-satisfying kiss.

When he let go, she swayed and touched her fingers to her lips. "Good night," she muttered and ran into the building.

NATALIE JABBED HER finger at the elevator button, her vision blurred, her limbs trembling and her lips tingling from Duff's kiss.

What was she thinking? She wasn't in Cancun to make love to a stranger. She was there to find her missing sister. If she hadn't run into Duff on the beach, whoever had been following her on the shadowy path might have caught up with her, revealing himself. Damn. It might have been her only chance to connect with one of the persons responsible for taking her sister.

The elevator door slid open and she stepped in. She punched the number for her floor and watched as the door slid closed.

A hand jutted through, stopping the door before it could close all the way.

Natalie's heart leaped into her throat. For a brief moment she thought it might be Duff, following her into the elevator for another of those earth-moving kisses.

A man—not Duff—stepped in.

Trained to observe, Natalie noted he was tall with dark hair, dark eyes and swarthy skin. He wore a white guayabera shirt, unbuttoned at the neck, with a gold chain around his throat. Dark trousers and polished black shoes completed his outfit. By the lay of the fabric of his trousers, she'd guess they were expensive and the thick gold ring on his right hand with the flashing white diamond marked him as a man with money.

She moved to the corner of the elevator.

The man started to touch a button on the elevator and dropped his hand without selecting a floor. The doors closed and the elevator rose.

A trickle of apprehension rippled through her. As far as Natalie was concerned, any man or woman at the resort could have had something to do with Melody's disappearance. Her gut instinct was to tackle the man and hold a gun to his head. But she couldn't do that to everyone she met. She'd be hauled off, thrown into a Mexican jail and left to rot.

Natalie knew that the sooner she found her sister the better. Time allowed the abductors the opportunity to move her to an undisclosed location or to sell her to the highest bidder, shipping her to who knew where.

On the edge, with every instinct telling her to slam the man against the elevator wall, Natalie clenched her fists and waited for the car to reach her floor.

The ping of the elevator bell announced their arrival. She was curious to see if the man got off the elevator or rode it up farther. Natalie stepped out and turned the opposite direction of her room, watching the elevator door in her peripheral vision.

The man's gaze remained on her as he leaned forward and punched a button. The doors slid closed and Natalie let go of the breath she'd been holding.

So he wasn't getting off at her floor or planning to attack her. It paid to be suspicious, but was she getting paranoid?

She stood for a moment in the hallway, watching the display above the closed elevator. The number changed from the eight to nine and paused.

What did that prove? Only that the man might have gotten off one floor above hers.

Shrugging, Natalie pulled her key card from her pocket and walked to her door.

The day had been long and she was tired. Her thoughts returned to her sister. Deep in her heart, Natalie knew her sister hadn't drowned or been eaten by a shark. She wouldn't give up until she either found Melody alive or… She gulped. Or she found her body.

STRIPPING OUT OF her clothes, Natalie stepped into the shower and let the water run over her face and hair. The warm liquid caressed her skin, trickling down her body, over her breasts and lower to the juncture of her thighs. If her sister wasn't in danger, if Natalie was really there on vacation, she'd have stayed longer on the beach, kissing Duff. She might even have spent the night making love to him. She wasn't a prude and she recognized chemistry when it hit her square in the chest. Or rather, when she hit him square in the chest.

Butterflies fluttered against the lining of her belly. Duff was a temptation she could ill afford.

Turning the warm water to cold, she forced back the desire stirring inside and concentrated on her next steps.

Natalie climbed into the luxurious bed and laid her head on the pillow, wondering where Melody was sleeping. With her sister missing, Natalie didn't expect to sleep at all. But once she closed her eyes, the exhaustion of worry dragged her into a deep, dream-filled sleep.

Throughout the night she suffered through nightmares of bad guys taking girls from their beds and herding them through the jungle. She also dreamed of Duff lying on the sand beside her, leaning up on one elbow to stare down at her. Then he was kissing her, nudging her legs apart with his knee. He lowered himself over her and thrust deep inside her.

Natalie woke with a start to the sound of her phone's alarm ringing in her ear. What she thought would be a sleepless night had passed and another day had begun.

She had to find Melody. She rose with renewed purpose, slipping into a bright pink bikini, sure to draw attention to her and her near-naked body. Hopefully the attention of whoever had targeted Melody. Setting herself up as bait seemed to be the only way she could lure Melody's captors out into the open.

A small group of young men and women gathered in

the hotel lobby, wearing swimsuits and carrying bags with towels and sunscreen.

A young woman with brown hair and brown eyes waved a clipboard above her head. "All those going on the Scuba Cancun dive excursion, if you've already checked in with me, please make your way to the bus outside. We leave in two minutes."

Natalie gave the woman her name.

"You're good to go. Find a seat on the bus."

With a quick glance around the lobby, Natalie hurried outside to the waiting bus. Once seated, she leaned forward, pretending to dig in her bag. She tapped the earbud in her ear. "Going silent as soon as we board the boat," she whispered.

"Roger," Lance responded. "Sure you don't want me out there as backup?"

"No. I can handle this."

"I have you on my GPS tracking screen. Be careful out there."

"Will do."

"Is this seat taken?" a deep, sexy voice asked.

Natalie jerked her head up and crashed into a strong, hard chin. "Oh!"

Duff Calloway clapped a hand to his jaw. "Sorry. I didn't mean to startle you."

"I'm the one who's sorry." She scooted over, allowing him to take the seat beside her. "I hope I didn't break anything. I've been known to be hardheaded."

Duff slid onto the seat, his thigh bumping against hers. "I've been hit harder in a barroom fight." He worked his jaw back and forth and then grinned. "I didn't expect to see you on this dive."

She shrugged. "Seemed like the thing to do in Cancun. My coworkers back home recommended the diving here."

"Have you dived before or is this your first time?"

"I have a couple of times," Natalie responded.

"Sounds like you and this guy have met before," Lance said softly into Natalie's ear. "If you want me to run a more thorough check on him, I can."

With one man in her ear and the other pressing against her leg, Natalie predicted this situation could get out of hand quickly. "So," she said. "What does Duff stand for?"

The man beside her smiled. "Dutton Calloway. Duff is the nickname my team calls me."

Lance chuckled in her ear. "I'll dig a little deeper into his background."

"Team?" Natalie turned toward him. "What kind of team?"

He glanced away. "Just the guys I work with."

Interesting. Natalie narrowed her eyes. "What kind of work do you and your team do?"

"We're kind of a search-and-rescue crew."

Natalie's eyes widened. "Like in the case of natural disasters?"

He shrugged. "Something like that."

"I bet it can be dangerous."

"You have no idea."

The bus lurched forward on its way to the dock and the boat waiting to take them out to the dive location.

"What about you?" Duff started. "You mentioned your coworkers. What do you do for a living?"

She smiled and glanced out the window. "I freelance as a journalist."

"Interesting." He tapped a finger to his chin. "What do you write about?"

She grinned. "Travel, people and places."

"I imagine you've been to more exotic places than Cancun?"

She nodded. "On occasion."

"Do you do much diving off the coast of Britain?" he asked.

"Not so much. The water is cooler and pretty choppy. I prefer to dive in warmer climates."

"You are an intriguing woman." Duff said. "And here we are."

All too soon the bus pulled to a stop at the marina where they boarded the boat that would take them to the reefs.

"Everybody choose a dive buddy," the excursion leader announced. "And remember, this person will remain with you at all times. If anything goes wrong during the dive, your buddy is there to ensure you get out of the water safely."

Duff grabbed Natalie's hand. "Got mine!" he said out loud, raising Natalie's hand into the air.

"Some wingman," Sawyer groused and glanced around for a dive buddy.

Natalie leaned closer to Duff. "What if I didn't want to be your dive buddy?"

"But you do, don't you?" He winked. "I promise not to make any moves on you while we're under water."

Natalie laughed. "I'm betting you have moves under water as well on dry land."

He tilted his head. "Guilty. I like to think variety is the spice of life, and live accordingly."

"You're hopeless."

The captain guided the boat out of the slip and into open water. Natalie excused herself, claiming she needed to stow her bag. Once separated from Duff, she made her way around the boat, identifying the two dive masters, the first mate and the captain. All were Latino men under the age of thirty, except the captain, who appeared to be an American ex-patriot in his late forties. Nothing in their faces indicated they were involved in a human trafficking operation. Hell, what did a human trafficker look like, anyway? But that didn't take them off Natalie's suspect list. She'd keep a close eye on them.

Duff had joined his friends at the front of the craft, staring out to sea, talking and laughing.

The crew was too busy opening boxes of equipment and checking the tanks and regulators to answer questions. The best Natalie could do was to introduce herself, which forced them to supply their names. She'd repeat them so that Lance would hear them clearly over the roar of the engine.

Using her cell, she snapped pictures of the boat, the passengers and the crew under the pretext of being an excited tourist on a fun excursion. When she had the pictures she needed, she shot them to Lance back at the hotel. He'd run them through facial recognition scans. Maybe he'd find someone with a record for abducting women.

By the time she was satisfied with her covert observations, she ditched the earbud into her bag, joined the guests on the deck and found her dive buddy.

While the dive master instructed the less proficient members of the excursion, Natalie grabbed a buoyancy control device—BCD—and a regulator and tank, slipping the straps over her shoulder. Then she selected a mask, snorkel and fins and sat on a bench to slip her feet into the fins.

Duff had his equipment on and tested well before Natalie. He held his fins in his hands and stood beside the men she'd seen him with the night before.

"Hey, Duff." The man with the black hair and brown eyes backhanded Duff in the belly. "You gonna introduce us to your dive partner?"

"Why would I do that?" Duff stepped between him and Natalie. "You'll just try to convince her to trade."

"Got that right. She'd be trading up." The man stepped around Duff and held out his hand. "Name's Sawyer. And you are?"

Before Natalie could reply, another man as tall as Duff with brown hair and green eyes shoved Sawyer aside. "You are beautiful. I'm Ben Raines, but you can call me Montana."

Once again, before she could reach out to take the man's hand, yet another man with black hair and blue eyes stepped in front of Montana. "Quentin Lovett at your service. Let's say you and me ditch these morons and team up."

Natalie laughed, her gaze searching for and finding Duff's.

His brows were angled toward his nose as he pushed through the hulking men. "Natalia and I are dive buddies. I suggest you find one of your own."

Natalie smiled at the men. "You're very flattering and it's nice to meet you, but Duff's right—we're dive partners."

"Lucky dog." Quentin groused good-naturedly. "If

she'd met me first, she'd know the difference between bottom skimming and quality."

The boat slowed to a stop and Guillermo, the dive master, directed their attention to the safety briefing. Once they had all been checked, one of the crew members went in first. The remaining passengers could either roll or step off the platform at the rear of the boat.

Natalie waddled to the edge, shoved her regulator into her mouth and breathed in. Good so far.

Duff stepped up beside her, took her hand and nodded. "On three." He put his regulator in his mouth, then raised one finger at time.

Natalie counted. "One...two...three."

Together they stepped off the platform and sank into the crystal-clear water.

The initial shock of breathing under water passed quickly and she settled into an easy breathing rhythm.

Duff fluttered his fins, pushing away from the boat.

Natalie followed to allow the others the space to enter without hitting them.

The dive master was the last into the water. He swam to the front of the group and led the pairs of divers, pointing out a sea turtle or an array of different kinds of coral clinging to rocks and crevices. The group stretched out along a rocky outcropping, following the master, moving slowly and scattering wide to see everything the ocean floor had to offer in the way of sea flora and fauna.

Natalie let the others pass her, stopping to admire a blue starfish clinging to the rocky ocean floor.

Duff swam ahead of her, glancing back every once in a while, giving her the hand signal for everything is okay. She nodded and returned the same.

The rest of the group had disappeared around the side

of an underwater cliff. Natalie eased along the rocky outcropping, admiring the colorful coral while searching for places a person could hide, jump out, drag a woman into a cave or crevice and effectively remove her without being seen by other divers or the crew in the boat above.

She passed a small cave, stopped and turned around. Was it just a cave or did it go all the way through the rocks to an opening on the other side? Natalie looked over her shoulder for Duff.

She could see the tips of his fins as he rounded the corner of the outcropping, swimming away from her.

If the cave was a tunnel, this would be a good place to snatch a woman and pull her away from the others, especially if she was lagging behind her partner.

Natalie's pulse quickened and she fluttered her fins, sending her toward the cave. She hadn't gone two feet into it before she could see it was a dead end.

A moray eel poked his head out of a hole, seeming to glare at her.

She swam out of his home and caught up with Duff around the outcropping only to find another shallow cave. After exploring it and finding it to be another dead end with a resident octopus, she began to despair. Where along this tour had her sister disappeared?

Ahead, the group passed through a narrow gap between two stony projections. By the time Duff and Natalie caught up, they'd move through what appeared to be a labyrinth of huge rocks and boulders. If the person in the rear didn't stay right with the ones in front, he could easily lose his way.

Natalie's gut clenched. This could be it. Her sister could have gotten lost in the maze of rocks on the ocean floor. Perhaps the authorities were correct in assuming she had drowned. She could have gone into a cave, gotten caught in the rocks and couldn't get out. If her partner had lost track of her, she wouldn't have known where to look.

Her heart sinking, Natalie didn't see the cave to her right until something snagged her regulator hose and yanked hard. The regulator popped out of her mouth, leaving her without the air she needed to breathe.

Panic threatened to set in. Natalie forced herself to be calm and reached over her shoulder, sweeping her arm to catch the hose and bring the regulator back to her mouth. Only the hose wasn't within reach. An arm slipped around her and unbuckled the straps holding her BCD and tank and yanked them from her shoulders.

That panic she'd held at bay set in.

Chapter Five

Duff stayed close to Natalia, keeping her in his peripheral vision up until that last huge boulder. When she didn't follow right behind him, he waited a second, then turned and retraced his path looking for her.

At first he didn't see any sign of Natalia or her equipment. Had she gotten lost in the maze in such a short amount of time? He'd seen her maybe fifteen seconds ago. She couldn't have gotten too far. Staying close to the last place he'd seen her, he checked behind one rock after another. Then he saw it lying half-buried in the sand. A single black fin.

His heart raced and he spun, searching all directions. A group of fish shot out of a large crevice in the rocks and skimmed past him as if hurrying away from a predator.

Surely, Natalia hadn't gone into the narrow gap between the rocks without her partner. She or her apparatus could get hung up. Without the assistance of a dive buddy, she could be stuck there until found or—

Duff kicked hard, sending his body flying through the water toward the crevice. At the entrance he pulled a knife from a scabbard on his leg, carved an X into the rock and then swam through. Once past the entrance, the gaps between the rocks widened, making it easier to maneuver.

He slashed an X on the rocks as he passed, marking his way back.

Something smooth and shiny caught his attention. As he neared, he could make out the metal around a regulator gauge and the bulk of a BCD and tank resting on the ocean floor.

He looked up, hoping to see Natalia at the surface, thirty feet above. She wasn't there. His heart racing, Duff hurried through the rocks. Where the hell was she?

Movement ahead made him kick harder. As he neared a large boulder, he saw fins kicking and flailing, the smooth, pale legs attached could be none other than Natalia's.

When he was close enough he could see that a man had hold of her around the neck and was feeding her a regulator. He had her arms wrapped in what appeared to be weight belts, her wrists secured behind her.

Anger spiked, sending a surge of adrenaline through Duff. He raced for the attacker, holding his knife in front of him. He'd kill the bastard if he hurt one hair on Natalia's head.

Natalia's attacker must have seen Duff. He shoved Natalia toward him and kicked away from them.

Duff wanted to chase after the man, but Natalia was without air and, carrying the weight of the belts, wouldn't be able to surface easily. Duff couldn't abandon her, nor did he want to.

She struggled, kicking her feet, trying to turn her body toward the surface. Without her arms to balance, she spun in a circle, sinking toward the ocean floor.

Duff grabbed her from behind and held her against

him. She fought, twisting her body in a frantic attempt to get free.

Finally, Duff spun her to face him, pulled the regulator from his mouth and shoved it toward hers.

She stopped struggling and opened her mouth, accepted the regulator, blew out the water and sucked in a deep breath.

Duff turned her, slipped his knife between her wrists and sliced through the heavy weaving of the weight belt material, taking several passes before he freed her hands.

When she was free, she grabbed hold of his BCD and anchored herself with him. Natalia took another deep breath and handed the regulator to him.

They buddy-breathed for a couple more minutes until she was once again calm.

Duff pointed to her apparatus and they swam together toward the pile of equipment resting on the sandy bottom. Together, they managed to get her back into her gear, tested the regulator and checked the gauges.

When he was certain she was okay, he pointed back the way they'd come, indicating she should go first.

Natalia swam ahead, looking back every few seconds as if she was afraid he'd disappear.

Following the marks on the rocks, he got her back through the maze. Sawyer, Quentin and Montana were swimming in a circle, looking for him. Soon the dive master and the rest of the group filled the narrow clearing.

Guillermo motioned for all to follow and they fell into a tighter string, moving through the rocks and out into the open. A shadow floated over them, indicating the location of the boat. One by one, they surfaced and waited their turn to climb aboard the boat.

Duff surfaced a second before Natalia.

When she came up, she spit her regulator out of her mouth and gulped in fresh air. She glared across at him. "Why the hell did you do that?"

He frowned. "What do you mean? I saved your life."

"I wasn't dying."

"If that man had his way, he'd have killed you."

"What's going on?" Sawyer swam up to them. "Why were you two so far back?"

"Someone attacked Natalia." Duff shook his head. "And for some insane reason, she didn't want to be rescued." He glared back at her. "Maybe you can explain."

"I didn't want you to rescue me. He was keeping me alive. I wanted him to *take* me."

"Are you out of your mind?" Duff bellowed.

"Shh." Natalie pressed a finger to her lips and glanced around. "I don't want everyone under the sun hearing you."

"What's wrong?" Montana swam up to them.

"Yeah." Quentin joined them, treading water. "What's with the pissing contest? They're waiting for us to get in the boat."

Natalia locked gazes with Duff. "Please, just keep this to yourself."

"Keep what?" Quentin asked.

Montana frowned. "Do you mind giving us a clue?"

Duff held up a hand. "All right. We'll save the question-and-answer session for later. After we get to shore."

"Okay." Natalia chewed her lip. "How do I know I can trust you and your friends?"

His lips twitched. "You don't."

"Hey." Montana splashed water at Duff. "We're the good guys."

Without releasing the lock on their gazes, Duff responded, "Just hold your thoughts until we get back."

Sawyer nodded. "You got it, Duff." He turned and headed toward the dive boat, followed by Montana and Quentin.

"When we get back—"

"I know. I owe you an explanation. It'll have to wait until we're on land." Natalia kicked her feet, aiming for the boat.

Duff fluttered his fins, sending him cleaving through the water, catching up to her quickly. While she climbed out of the water, he held her fins. She reached for them and took his, too.

Once on the boat, Duff helped Natalia out of her apparatus and set it aside. He wanted to get to the bottom of whatever craziness she had in mind.

The ride back stretched for what seemed like an hour when in fact it was fewer than thirty minutes. The passengers compared experiences of what they'd seen or encountered on the reef tour. All except Natalia.

She stood alone at the rear of the boat, staring back at where they'd been retrieved. She'd slipped a cotton sundress over her swimsuit, but the breeze from the moving craft plastered it against her curves, outlining her incredible form beneath. Her brows pinched in the middle, a faraway, melancholy look made her appear even more distant. She ignored the lively chatter of the other divers, her back to them, cut off from the normal excitement of having been on some of the most incredible reefs off the coast of Mexico.

After a few minutes the rest of the passengers grew quiet, their sunburned faces staring out over the water.

No matter how hard Duff tried, he couldn't make sense of Natalia's desire to be captured by a stranger and her refusal to bring the attack to the attention of the crew.

Duff paced the length of the boat until they pulled up to the dock and off-loaded passengers. He refused to let Natalia get away without cluing him in on her unbelievable statement.

NATALIE SPENT THE remainder of the excursion staring out at the ocean, wondering if what had almost happened to her was the exact scenario Melody had been subjected to. If so, she would have been just as helpless to free herself from her captor. Thirty feet beneath the surface, without air, she would have been forced to rely on her captor's regulator until they surfaced. But where?

Her gaze took in the shoreline, memorizing every detail she could. As soon as she could, she'd rent a boat and return. Perhaps she'd find the spot the attackers had been waiting. Maybe finding the location would shed light on who they were and ultimately lead her to her sister.

One thing the attack had proved was that her gut had been right. Melody was alive. She hadn't been swept away by a current and lost at sea. Someone had taken her, most likely from the same location.

As soon as the boat docked, Natalie was the first passenger off. She hurried down the wooden boardwalk, searching for a boat to rent. Where the excursion boats were moored, the vessels were large, designed to take numerous passengers to parasail, fish or dive. Farther along the marina area, Natalie spotted individual boats, smaller than the rest. She turned to the left and headed for them.

"Hey." A hand clamped on her arm. "Not so fast."

She stared down at the hand on her arm and then up into Duff's face. "Let go of me."

His three friends stood behind him, all muscular, some tattooed, each ready to champion their friend's cause.

Duff's jaw tightened. "You owe us an explanation."

"I told you. I didn't want your help."

"Woman, you're not making sense." Duff gripped both of her arms, frowning down at her, his brow furrowed. "A man tries to abduct you and, when I try to help, you tell me to butt out. I don't get it. Why would you want to be abducted?"

She glanced around, noting one of the deckhands from their dive boat holding a cell phone to his ear, staring at her.

Natalie grabbed Duff's arm and dragged him away from the boat and the prying eyes. His friends followed.

Once she had him out of earshot, she leaned close. "I wanted him to take me to where he hides the women."

Duff shook his head. "What women?"

With a sigh, she stared into his eyes and dropped any hint of an English accent. "The women who've disappeared from this area over the past few days. One of them was my younger sister. Melody."

Duff's eyes flared, his lips pressing into a thin line. "When?"

"Two days ago. She disappeared on the same dive boat. I'm betting in the same manner in which I would have disappeared if you hadn't been so heroic and saved me." She squared her shoulders. "Now, if you'll let me by, I need to rent a boat."

Duff shook his head, his body blocking her way. "Why are you renting a boat?"

"I have to go back to see if I can find where my attacker surfaced."

Again the big man shook his head. "You can't. We were among huge rocks that protruded above the surface. A boat would be smashed against those rocks."

"If they got in there, I can get in there," she returned.

"You're not going alone." Duff glanced over his shoulder at his buddies. "Right?"

"We're with you," Sawyer said.

"Whatever it is you have in mind," Quentin agreed. Montana nodded.

"I can't go boating with four big guys. I came here hoping to put myself up as a target for whoever is abducting women. If I'm seen with four hulking men, they'll look for easier prey." Natalie snorted. "Then again, after Duff rescued me on the dive, my gig might be up anyway."

Duff chuckled. "And here I thought I was helping. You really think we're hulking?"

Natalia rolled her eyes. "That's all you got out of what I just told you?"

He held out his hand. "Let me make it up to you. We'll go out on a boat to see if we can find the pickup point." He gave his friends a look. "Just the two of us."

"Hey." Sawyer frowned. "I was almost beginning to think this vacation was getting interesting."

"You three can split up and follow the crew members of the boat." Duff gave them a stern look. "And don't make it obvious. And, for the love of Mike, don't beat the crap out of one of them for the information."

Quentin shook his head. "You're taking the fun out of it, dude."

Duff grabbed her hand. "Come on, we'll make this look like a date. Just me and you."

Natalie wasn't sure she liked the idea of being alone with the man. "How do I know you're not involved in this abduction operation?"

Sawyer barked out a laugh. "Duff doesn't need to abduct women, they usually come to him willingly."

Quentin added, "In droves."

Duff shrugged. "We weren't here two days ago. You can check our flight records. We arrived yesterday."

"And before that?" she asked.

He shook his head. "Sorry, can't divulge that information. We were conducting black ops."

Natalie's belly tightened. "What do you mean? Secret operations?"

Sawyer leaned close. "We're Navy SEALs. Our missions are classified." He winked.

Duff shoved him away from Natalie. "You guys better go. Some of the crew members are leaving the boat now."

Sawyer, Quentin and Montana spun and hurried away.

Natalie glanced up at Duff. "And I'm supposed to feel safe with you just because you say you're a Navy SEAL?" She tilted her head to the side, studying him. "You could be feeding me a line."

"Take it or leave it." He held out his hand. "Right now we need to secure a boat and get back out to where we were diving. Something else that might be of interest to you, but might mean nothing, is that I saw a fin in the maze of rocks. I thought it was yours, but you managed to come back with both of yours."

Natalie's breath caught and held for a moment then she released it. "It could have been Melody's." She took his hand. "Let's go."

Farther along the marina they found a man willing to let them rent his small fishing boat for a crazy amount. Natalie didn't care. Melody was in danger. The sooner they found her the better.

Duff insisted on paying, then handed her into the boat. "Wear your life jacket," he ordered.

Natalie bristled but didn't argue. She buckled herself into the jacket and settled back in her seat.

The boat owner untied the mooring line and waved as Duff shifted the throttle forward and they eased out of the marina. As soon as the craft cleared the no-wake zone, Duff shoved the throttle forward and they sped out into the open water, bouncing over the waves toward the island reefs and the area where they'd been scuba diving.

Duff seemed competent and confident at the helm. Natalie was a trained agent, but she'd never had the opportunity to handle a boat in a lake, much less on the open ocean where the stretch of water was so vast a person could easily get lost.

"Where did you learn to handle a boat?" she asked.

"I grew up on a ranch." His lips twitched.

She shook her head. "Seriously. What did you ranch? Fish?"

He glanced in her direction, a twinkle in his eyes. "I grew up on a ranch near Port Aransas, Texas. When we weren't taking care of cattle, we were fishing. My dad taught us how to ride horses and fish before we were three years old. Mom cringed and let him. With four boys to look out for, she couldn't tell him no."

"No sisters?"

Duff shook his head. "No. Mom was outnumbered from the get-go."

"Why didn't you stay and ranch?"

"My older brother followed in my father's footsteps. My younger brothers and I all joined the military."

"All Navy SEALs?" Natalie asked.

"No. My brother Jack joined the army and went into the Special Forces. Gabe joined the air force and flies F-16s."

"So, you're really a Navy SEAL?" Natalie stared at his arms and the tattoos laced across his shoulders and back.

"I am."

"And you're on vacation, not some operation you can't tell me about or you'd have to kill me?"

He grinned. "We're really on vacation."

"Lucky you to run into me." She stared ahead.

"And the English accent?" Duff prompted.

"Completely fake."

"The name?"

"Close. Instead of Natalia, I'm just plain Natalie."

Duff's lips quirked on the corners and he stared across at her, as if assessing her. "I think it fits you better."

His smile warmed her insides. "I thought it would throw off the abductors long enough to think I'd make a good target."

Duff frowned. "Why would you set yourself up as a target? What makes you think you'd have a better chance of escaping once they had you?"

She didn't answer right away. Still unsure whether to trust him, Natalie didn't want to reveal she had a GPS tracking device embedded beneath her skin. It would lead to a lot more questions and answers she wasn't ready to give.

She glanced at the island shoreline, recognizing the shape and features. "We're getting close."

The coastline grew unfriendly and rockier.

"There." Natalie pointed to the rock formations jutting out of the water.

"Looks like the location." Duff slowed the boat and made a wide sweep around the rocky shoreline. Waves lapped at the jagged pillars, making it very dangerous for a small boat to weave between them. Anyone who tried would smash against the rocks and sink.

"Look." Duff pointed toward an opening nearer the shore protected from the waves by a long barrier of boulders. He eased the little fishing boat into the opening to find a small lagoon on the other side leading into a hidden cave.

Natalie stood, holding on to the windshield. "Damn. It's a perfect location for hiding prisoners."

"Surely the locals know about it."

"That makes me wonder why the authorities hadn't found it when they were searching for my sister." Her eyes narrowed. "Unless the investigator was in on this whole abduction deal from the start."

Natalie glanced around the sandy shore on the edges leading into the cave. She didn't see any footprints, but the tide had risen, sweeping across the sand in gentle waves.

Duff pulled the throttle back to the idle position near the entrance to the cave. "We don't know what we'll find in the cave. Whoever attacked you could be in there."

"Then let's go in," Natalie said.

He shook his head. "What if they're armed?"

Natalie's lips pressed together. "I'll take my chances. I need answers. If we could get hold of at least one of the people involved, I'd be that much closer to finding my sister."

He touched her arm. "And if they shoot you before you get your answers, who will save your sister?"

Her fingers clenched into fists. "We won't know if they're even in there if we don't go in and find out."

Duff backed the boat away from cave entrance and shifted it into idle. Then he stepped away from the steering wheel. "It's yours."

She frowned. "What are you going to do?"

He winked. "I'm going for a swim."

"What?" Natalie stepped behind the steering wheel. "What if you don't come back out?"

"Give me fifteen minutes. If I'm not back by then, go to my friends and let them know what happened. Don't come in after me. Someone needs to stay with the boat."

"But—"

"I'll be all right." He slipped off the end of the boat, dropping silently into the water. He swam toward the cave entrance, his arms cutting through the water with smooth, even strokes.

Natalie held her breath, her heart pounding.

When Duff reached the cave entrance, he dived beneath the surface and disappeared.

Chapter Six

Duff swam beneath the surface until the water darkened, past the point where sunlight streamed through the cave entrance. He eased to the surface enough to bring his eyes and nose out of the water and stared around the small cave, waiting for his vision to adjust to the darkness.

Nothing moved and he couldn't see any boats tethered to the rocks. The cave was empty.

At the far end of it he found a rocky ledge large enough to hold several people. A railroad spike had been driven into it as a possible place to tie off a boat while a diver slipped away to perform nefarious tasks.

Duff pulled himself up onto the ledge where he found a discarded soda can and a few candy wrappers. They might be able to lift fingerprints if he could get the items back to the boat without destroying the prints. Lifting them carefully so as not to leave his own prints, he stuffed them into his pocket. Though, being in Mexico, if the perpetrator was Mexican, they probably didn't have fingerprint databases like the ones in the States. Still, any evidence might be of use.

He glanced around the rest of the cave. No other landing point existed, just the ledge. He scoured it for any other evidence and turned to leave when he noticed a small gold chain protruding from a rocky crevice. He hooked his finger through it and eased it out.

At the end of the chain was a gold pendant in the shape of a dove.

Duff slipped the necklace into his other pocket. After another quick look around, he swam back to the cave entrance.

When he emerged, Natalie eased the boat forward.

"I thought you'd never come back out."

When he stood beside her, he pulled the items from his pocket, laying the can and candy wrapper on a seat. "I'm hoping we can lift prints from these." He reached into his other pocket, dragged out the chain and held it up. "Do you recognize this?"

Her face blanched and her eyes swam with unshed tears. Natalie took the necklace from him, nodding. "I gave this necklace to Melody when our parents died. She never took it off."

"Maybe she left it as a sign."

Natalie slipped the chain over her head and settled it around her neck. "She's alive. We just have to find her."

Duff's heart squeezed at the ready tears filling Natalie's eyes. He pulled her into his arms and held her.

She rested her fingers against his chest, her body shaking. "She's the only family I have left."

"We'll find her," he said, smoothing his hand over her long, blond hair.

For an extended moment he stood in the gently rocking boat, Natalie held close in his arms.

When she straightened and pushed away from him, he brushed a strand of her hair behind her ear. "We'll find her."

"I hope so." She sniffed. "Before it's too late."

"I'll help in any way I can." Duff took over at the helm, easing the boat through the narrow channel and back into the open. As they cleared the watery field of rocks, Duff took in a deep breath and let it out. Though protected from the waves while navigating the secret entrance, there could have been underwater hazards he didn't know about. Having emerged unscathed was a huge relief.

He dragged in another breath, turned toward the mainland and shoved the throttle forward.

The roar of the engine masked any other sound. Something hit the windshield so hard and fast it left a round hole and cracks spreading out like a spider's web.

Damn, it was a bullet hole.

"Get down!" Duff yelled and ducked low in the boat, only raising his head high enough to see over the dash.

Natalie slipped out of her seat onto the floor of the boat and glanced to the rear. "We have a tail."

Another bullet shot through the glass right where Duff's head had been a moment before.

He swerved and shifted the throttle all the way down, running the engine wide-open.

"They're catching us," Natalie yelled over the sound of the engine.

Duff couldn't make the boat go any faster. The best he could do was to escape and evade being killed. He chanced a glance to the rear. As Natalie had said, their pursuer was quickly catching up to them in a newer, higher-speed vessel. They'd be on them in seconds.

Natalie crawled forward into the front of the boat.

Duff didn't know what she was doing but at least she was getting farther away from the approaching shooter.

She dug in one of the storage wells and pulled out an

anchor. Carrying the anchor, she worked her way toward him. "Let them catch up. I have an idea."

He had an inkling of what her plan might be, but it would be dangerous. Hell, it couldn't be any more dangerous than being on a slow boat, unarmed and pursued by a speedboat with men shooting at them.

When the other vessel had nearly caught up with them Duff pulled back hard on the throttle, bringing it to the neutral position. The fishing boat slowed immediately.

The other boat, so close behind them, swerved to miss hitting them. The shooter was too busy holding on to aim. They slid past, barely missing the fishing boat.

Natalie lunged to her feet, slung the anchor into the back of the other boat and ducked back down.

Duff shoved the throttle forward and turned sharply away from the speedboat.

Natalie had secured the anchor line to a cleat on the side of their fishing boat. When the line played out completely, it snapped tightly and yanked both boats hard.

The other driver was already turning toward them so quickly the boat tipped up on one side. The pull from the anchor dragged the speedboat over even farther, flipping it upside down.

Duff stopped immediately and backed up enough that Natalie was able to untie the line from the cleat.

Free of the other boat, Duff drove off.

"Wait!" Natalie yelled. "We should go rescue one of them. They'll know where Melody is."

"Or they'll have another boat full of shooters on their way. Or their weapons will fire fine wet. We need to get the hell out of here."

"We can't just leave them. They might be our only chance to interrogate."

Duff turned the boat around and slid up close to the capsized craft. One man floated facedown in the water, unmoving. Another cried out and swam toward their little fishing boat.

Already, Natalie was leaning toward the man as he came up along the starboard side.

"Take the helm," Duff commanded.

Natalie glanced up.

"I can get him on board quicker." Duff left the steering wheel and passed Natalie as she took his seat.

Duff reached for the hand of the survivor.

The man's fingers curled around his and Duff dragged him up the side of the boat. He almost had him over the lip when a shot rang out. The man jerked and his grip slackened.

"Get us out of here!" Duff shouted.

Natalie pushed the throttle wide-open and the little boat surged toward the capsized one.

Duff tightened his hold and dragged the man onto the boat as the craft slid to the side, nearly knocking into the doomed boat.

Flexing his arm to ease the strain of dragging a dead weight on board, Duff squatted next to the man and felt for a pulse.

Deadweight was correct. Their witness wouldn't be spilling any secrets.

Natalie glanced back. "Is he—?"

"He's dead," Duff confirmed.

"What should we do with him?"

"I don't feel like spending my vacation in a Mexican jail."

Once they were out of shooting range of the capsized vessel, Natalie slowed the fishing boat and brought it to a stop. She joined Duff, next to the body. "Should we dump him?"

Duff scratched his head. "That's my vote."

Natalie reached for her oversize purse and pulled out her cell phone. "Could you turn him over so that I can get a clear shot of his face?"

Duff did as requested. "Do you always take photos of dead men?"

"Only when I think it might help me find my sister." She snapped a few shots of his face, his profile and the tattoos on his arms. Then she texted someone.

"Did you just send those pictures to someone?"

She nodded without looking at him.

"You're not going to tell me who, are you?"

"If I did, I'd have to...you know..." She sliced a finger over her throat and glanced at him with a challenge in the lift of her brows.

Duff's mouth twisted into a wry grin. "I have a feeling you have as many secrets as I do. Do I want to know them?"

"Probably not."

"Fair enough...for now." He didn't like being in the dark with Natalie. "Promise me you'll clue me in if it means the difference between life and death."

"Deal."

Duff went through the man's pockets, searching for any form of identification. As he expected, he found none. He glanced around at the huge expanse of water surrounding them.

"All clear," Natalie said.

Duff hooked his hands beneath the man's arms and

Natalie grabbed his feet. Together they maneuvered him over the side of the boat. He landed with a small splash in the water and slowly sank.

"Let's get out of here." Duff assumed control of the helm and headed back to the shore.

When they turned in the boat, between Natalie and Duff, they gave the owner a hefty tip for the damage to his windshield and the loss of his anchor. He didn't ask questions, took the money and drove the boat out of the marina, looking right, left and over his shoulder as he left.

Natalie's gaze followed the little fishing boat out of the marina. "Do you think I'll ever find my sister?"

Duff slipped an arm around her waist. "We will," he promised.

Whether or not she'd be alive when they did find her was another question entirely.

NATALIE LET DUFF hold her hand all the way out to the main road where they flagged down a taxi and climbed in. The stress of the day weighed heavily on Natalie. As independent as she considered herself, she couldn't help the feeling of relief it was to have Duff at her side. She leaned against his muscular shoulder, absorbing some of his strength.

"What next?" he asked.

She tapped the evidence they'd wrapped in a plastic bag. "I'll get these to someone who can lift prints. But I'm worried about my sister's friends. If these guys are getting brave enough to go after me two days after nabbing my sister, who's to say they won't take one of her friends?"

"Were those the young ladies you were partying with last night?"

Natalie nodded. "Two left to go home, but the others are here for a few more days. They couldn't get their flights changed."

"Then we stick with them."

"We?"

"Okay, you. With the Navy SEALs as backup. We can hang back, but be there if you need us."

"I can't follow all of them."

"No. If one strays from the pack while you're not watching, one of us can follow and make sure they're okay."

"My sister and her friends were supposed to go to Chichén Itzá tomorrow. I think her friends were planning to cancel after losing Melody."

"Your point?"

"One of the missing women disappeared on a hike around the ruins." Natalie caught his gaze. "I could take my sister's reservation and see what happens."

"Please tell me you're not going to put yourself out there as bait again. They might think you're too much trouble and shoot you instead, since you got away twice."

She tapped a finger to her chin, thinking. "You could be right."

"And if your sister's friends decide to go on the excursion with you, they could end up as collateral damage."

"What if they decide to go anyway?"

"Then you have to go. And the SEALs will be there, as well. Only we'll follow in a rental car instead of taking the guided tour."

She stared across at him, her eyes narrowing. "Why are you so eager to help?"

"It's the right thing to do." He reached for her hand and curled his big fingers around hers. "And I like the strong, sassy type."

Again her insides warmed at his compliment and she curled her fingers around his, glad she didn't have to do this alone.

Having Lance follow her with the GPS tracking device gave her a certain sense of security. Having a Navy SEAL as her physical backup was even better. She wasn't sure she'd have made it away from the cave island alive had she gone there alone.

The taxi driver dropped them off at the entrance to the resort.

"We shouldn't be seen together any more than necessary," Natalie said.

"Why not? We've shared a breathing apparatus, a fishing boat and a taxi. That makes us practically a thing." He winked.

"Still. If there's a chance of me being taken rather than one of the other girls, I'd rather it was me."

Duff touched her cheek. "Again, they might not take you. Since we returned to the cave and those thugs fired at us, I'd say there is a strong possibility they'd shoot you rather than take you as a hostage."

"How else am I supposed to find where they hid my sister? I can almost bet they won't tell us if we ask."

"Then we have to find a way to follow them to where they are hiding your sister and the other girls."

Natalie cupped her hand over his and leaned her cheek into his palm. "The longer she's missing—"

"We'll find her." Duff tipped her chin upward and lowered his lips to hers. "I promise."

When his lips met hers, Natalie forgot what she'd

been about to say, the plastic bag she'd been carrying slipped from her hand. Electric shocks emanated from where their mouths connected and spread throughout her entire body.

She should have pushed away and run inside to the sanctuary of her room. But she couldn't. Instead she leaned up on her toes and deepened the kiss, opening her mouth to him.

His tongue swept in, claiming hers, caressing in a long, slow, slide. Duff slid his hand across her cheek, down the column of her throat and lower to the small of her back where he applied enough pressure to press her against his naked chest and snug her hips up against his. The hard evidence of his desire nudged her belly. An answering fire curled low inside her, making her ache in ways she hadn't in a very long time. Her fingers pressed into the hard plains of his muscles and she could smell the sun and salt from the ocean.

He tempted her sorely and she would have followed him to his room in a heartbeat if her sister's life wasn't hanging in the balance.

When at last he lifted his head, she dragged in a deep breath, filling her lungs. "I should go find the other girls."

"I'll see you tonight at the cabana bar?"

"If Melody's friends go there."

He nodded. "I'll find you."

Reluctantly she lifted her fingers from his chest. "If your friends discover anything..."

"I'll let you know whatever they found as soon as I can."

She took a step away and forced her hands to fall to her sides. "Thank you for saving my life twice today," she whispered. Natalie turned, scooped up the plastic bag and walked into the building, afraid if she looked back, she wouldn't go without Duff.

The man was growing on her. He had a way of being in the right place at the right time. From rescuing a drowning woman to saving her not once but twice. Her luck was bound to run out soon. She hoped she found Melody before that happened.

Natalie didn't go straight to her room. Instead she wound her way through the lobby, wandered into a lounge, bought a fruity drink and headed outside. In her roundabout way, she found her way to the bungalow where Lance was set up.

After a quick glance around she knocked on the door.

It opened before she could knock more than once.

Lance grabbed her arm, dragged her in and shut the door behind her. "What the hell happened after you got on board the boat? And how did you end up with a dead guy on a scuba excursion?"

"Sorry. It's been a helluva day." She handed him the drink.

He pushed it back at her. "You look like you need it more than I do." He backed up, propping his hip on the sofa. "I got nothing on the deckhands from the boat, but the dead guy is a thug who works for a man named Carmello Devita, a well-known drug runner who likes to dabble in other dangerous and lucrative pursuits."

"Like human trafficking?"

"Like hostage ransoming."

"Why would he take Melody? She has no family other than me and I'm a long way from being rich. And the other girls who were taken weren't from rich families."

"Maybe he's diversifying into human trafficking." Lance flung out his hand. "Either way, your dead man is a known gun-for-hire working for Devita."

"Great. At least we have a starting point. Where can I find Devita?"

"That's the sixty-four-million-dollar question. The DEA has been searching for him over a year and they have no leads."

Natalie tilted her head. "And you know this how?"

"Royce is the man with the contacts."

"So what you're telling me is that we're no closer than when we got here?" Her shoulders slumped.

"I didn't say that." Lance slipped into his chair in front of the computer screen. "At least you eliminated one of his gunmen."

"We didn't eliminate him. One of his men did."

"We?"

Natalie sighed. "Duff and I."

Lance's lips curled upward. "Good news is that I did a search for him in the criminal databases and didn't find a match."

"Because he's not a criminal. Turns out my dive buddy is a Navy SEAL." She pointed to his screen. "Look up Dutton Calloway, U.S. Navy, to verify."

Lance's fingers flew over the keyboard. A minute later a screen popped up with a picture of Duff.

Natalie's chest tightened and her lips tingled. "That's him."

"Sweet," Lance said. "What's he doing here?"

Natalie filled him in on what had happened during the dive and the boat trip back to the dive location.

"You trust him?" Lance asked.

"He's saved me twice. How could I not trust him?"

"It's nice to know you have someone in the field covering your six."

"I suppose. Only I don't want anyone else to be collateral damage while I'm searching for Melody."

"Count your blessings, woman. If I weren't tethered to this computer, I'd be with you. If he offered to help, take him up on it."

Chapter Seven

Duff knocked on Sawyer's door. A moment later it opened.

Sawyer held it for him. "What did you find?"

"A cave where the attacker hid his boat and a necklace belonging to Natalie's sister. Then we were shot at, almost run over by another boat, capsized it and then hauled a man on board who was promptly shot and killed before we could question him."

Sawyer grinned and clapped him on the back. "All in a day's work." Then his smile disappeared and he grew serious. "You weren't kidding, were you?"

Duff's jaw clenched. "I wish I were."

"Wow. Pretty impressive," Quentin said. "But did you have to go and shoot the guy? We could have interrogated him, maybe gotten some useful intel from him before you killed him."

"I didn't shoot him," Duff said. "One of his own guys got him when he saw me pulling the man into our boat."

Sawyer whistled. "They didn't want him spilling the beans."

Duff nodded. "What did you learn?"

Sawyer shook his head. "Not much."

Montana sat on a couch, his long limbs stretched out

in front of him. "We followed the men from the boat and got nothing. My guy went home for lunch with his wife and five kids."

"Mine ended up in a bar," Quentin said. "He drank three Coronas and returned to the boat for the afternoon excursion."

"The captain stayed on the boat," Sawyer finished. "I went back to the booking desk here at the hotel, thinking maybe the booking agent was feeding the attackers information about the women going on the excursion. The agent had clocked out for lunch. She'll be back later this afternoon."

"So what the hell are we doing?" Quentin asked. "I thought we were here on vacation, not on a mission."

Duff shoved a hand through his hair and paced across the short length of the bungalow Sawyer had rented for his stay in Cancun. Each of the men had rented one away from the main resort hotel, preferring the isolation and the closeness to the beach. They'd secured rooms to themselves in case they did manage a little romance while there.

"I don't know much more than you. Natalie's sister disappeared two days ago on a dive trip from the same boat we went out on today. You know the rest from what happened."

"That wasn't my question." Quentin pushed to his feet. "Why are you getting involved?"

Duff stared at Quentin. "If I don't, she'll do it on her own. You heard her. She actually wanted to be captured, hoping her attacker would take her to her sister."

Sawyer whistled. "Yeah. That's insane."

"All the more reason you should step back and look

at this logically." Quentin planted himself in front of Duff, forcing him to stop pacing.

"And what?" Duff's fists clenched. "Leave her to be captured by whoever took her sister and two other women?" He shoved Quentin's chest. "Is that what you would do? Leave a woman defenseless? It would be one thing if I didn't know any better, but I do. I can't let Natalie waltz into enemy territory alone."

"Can't she take it to the authorities?" Montana suggested.

Duff snorted. "She got no help from them. You know the Mexican government isn't necessarily in control. The drug cartels have been calling the shots for so long, nobody has faith in the authorities anymore."

"We're only here for two weeks. What if you don't find the sister in that time?" Sawyer asked.

Duff crossed his arms over his chest. "All the more reason to find her and get back to that relaxing vacation we've earned. Anyone have connections in the DEA? Maybe we can get them involved."

Sawyer's jaw tightened. "I might know someone."

"Call." Duff waved a hand in his direction. "The sooner we have someone working it, the better chance we have of finding those women."

Sawyer pulled his cell phone from his pocket and stepped out of the bungalow to make his call. He was back inside a minute, his face ruddy-red and his nostrils flaring. "Sorry. My source was less than helpful."

Duff cursed beneath his breath. "Look. I'm not asking any of you to get involved in this. I'll do this on my own. You guys stay and enjoy your vacation." Duff headed for the door.

Sawyer stepped in his way. "I'm in. Just tell me what I can do to help."

"I'm in." Montana shoved to his feet and dug his hands into his pockets. "A man can only take so much sand and sea before he gets bored."

Quentin stared from one man to the next and finally shrugged. "I'm in. I could use a little excitement myself. Can't have Duff here dodging *all* the bullets."

Duff smiled at his teammates. "Thanks."

"So what's next on the agenda?" Sawyer asked.

"We go to dinner and show up at the cabana bar tonight to watch for anything strange. Natalie thinks her sister's friends might be targeted since they didn't get her."

Quentin clapped his hands. "You said the magic word. Bar. I'm there."

Montana rubbed his flat belly. "I'm for a steak and seafood, then the bar."

Duff glanced toward the door. A smart man would walk away from Natalie and let her handle her investigation on her own. But since when was he smart? He'd joined the Navy SEALs, a surefire way to end up in a body bag. Besides, his father had taught him better than that. You don't back away from a difficult situation. You meet it head-on. "I'm going for a walk, then a shower. I'll see you all in an hour for dinner. Save a place at the table for me."

Sawyer stepped out the door with Duff. "Is that it?"

"Is what it?"

"You feel like helping a stranger because it's the right thing to do?"

"Yeah. So?"

Sawyer's lips quirked. "You sure it doesn't have anything to do with the fact she's a knockout in a pink bikini?"

Duff's cheeks burned. "No, it doesn't."

Sawyer's brows climbed up his forehead.

With a sigh, Duff nodded. "Okay, maybe a little."

"She's hot."

"And smart, and not afraid of much," Duff added.

"Careful, old man. You came for fun in the sun and a fling. If you aren't watching, you'll fall for this woman and complicate the hell out of your life."

"I know." Duff sighed. "And we don't need complications."

"Not in our line of work."

Duff rocked back on his heels. "Sawyer, you ever think of doing something else besides being a SEAL?"

Sawyer's mouth tightened. "Haven't really thought about it."

Glancing away, Duff stared through the palm trees, catching glimpses of the ocean. "Do you ever want to settle down and raise a family?"

Sawyer snorted. "My family left a bitter taste in my mouth. I can't imagine me and a family being a good idea."

"You're great with your brothers in arms. Why don't you think you'd be a good father or husband?"

"My father isn't like yours. He didn't teach me to fish or ride a horse. Hell, he was never around long enough to teach me to walk. When he was, it was always to tell me everything I was doing wrong in my life." Sawyer shook his head. "If I'm anything like my father, I don't want to put that burden on any kid."

"But you're not like him. You get along with everyone. Every man on the team would take a bullet for you."

"And I would take a bullet for them. Even Quentin." Sawyer smiled. "All of you are my real family. I don't know what I'd do without you."

"You need to start thinking about a life after the Navy. We won't stay young forever, and this job is hard on a body and soul."

Sawyer stared into the distance, then shook as if to pull himself out of his thoughts. "I think you're deflecting the real issue. What's up between you and Natalia?"

"Her real name is Natalie. And nothing. I just want to help."

"Okay. I'll take it at face value. If you need to talk about it in the future, you know where my bungalow is." Sawyer patted Duff on his back. "Go for your walk. Maybe you'll run into your pretty damsel in distress."

Duff left Sawyer and headed for the beach, away from the hotel and away from Natalie. Were his friends right? Was he getting in over his head with something he had no business getting into? Or was he getting in over his head with a female who could easily derail him with a flash of her pretty blue eyes?

Whatever it was, he couldn't leave Natalie to fend for herself against forces much more powerful than one lone woman. The look on her face when he'd handed her Melody's necklace had sealed that deal. Melody was her sister. She'd do anything to get her back.

Duff loved his biological brothers as well as his brothers in arms. He'd do as much or more for them as Natalie would do for her sister.

NATALIE LEFT LANCE'S BUNGALOW, careful to check for anyone lurking in the shadows. She hurried back to her room, stripped out of her suit and wrap and stored her sister's necklace in her suitcase. Then she showered and changed into a soft, figure-hugging, short dress and strappy, spike-heeled sandals. After one last glance in the mirror, she went in search of Melody's remaining friends.

A knock on the door to the room a few doors down yielded Kylie, wearing her pajamas, her face lacking any makeup and her hair still crinkled from lying in bed. "Oh, Natalia, I didn't expect you."

"Did Jodie and Lisa leave this morning?" Natalie almost forgot to layer the English accent. Since she'd revealed her charade to Duff, she hadn't felt it necessary to continue. But with her sister's friends, she couldn't really let it drop yet. Not if they were being watched by potential kidnappers.

Kylie turned and padded barefoot back to the bed where she sat and pulled a pillow up to her chest in a hug. "I miss them already."

"They were your roommates?"

"And Melody." She gave Natalie a weak smile. "I'm beginning to think I'm the jinx."

Natalie sat beside her and put an arm around the young woman's shoulders. "You most certainly are not. You could not have caused this situation to happen." She tightened her hold on the girl. "When are you due to fly out?"

"Not until the day after tomorrow with the rest of the group."

"Then you have to do something to cheer yourself up."

"I wish there was something I could do to find Melody. I don't feel right going home without her." She buried her face in her hands and sobbed.

Natalie held her just as she'd held Melody when their parents had died. A lump knotted in her throat and she fought to hold back the ready tears when she thought of the horrible things that could be happening to her baby sister.

When Kylie had cried herself out, Natalie hugged her once more and gripped her shoulders, forcing the girl to look at her. "You aren't doing anyone any good holing up in your room. Your friend Melody wouldn't want you to get depressed and mope. You have to get out and at least pretend you're having a good time."

"I can't. All three of my friends are gone."

"Where is the rest of your group?"

"They came by earlier and asked if I wanted to go to dinner." Kylie rubbed a hand across her face. "I told them I didn't feel like it."

"When were they going?" Natalie asked. She didn't like the idea of the group of young women splitting up. They needed to stay together for safety's sake.

Kylie glanced at the clock. "Fifteen minutes ago."

"Get up." Natalie grabbed Kylie's hands and pulled her to her feet.

"Why?" Kylie resisted.

"You're going to dinner with your friends."

"I told you, I don't feel like it," she whined.

"Wash your face and put on a little makeup. I'll straighten your hair." She herded Kylie into the bathroom, wet a washcloth with cold water, wrung it out and handed it to the younger woman. "Get moving. Melody would want it this way."

Kylie took the cloth. "She would?"

"If you were Melody, would you want all your friends to sit around and cry over you?"

Kylie sniffed. "No." She pressed the cool cloth to her swollen, red-rimmed eyes. When she set it on the counter, Natalie slapped a concealer stick in her hand.

"That should help hide those puffy eyes." She smiled gently and plugged in the flat iron.

While Kylie applied makeup, Natalie smoothed the kinks out of her hair. A few minutes later, they left the bathroom.

Kylie had more of a bounce in her step. "I am a little hungry."

"Good, maybe we'll catch your mates in the restaurant and order something quick and easy."

Kylie hugged Natalie. "Thank you for being here for me. Somehow, I feel closer to Melody." She tilted her head. "You're a lot like her. Isn't that strange?"

Natalie smiled and resisted the urge to tell Kylie the truth. Better to find Melody first. If keeping her real identity a secret helped, then she would continue to do so.

Kylie stripped out of her pajamas and stepped into a flirty, pastel-pink dress of sheer fabric with an underslip of shiny, silky pink. She slid her feet into low-heeled sandals bejeweled in sparkling clear rhinestones. After a glance in the full-length mirror, she gave Natalie a soft smile. "I do feel better."

"Good. Then let's catch up with the others." Natalie gripped Kylie's hand and led her through the door, closing it firmly behind them. She'd have to do something about Kylie's sleeping situation. The young woman needed a friend in her room. A lone female in a foreign country would be a target to the kidnappers.

The four other young women were lingering over their meal in the resort restaurant, talking quietly, their expressions somber.

Natalie led Kylie up to the table and smiled brightly. "Do you have room for two more?"

"Of course," said an auburn-haired woman Natalie recognized as the one they called Allison as she jumped to her feet and dragged two more chairs to the small table.

It was a tight fit, but Natalie didn't care. At least she was close to them and included in their group. She'd have a better chance of keeping them safe.

"Like Kylie, are you all staying one more day before flying out?" Natalie asked.

They nodded as one.

"We were all scheduled to fly in and out on the same plane," said Brianna, a black-haired, petite beauty.

"Yeah." Chelsea, the sandy-blonde, sighed. "We even had seats all grouped together."

"It doesn't feel right without Melody, Jodie and Lisa here," Hanna said. She pushed a strand of light brown hair back behind her ear.

"You have two more nights here and one whole day." Natalie glanced around at the sullen faces. "You can't spend it in your hotel rooms moping."

"We were all supposed to go on the excursion to Chichén Itzá tomorrow," Kylie said.

"We were so looking forward to visiting the ancient Mayan pyramid. Especially Melody."

Natalie remembered how excited her sister had been. She had been working toward a minor in archeology in college. Chichén Itzá had been on her radar since she'd first read about it in a *National Geographic* magazine when she was eight years old. Their parents had promised to take them when they were older.

That dream had almost died with their parents.

Natalie had been so happy for Melody to have this opportunity. Now it seemed as though her sister would never get that chance.

The hell she wouldn't.

"Aren't you going?" Natalie asked.

"We hadn't planned on it," Chelsea said.

Kylie's lips twisted. "Although we paid for the trip in advance and they won't give us a refund."

"Then go." Natalie searched their faces. "Otherwise tomorrow will crawl by. There's no reason you shouldn't see the ruins."

"What about Melody?"

"Go for her," Natalie urged.

Kylie nodded. "I don't feel any better for having stayed in my room all day. The time dragged." She nodded toward Chelsea. "What do you think?"

Chelsea was already nodding. "We should go. It will make the day fly. Then, before we know it, we'll be on our way home."

"Without Melody…" Allison said.

"Do you think they'll ever find her…you know… body?" Brianna asked, her voice a soft whisper.

"I hope so," Chelsea said. "Her family will want closure."

"She only had a sister," Kylie said. "I can't imagine how terrible it was for her to get that call." Her eyes filled again.

Natalie fought the urge to cry with Kylie, but she wasn't ready to give up on her sister. Melody was alive and—damn it—she was going to find her, if it was the last thing she did.

Kylie sniffed and pushed away from the table. "I

don't know about the rest of you, but I could do with one more drink before we leave."

"Me, too," Chelsea said. She, Brianna, Allison and Hanna stood as one.

The six women paid for their meal and left the restaurant, walking out the back door of the hotel to the cabana. People were drifting into the bar as the sun set, cloaking the resort in semidarkness displaced by the lights from the hotel and the blue glow of the pool. Twinkling lights hung from the ceiling of the cabana, giving just enough light to see without being so bright it disturbed the ambience.

Natalie shot a glance around the bar. So far her Navy SEAL protector hadn't showed up. It was just as well. She didn't want the other men in the bar to think she was with him, in case one of them was scouting potential victims.

The music was played loud, limiting the amount of talking between the girls. They all ordered frozen strawberry margaritas and, as the night before, made a toast to their missing friend.

Natalie raised her glass to her lips, the sugar and frozen concoction melting in her mouth.

The music slowed and some of the dancers left the wooden dance floor to refresh their drinks. Others swayed to the rhythm of the band, pressing close together, hips rubbing against hips.

"Would you like to dance?" a voice said over her shoulder.

With a start Natalie turned on her chair and stared up into gray eyes. A nice-looking man with short-cropped blond hair smiled down at her.

"Excuse me?"

He chuckled. "I asked if you would like to dance."

She glanced at her sister's friends.

They all stared at the handsome man.

"Go on. We'll save your drink for you," Chelsea said.

Natalie didn't feel much like dancing with the stranger but, as last night, being out on the dance floor would put her in the line of sight of anyone scoping the crowd for likely victims.

"Okay," she said and laid her hand in his.

His grip was strong and he practically lifted her out of her chair.

Natalie followed him to the dance floor, her gaze darting toward the entrances. Where were the SEALs?

As the stranger pulled her into his embrace, Duff and his friends entered the cabana.

A thrill of recognition and anticipation zipped through Natalie. Duff's large form and broad shoulders would make any woman's heart flutter. The man was gorgeous and looking her way.

Duff's gaze found hers and he frowned.

Natalie sucked in a quick breath and stumbled.

"Careful," said the man holding her in his arms. "I've been known to be all left feet."

"No. I lost my step." She dragged her gaze from Duff's and looked up into her partner's eyes.

"I'm Rolf Schwimmer." He winked and spun her around in a fancy dance move.

"I'm Natalia."

He dipped his head. "A pretty name for a lovely woman."

"Thank you."

"Are you here on vacation?" he asked.

"I am."

He nodded toward Melody's table. "With your friends?"

She glanced toward the girls. "No, I met them when I got here. But they've been good enough to allow me to join them."

"What part of England are you from?"

"Oxford. And you?"

"I'm not from England." He smiled, his eyes twinkling.

"Obviously. Your accent is American."

"Guilty," he said. "I'm originally from Minnesota."

"A long way from home."

"As are you," he pointed out.

"Are you on vacation?" she asked.

He shrugged. "Not so much. I only wish I was here for pleasure. Alas, I'm here to conduct a little business."

"What kind of business?"

"I'm in securities and acquisitions."

"Like buying assets?" she asked, her mind going to what this man could be doing and if it had any relation to her missing sister.

"Something like that."

He didn't look down at her. Instead he danced her around the floor in a tight hold, molding his body to hers. For a while he didn't speak. When the song ended, he held on to her hand. "Stay for another? You're the only person I know."

She laughed. "I don't know you."

"Okay, so you're the only person who hasn't turned me down." He winked. "Dance with me again."

"One more time then I want to sit with my new friends."

The song was fast-paced and required skill at the

salsa. Natalie backed up a step. "I'm sorry, but I'm not good at this dance."

"Then we'll look terrible together." He swung her away from him and back into his arms. "See? You're a natural."

Natalie narrowed her eyes but didn't have time to study his face before he swung her out and back again. She laughed. "You've obviously done this before."

"Maybe." His feet kept time with the music, stepping forward and back, his hips swaying. "Don't let my blond hair fool you. I've spent a lot of time in Mexico. And when in Mexico, you learn to salsa."

By the time the song ended, Natalie was breathless. "Thank you."

"Please." He bowed over her hand. "Let me thank you." He walked her back to the table, nodded to Melody's friends and then left her to take a stool at the bar.

"Wow," Kylie said, her gaze following the man. "He was dreamy."

"You ladies should dance." Natalie took a seat and dabbed at her cheeks with a bar napkin.

"It would be nice to be asked." Chelsea looked around the bar. "Aren't those the guys from last night?" She tipped her head toward Duff and his Navy SEAL friends.

"Didn't you dance with one of them?" Kylie asked.

Natalie nodded, steeling herself from looking that way. No matter how good-looking, the man she'd just danced with didn't have the same rugged appeal as Duff with his slightly shaggy hair and tattoo-laced shoulders and arms.

Her body shivered with anticipation, hoping Duff would ask her to dance again.

"You guys, don't stare." Chelsea turned away. "You'll look pathetic and too eager."

"Here comes one of them," Hanna whispered excitedly.

Out of the corner of her eye Natalie saw a man moving toward them. Her heart skipped several beats and settled back to a normal if somewhat disappointed beat when she realized it wasn't Duff.

Sawyer walked across the barroom, stopping in front of Allison. "Wanna dance?"

Allison beamed and leaped from her seat. "Yes." She grabbed his hand and practically dragged him to the dance floor.

"So much for playing hard to get," Chelsea muttered.

One by one the young women were asked to dance.

Natalie kept a close eye on them and the men they were with. She'd be damned if her sister's friends were the next victims of the kidnappers.

"You're scaring the natives with that frown," a deep voice rumbled next to her ear.

Natalie turned to look up into green eyes and her pulse rushed. "Hi."

"The girls seem to be enjoying themselves despite missing their friend."

"I had to convince them to come out tonight."

When he held out his hand she slipped hers into it, liking how small he made her feel. Not in an intimidating way but in a way that made her feel protected. "Did your guys learn anything from the boat crew?"

"Nothing." He pulled her to her feet and led her toward the dance floor. "Who's the guy you were dancing with?"

"Rolf from Minnesota."

"What's he doing in Cancun?" Duff asked.

"He said he was here on business."

"What kind of business?"

"Securities and acquisitions." Her brow furrowed. "He's American."

"So? Our abductor could be a greedy son of a bitch looking for a quick score." Duff pulled her close and spun her around, putting her back to the man in question. His gaze swept over the top of her head. "Don't trust him."

"Got it." She rested her hand on his chest. "I'm worried."

"I know," he said, his gaze dropping to hers and softening.

"I'm no closer to finding my sister than I was when I arrived in Cancun."

"What next?"

"I don't know." As she danced in a circle, rocking back and forth, Natalie counted the five girls she felt somewhat responsible for. Three of them danced with Duff's friends, which made her feel a little better about their safety. But the other two were dancing with men she didn't know anything about.

Chelsea was dancing with Rolf, the handsome American, who'd asked Natalie to dance first.

Kylie was with a dark-haired man with an easy smile and classy clothing from his button-up starched shirt to dark, tailored trousers. Natalie watched as Kylie gazed up at him, her eyes shining despite the earlier tears.

Could he be one of the kidnappers?

Natalie glanced around the room. Men lounged with their backs to the bar, watching the action in front of the band. Were they part of the kidnapping operation?

"You're thinking too hard," Duff said, his lips so close to her ear she could feel the warmth and smell the minty freshness of his breath.

"It's my sister I'm trying to find. If it was one of your family members, what would you do?"

His grip tightened on her waist. "Probably rip the place apart until I found who was responsible."

"Right." The music came to a stop.

The band announced a short break and laid down their instruments.

Natalie scanned the room, locating each of Melody's friends heading toward their table. One, two, three, four— Where was Chelsea? Her pulse ratcheted up. "I've lost one." She stepped away from Duff, panic rising in her chest.

"Lost one what?" Duff asked, his gaze sweeping the room.

"Chelsea." Natalie hurried toward the table where the other four had congregated.

Duff followed.

"Where's Chelsea?" she asked, trying her best not to show her apprehension.

"I don't know. She was dancing when we were." Kylie glanced around. "Maybe she went for a walk with her dance partner," she offered.

Natalie stared at each of the four, quickly pinning them, one at a time, with an intent look. "Do me a favor and don't walk off with anyone other than one of your friends tonight."

"Why?" Kylie's brow dipped.

Natalie forced a smile. "You're in a foreign country known for drug wars and kidnapping. You never know if you're with a good guy or a bad one."

Allison's face blanched. "I thought Cancun was safe. Well, other than what happened on that scuba dive."

"You never know how secure you are. It's just safer in numbers."

"She's right," Hanna said. "Now you're making me worry about Chelsea. You don't suppose she went for a walk with her dance partner, do you?"

"Duff and I'll go look," Natalie offered.

Kylie stared hard at Duff. "How do you know he's one of the good guys?"

Natalie smiled. "He saved Lisa's life, didn't he?"

Kylie nodded. "I guess he is a good guy. But be careful, will ya?"

"I will." Natalie touched Kylie's arm. "Stay here with the others while we check the bathroom and the other usual places."

Damn. She'd let one of them slip out of her eyesight.

Dear God, she hoped Chelsea was okay.

Duff took her hand and led her toward the bathrooms behind the bar. "It's going to be okay."

How? She had no idea where her sister was. Now she'd lost one of Melody's friends.

Chapter Eight

Duff went with Natalie to the bathroom. When she came out, shaking her head, he took her hand and led her back into the bar.

Sawyer spotted him and raised his chin as if to ask if all was okay.

Duff gave a slight shake of his head and tipped it toward the exit, leading out to the pool and the beach beyond.

Sawyer rose from his bar stool and stretched, turning to his teammates to pass the word. One of them would stay at the bar, keeping a close watch on the four women still there.

With his friends covering his six, Duff left the bar, following Natalie out to the pool. A couple lay on one of the lounge chairs kissing, their bodies entwined, completely unaware of anything other than the pheromones and lust driving them.

Natalie hurried past and down the steps to the narrow boardwalk leading through the palms to the beach beyond.

"I think I see someone ahead," Natalie said.

A muted scream penetrated the darkness over the sound of the waves washing up on the sand.

Natalie kicked off her high heels and ran toward the sound.

A woman ran along the beach, heading toward them.

A man chased after her.

When she reached Natalie, she crashed into her arms.

Natalie staggered backward, absorbing the impact. "Chelsea, honey, what's wrong?"

"I was…walking…on the beach…with Rolf…" Chelsea gulped back a sob. "And I was attacked."

Rolf ran and stumbled across the beach toward them.

Duff lunged past Natalie, fists clenched, ready to take on the man.

"Wait!" Chelsea turned toward Duff and Rolf. "What are you doing?"

"I'm going to wipe the beach with this man's face," Duff said.

Rolf ground to a stop and dropped to his knees in the sand, blood dripping down the side of his face from a gash on his cheekbone.

"*Rolf* didn't attack me. A couple of men did." Chelsea dropped to her knees beside the handsome man. "Oh, God. They hurt you." She reached out to touch his cheek.

Rolf flinched away. "I'm okay. Are you?" He rose to his feet and held out a hand to her.

She took it and let him pull her up. "I'm okay. He only knocked me down."

Sawyer and Quentin skidded to a stop on the sand, their fists raised, ready for anything.

"What's going on?" Sawyer asked.

Duff nodded toward Chelsea. "The girl was attacked."

Sawyer stepped toward Rolf. "Do we need to take care of business?"

Quentin moved up beside Sawyer.

"Not yet," Duff said. "Seems someone else did the attacking. This guy fought them off."

Sawyer and Quentin didn't back down, placing their bulk between Rolf and Chelsea.

"Chelsea, why did you leave the others?" Natalie glared at the man who'd taken her out to the beach.

"I needed some air. All of a sudden everything got to me and I had to get outside. Rolf was good enough to follow me to make sure I would be all right."

"I wasn't sure what was wrong or why Chelsea felt a need to be outside," Rolf said. "But it's not safe for a woman to walk the trails or the beach alone at night."

Duff nodded, not willing to give the man the full benefit of a doubt. For all he knew Rolf could have been part of a scheme to take Chelsea but had been bested by someone with the same idea.

"Come on, Chelsea, let's get you back to the hotel." Natalie slipped an arm around the girl. Chelsea let Natalie lead her back to the others.

The four girls waiting at the bar surrounded their friend and left for the hotel.

Natalie hesitated, her gaze swinging to Rolf. "You should have one of the hotel staff see to that cut."

"I can manage." He raised a hand to the injury and winced. He made a move to follow the five young women. "After I make sure Chelsea makes it to her room."

Duff, Quentin, Montana and Sawyer stepped in the man's way.

"We'll see to it," Duff said.

Rolf's eyes narrowed and he straightened. "Okay." Then he performed a smart about-face and marched away.

Duff's gaze followed the man for a moment. "I'm not sure I trust that man."

"Me neither." Natalie glanced up at Duff. "I'm going to follow the girls to their room."

"I'm coming."

She shook her head. "That's not necessary. We'll be in the hotel with all security cameras."

He held up a hand. "Humor me, will ya?"

She nodded, a smile slipping across her pretty lips. "Okay." She glanced around the bar, wondering if being with Duff would keep the abductor from targeting her. At the same time, she didn't care. She liked having him close.

"What do you want us to do?" Sawyer asked.

"Keep your eyes open and have another beer." Duff left his buddies in the bar and hurried after Natalie and the bevy of females. Whatever the hell was happening was getting entirely too close to Natalie and her sister's friends. He'd have to stay a lot closer to them to protect them. His bungalow was too far away. Perhaps he could have the reservation desk move him to the same floor.

Making a mental note to check on his way back to the bar, he stepped into the elevator with the women and rode up to the eighth floor.

Chelsea pulled her key card from her purse and slipped it through the lock. When she reached for the door handle, Duff brushed her hand aside. "Let me check first."

Chelsea stepped back and let Duff enter ahead of them. He walked through the small room, stepping over suitcases, discarded clothes and cosmetic cases. After he'd made certain there weren't any bogeymen hiding in the closet or bathroom, he held the door open for the women to enter, stepping outside before he was completely overwhelmed with estrogen. He held the door open a moment longer. "Do you ladies need anything before I leave you?"

Natalie nodded toward one of the girls. "We need to get Kylie's things moved in with her friends. I don't think she wants to be alone tonight."

"I don't," Kylie agreed.

Duff helped move Kylie's things into the room with the other girls. "Kylie, if you'll give me your key, I'll stay on this floor. If you need anything, I'll be less than a shout away." He held out his hand. "If you trust me."

Kylie held her key card clutched in her fingers, staring from Duff to Natalie.

Natalie nodded. "I'm on the same floor, too."

Kylie handed over the key card. "Are you going on the excursion to Chichén Itzá, tomorrow?"

Duff glanced from Natalie to Kylie and back. "What excursion?"

"Kylie and the rest of the girls had planned a visit to the Mayan ruins, before their friend went missing. Their reservations were nonrefundable." Natalie gave Duff a slight smile. "I told them they might as well go. It beats sitting in their rooms all day." She chewed on her lip. "But after what happened to Chelsea…I'm not sure it's a good idea."

"My guys mentioned wanting to see the ruins. What if we went along?"

Kylie frowned. "We have three extra paid slots from Melody, Lisa and Jodie's tickets."

"I'll go," Natalie volunteered.

"I will, too." The thought of Natalie and the other young women going off into the Mexican jungle didn't sit well with him. "If you think we can take your friends' places on the tour, I'll go, and bring one of my buddies along."

Sawyer would come. If the other two wanted to join them, they could follow in the rental car.

Kylie nodded. "Okay, then. I guess we'll go." She gave them a weak smile. "Thank you for being there for us. I can't imagine our troubles are making your vacation better."

"Don't you worry about it. We'll have a nice time seeing things we wanted to see anyway." Natalie hugged Kylie. "Only with better company."

Kylie entered the shared room with her friends and closed the door behind her.

Natalie's smile slipped from her lips. "I don't know what's going on." She glanced up at Duff. "Should I advise the girls to stay in their rooms until their flights leave the day after tomorrow?"

"They should be all right, as long as they stick together."

"You don't have to come along, you know."

He touched her cheek with the backs of his knuckles. "Neither do you."

"I couldn't stand it if something happened to them."

"In the meantime, what's your plan?"

"I'm going back to the bar. If I'm not watching out for the others, I'll have time to study the patrons."

Duff's brows knit together. "I'll go with you."

"I'm not sure that's a good idea."

"I don't care if it's a good idea. Someone tried to take you once already."

She smiled. "Under water. And I'm capable of taking care of myself."

He shrugged. "Then I'll move my things into Kylie's room, in case they need help tonight."

"Thank you."

"And about tomorrow—"

"You and your friends don't have to go," she said.

"I know. But after what happened on the dive and then the attack on Chelsea, I think those girls need all the protection they can get."

"What's in it for you?"

He chuckled and brushed her mouth with his thumb. "The pleasure of your company."

Natalie snorted softly. "Please."

"That's right. That's what I wanted to hear." He bent and brushed his lips across her. When she didn't slap his face he slipped an arm around her waist and dragged her body up against his.

If she'd pushed him away, he would have stopped immediately. Instead her fingers curled into his shirt and she leaned up on her toes to deepen the kiss.

His blood thrummed through his veins, searing his insides with a desire so potent he struggled to keep it at just a kiss. He slid his tongue across the seam of her lips.

Natalie opened to him, her tongue meeting his, twisting and gliding along the length of his. Her fingers crept upward, locking behind his neck, bringing him closer. Her breasts pressed against him and a slim leg curled around the back of his calf.

Duff's groin tightened. If he didn't break it off soon...

With herculean effort, he dragged his lips free and

rested his forehead against hers. "Definitely the pleasure of your company."

She let her hands slide away from his neck and down to his chest. "We probably shouldn't do that again."

"Why?"

Natalie sucked in a deep breath and let it out slowly. "I'm here to find my sister. You're—" her eyes narrowed as she gazed up at him "—a distraction."

He grinned and grazed her cheek with his lips. "I'll take that as a compliment. Now, I'd better get my toothbrush and shaving kit. And you'd better go check out the bar for potential kidnappers."

They stepped into the elevator at the same time and the doors closed.

If Natalie made one move toward him, Duff would be completely helpless to resist.

NATALIE WATCHED THE doors slide closed, trapping her in the small, intimate space with Duff. Her lips tingled and her core throbbed with the prospect of what could have happened had he not stopped kissing her when he did. She shifted, her shoulder bumping against his.

He reached for her hand.

She let him take it, her fingers curling around his, her pulse speeding as the elevator car started downward. "Really, we shouldn't—"

He tugged her hand and turned at the same time, his other arm slipping around her. "I know. You made that perfectly clear." With her body clamped against his, she couldn't move, was powerless to resist when his lips crashed down onto hers.

She met him with the passion roiling up inside, threatening to consume her.

When the bell dinged, indicating they'd reached the ground floor, she stepped back and dragged the back of her hand across her lips. This was not how an SOS agent acted. Twice now she'd lost control with this man.

He turned to face the doors as they slid open. "Sweetheart, you're as much of a distraction as you claim I am." He swept his hand forward. "After you. And I'll do my best to help you stay focused. I get it that you're here for your sister."

Natalie hurried past him, careful not to touch him. Afraid, if she did, they'd end up in another mind-bending, soul-stealing embrace.

He stepped out of the elevator behind her and stopped.

Natalie glanced over her shoulder, her gaze questioning.

"I'll let you have a head start." He gave her a strained smile, his trousers fitting tightly over a telltale bulge.

A surge of something akin to power burned through her. She'd had that effect on him. As she strode across the lobby, her step was lighter, her body still sizzling with the desire he'd inspired. The man was a huge distraction.

Back in the cabana bar, the crowd had thinned. Duff's friends sat at a table away from the dance floor, their heads together, each with a hand wrapped around a bottle of beer. They spotted her as she entered and turned toward her.

She dipped her head slightly and headed for the bar, slipping onto an empty stool.

Two men sat on stools farther down. One of them turned and tipped his head toward her. Natalie recognized the blond hair and the bandaged cut on his cheek.

"Is Chelsea all right?" Rolf asked.

"She's a little shaken, but fine." Natalie nodded toward his cheek. "I see you got that taken care of."

"Had bandages in my shaving kit." He stood and moved closer, taking the stool at her side. "I wouldn't have let her walk out on the beach had I known this area was that dangerous."

"She was pretty distraught. I'll bet she'd have walked out there with or without you." Natalie motioned for the bartender.

"Could I buy you a drink?" Rolf asked.

"Thank you." She ordered a glass of wine. When the bartender set it on the counter, she lifted it. "To interesting vacations."

Rolf raised his beer, touched it to the rim of her glass. Then he downed a long swallow.

"How long have you been in Cancun?" he asked.

"I got here yesterday."

He nodded. "I arrived this morning."

Natalie shook her head. "Nothing like adventure on your first day."

"I don't understand. I thought they had sufficient security at the resort. Have there been other attacks in the area?"

"I wouldn't know." She didn't tell him about the diving incident. If her attacker wanted to try again, she'd make sure it happened this time. Lance had her back with the embedded tracking device. Hopefully, Duff wouldn't interfere this time. However, Melody's friends didn't have embedded devices. Natalie needed all the help she could get to see to their safety. She'd need to be at her sharpest. One of the women who'd disappeared had been at the Mayan ruins when she'd gone missing.

"I'd better call it a night." Natalie drank the last of her wine and stood. "Thank you for the drink."

Rolf touched her arm. "Would you like for me to walk you to your room?"

She smiled. "Thanks, but the last time you walked somewhere with a woman, you got the worst end of the deal. I can get from here to the hotel by myself. But thanks." As she headed back, she cast another glance around the bar. Two couples danced to a slow song, the SEALs were scooting back their chairs and rising and no one else appeared to be prime candidates for kidnappers. Perhaps they'd moved on to another hotel.

Duff's friends exited out the opposite end of the bar, heading toward the bungalows.

Natalie considered checking in with Lance one more time, but decided a radio check in her room was good enough. As she walked through the lobby, she couldn't help but look for Duff. He should be back in Kylie's room by now. Her heart fluttered. Kylie's room was next to Natalie's. She and Duff would be sleeping only a few steps away from each other.

Out of the corner of her eye she spotted the dark-haired man Kylie had danced with earlier—the one with the button-up shirt and tailored trousers. He hurried toward an exit, his body tense, his gaze swinging side to side.

Natalie's pulse jumped. Something about the way he moved made her hackles rise and her nerves leap to attention. As he ducked through the door, Natalie altered her direction and followed.

The man entered a hallway marked Employees Only off the side of the huge lobby.

Natalie stopped short of the restricted-access hallway.

The man walked quickly to the end of the corridor and out the exit door at the end.

Natalie looked around to make sure no employees were wandering around, then jogged down the hall to the end where a large metal door with a red sign above it read *salida*. She eased through and caught a glimpse of the man.

He walked quickly through a dark alley between the main building and what appeared to be the utilities building housing the air-conditioning units. Natalie gave him time to reach the end of the building before she stepped through.

Once outside the hotel, Natalie slipped into the shadows and scanned the area for movement. For a moment she thought she'd lost track of the man.

Then she spied a trouser leg rounding the corner of the hotel toward the bungalows. Why would a man sneak through the employee-only area of the hotel and then out the employee exit? Perhaps he was one of the staff members or...he had something to hide.

With no weapon tucked beneath her minuscule dress, and her headset back in her room. She had no way to call for backup if something went south. But if Sneaky Dude was someone important to her sister's disappearance, she owed it to herself and to her sister to follow him.

She slipped out of her high heels and tiptoed to the edge of the building, wishing she had worn something dark, covering her arms and legs and hair so that she would blend better with the shadows. If the man thought someone was following him and turned, he'd see her light blue dress like a ghostly figure hovering nearby.

She stayed back far enough he wouldn't see or hear *her*, but close enough she didn't lose *him*.

He disappeared into the bushes.

Torn between running to catch up and revealing her position, Natalie moved silently in the shadows until she reached the stand of bushes.

Parting the branches, she peered through to the path leading to the bungalows.

A dark figure moved along the edge, fifty feet to her right.

Natalie eased through the branches and waited beside the bush until her quarry stopped outside the door to one of the bungalows. After a quick knock, the door opened, shedding a triangle of light onto the stoop. Slim, pale arms reached out, wrapped around the man's neck and dragged him over the threshold. The door was closed, pitching the path into darkness again.

Natalie hurried toward the bungalow so that she didn't lose track of which one it was. When she came abreast of the building, she memorized the number. She'd run it by Lance to find out who was registered there.

A tiny ray of light shone from one of the windows on the side of the bungalow. Natalie eased up to it and peered inside.

The man and woman were locked in a tight embrace. Feeling like a Peeping Tom, Natalie backed away and ran into another wall. She swallowed her gasp. Hands locked on her arms and spun her around.

Chapter Nine

Natalie stared up into Duff's smiling face. He leaned close and whispered against her ear, "We have got to stop meeting like this." He slid his fingers down her arms.

Natalie sucked in a breath and willed her heart rate to slow. "You scared a year off my life." Natalie grabbed his hand and pulled him along the path, back toward the hotel.

When they were far enough away from the bungalow with the embracing couple, he pulled her to a stop. "Why were you following that man?"

"He was acting suspicious," she said, glancing toward the bungalow.

"He might have been meeting his lover."

Natalie sighed. "You're probably right. The way they were carrying on…"

The door to the bungalow opened and light spilled out onto the stoop again.

"Damn. He's coming out." Natalie grabbed the front of Duff's shirt and rose up on her toes. "Kiss me."

He dropped his duffle bag and complied, crushing her mouth with his. Duff circled her waist with his hands and pulled her closer.

Natalie wrapped her arms around his neck and deepened the kiss, one eye open, her gaze on the man leaving the bungalow.

He stopped, hesitated and turned away, walking fast toward the beach.

Natalie really had no idea when he disappeared out of sight. The kiss that had started as a ploy to hide the fact she'd followed the guy out to his secret assignation had turned into more than subterfuge.

Duff slid his hands low on her waist.

Natalie curled her leg around his calf, leaning into him, her center rubbing against one of his thick thighs. Her short dress hiked up.

Duff cupped her bottom, his fingers digging into her.

If she hadn't been fully dressed, they might have taken it all the way.

What might only have been seconds stretched into a lifetime. Finally, Duff pulled away, his hands rising to grip her arms. "You're here for your sister."

"Right." Natalie ran her tongue across her lips, moistening them after another incredible kiss. Her head spun and her knees wobbled. "I should go to bed." *With Duff.* "Alone."

A grin spread across his face. "And here I thought you were coming around." He kissed her forehead, grabbed his duffle bag and took her hand. "Come on. I'll walk you back."

They didn't speak all the way back to the hotel, but her hand felt warm in his and she liked how work-roughened it was. This man wasn't afraid of getting his hands dirty. Hell, he probably killed people for a living. And rescued them. From what she'd read about SEALs, they did whatever task assigned: destroying enemy arsenals or strongholds, assassinating enemy leaders and rescuing hostages.

Right at that moment Natalie could have used a little rescuing from herself. With the worry of her sister's disappearance weighing heavily on her, and no clear leads, she shouldn't be thinking about getting naked with a virtual stranger. Especially one as lethal as Duff.

Strengthening her resolve to fight her desires and get a good night's sleep, she stopped at the entrance to the hotel. "Good night, Duff."

Duff was standing closer than she'd anticipated and the scent of his aftershave wafted up to her nostrils, tantalizing her, making her forget that fresh resolve, opting for immediate gratification in someone to hold her through the night.

She raised her gaze to his and fell into his green eyes.

He lifted a hand to cup her cheek and bent, capturing her mouth with his.

Natalie kissed him back, her heart pounding, sending a rush of blood through her body and heat pooling low in her belly.

"Good night, Natalie." He brushed her lips with his, this time in a feather-soft touch that left her wanting so much more.

When he straightened and opened the door to the lobby, she hurried inside and headed for the elevator bank.

Feeling as if she'd escaped what could have been a big mistake or the best decision she'd made in her life, Natalie oscillated between continuing on her march to a lonely bed and going back to invite Duff to join her.

Before she could do the latter, she stepped into the elevator and pushed the button for her floor.

The doors started to slide closed when an arm jutted between them and forced them back open.

"Did you forget we were going to the same floor?" Duff grinned and stepped into the car with her, letting the doors close behind him.

Natalie's eyes narrowed. "Then why did you let me go outside the hotel?"

He held up a hand. "You seemed in a hurry to get away from me."

"It's not you, per se."

He crossed his arms and leaned against the wall of the elevator as the doors closed, locking them into the confined space. Alone. "Not me? Then who are you trying to get away from?"

Natalie bit her bottom lip and faced the door, not Duff. "No one. Forget it." She wasn't about to tell him she was running away from the raging desire he'd inspired in her from the first time she'd seen him.

Duff's broad shoulders filled the elevator car and made Natalie's heart thump against her ribs. If he didn't know Kylie's room was beside hers before, he'd know when he walked her to her room.

They rode in silence, neither one touching the other, though Natalie had the strongest urge to reach out and grab his hand. And a lot more than his hand. The man had her tense, on edge, ready for…what? Another kiss?

A kiss didn't seem to be nearly enough where Duff was concerned.

When the elevator door slid open, Duff waited while Natalie stepped out.

In the corridor Natalie led the way, stopping in front of Kylie's room.

Duff raised his brows. "Which room is yours?"

She tipped her head toward the one next door.

The corners of Duff's lips turned upward. "Afraid I'll steal into your room while you sleep?"

"No, I'm more afraid you won't." Oh, hell, had she really said exactly what was on her mind?

He held out his hand. "Your key."

She removed it from a hidden pocket in her dress and gave it to him.

"Nothing is going to happen tonight," he said, opening the door for her.

Natalie straightened her shoulders, definitely disappointed by his announcement.

As she started past him he added, "Unless you want it to."

She stumbled. "Pardon me?"

He cupped her chin as he had downstairs. "You heard me."

Already, Natalie was lost. She leaned into his open palm. "You had to do it, didn't you?" she muttered.

He chuckled. "Do what?"

She slipped her hand in his and led him into her bedroom, closing the door behind him. "You had to make me want you."

It might be the worst decision she'd ever made on the spur of the moment, but it was the only one she could consider. She wanted him. Wanted his body next to hers, his fingers touching her in her most private places. That hard ridge beneath his jeans indicated he was as excited as she.

Duff stopped. "Are you sure?"

Natalie nodded. "I am." She reached behind her, unzipped her dress and let it fall to the floor. "Now, don't make me wish I'd had the good sense to send you away."

"Sweetheart, I'll make you wish for a lot of things…" He threaded his fingers through her hair and pulled gently, tilting her face up to receive his kiss. "But not to send me away."

With the heat of his lips on hers, she could feel the truth in his words. She opened her mouth and her body to him, refusing to back down or to second-guess her decision.

Duff ran his hands through her hair and down her naked back, flipping the hooks loose on her bra. He slid the straps down her arms and flung the garment to the side.

A shiver of anticipation rippled across Natalie's skin as Duff palmed her breasts, covering them with his big, rough hands.

She arched her back, pressing them harder into his touch.

"You're beautiful," he whispered into her ear, nipping at her earlobe.

Natalie tipped her head to the side, giving him better access to her throat and the pulse beating like a snare drum at a parade. "You're overdressed." She made quick work of loosening the buttons on his shirt and dragged it over his broad shoulders.

Ah, yes. Those shoulders were drool-worthy and shouldn't be covered. Natalie traced the tattoo on his right arm and bent to taste his skin there. Slightly salty and purely male. Sweet heaven, he was turning her inside out with the need to see all of him.

With that in mind, she jerked the button loose on his jeans and ran the zipper down. His shaft jutted out. The man went commando.

Her core melted into molten heat, making her throb

and ache for more. Natalie slid her hands over his backside, easing the jeans from his hips while clenching her fingers around his taut bottom.

Duff groaned and trailed a path of kisses down the long line of her throat, pausing at the insanely beating pulse at the base. He tongued it once, then lowered his hands, cupped her bottom and lifted her, wrapping her legs around his waist.

Three long strides brought them to the bed where he eased her onto her back. With a swift tug he removed her panties, exposing her moist entrance.

Duff's eyes and nostrils flared as he stepped between her legs. He skimmed his hands across her thighs toward the apex and the tuft of hair covering her sex. "Stop me if I'm going too fast," he said through clenched teeth.

"Please," she said. "You're going too slow."

With a soft chuckle he dropped to his knees, draped her legs over his shoulders and feathered his fingers along her inner thigh, searing a path to her core.

"Please," she moaned, digging her nails into the comforter, her body writhing. If she didn't have him soon, she'd come apart in a million pieces.

"Patience, Natalie." Duff slipped a finger between her folds and strummed the strip of flesh hidden between.

Electric shocks ripped through her, making her even more aware of the man and everything he was doing to her.

Duff dipped his finger into her channel, swirled it around and up through her folds to stroke that special bundle of nerves, igniting her in a firestorm of sensations.

Again and again he stroked her, bringing her to

the edge of sanity. When he parted her folds with his thumbs and bent to tongue her there, he took her to an entirely new dimension. He continued his assault until she thought she would die from pleasure.

Then he was on his feet, fumbling for his wallet in the back pocket of his jeans. Duff pulled out three foil packages, dropping two on the floor. Without bending to retrieve them, he ripped open the third packet and rolled the content over his pulsing shaft. He scooted her back and climbed onto the bed, parting her legs for him to slide in between.

Past her ability to control her impatience, Natalie bent her knees, locked her legs around Duff's waist and buried her heels into his bottom.

He drove into her, burying himself to the hilt. For a long moment he stayed deep inside her, giving her time to adjust to his width stretching her inside.

Natalie closed her eyes, taking all of him. She curled her fingers around his broad shoulders, digging her nails into his skin. This was what she'd been craving from their first kiss.

Duff eased out and back in, repeating his moves over and over, settling into a firm, thrusting motion, gliding in and out.

Natalie dropped her heels to the mattress and rose up to meet him, the tingling sensations returned, spreading from her center outward in waves. She rode the tide, her breath caught in her throat, her heart hammering.

Duff thrust one last time and remained buried deep inside her, his shaft throbbing, his body rigid with the extent of his release.

When at last he relaxed, he dropped down on top of

her, then rolled to the side, taking her with him, without severing their intimate connection.

Natalie rested her head in the crook of his arm and took in a ragged breath, his masculine scent filling her with intense satisfaction and the realization once would never be enough with Duff.

For a long time he held her against him, his hand drifting over her skin, stroking her in gentle tribute to what they'd just shared.

"That was incredible," she said when she could finally form thoughts in her sex-fogged brain.

"Why do I feel there's a 'but' coming?" He chuckled, his fingers curling into her bottom, pressing her closer.

She gave him a sad, halfhearted smile. "But this isn't helping me find my sister."

"Tomorrow we'll turn this resort town upside down."

She shook her head. "Whoever has her and the other women will not be that obvious. And there could be so many different places they could be hiding."

"One thing is certain," Duff said. "They tried to take you."

She nodded.

"They might try again."

Natalie shook her head, running her hand along the rigid muscle of his arm. "Not with a hulking SEAL following my every step and now sleeping in my room."

He brushed the hair out of her eyes. "I can't help it. I don't like that you're using yourself as bait."

"What other option do I have? They seem to be taking blondes."

"Surely there are other blondes they can target."

Natalie chewed on her bottom lip. "Do you think Chelsea was one of their attempts?"

"Maybe." His jaw tightened. "I'm not sure I trust the man she was with. What do we know about Rolf? What if he staged that scene to throw us off?"

Natalie had been thinking along the same lines. Now would have been a good time to tell Duff that she had a man working with her who could identify Rolf and others frequenting the resort.

She opened her mouth to admit she was not alone and had a backup plan.

A soft knock at the door made them both stiffen.

"Natalia?" a woman's voice called through the heavy door.

Natalie rolled out of the bed, grabbing for her discarded dress. "Who is it?"

"Kylie. Could I come in?"

"Just a minute. I was about to get into the shower."

"I'm sorry to disturb you. I just…just…"

"Hold on." Natalie shoved Duff's clothes at him and pushed him into the bathroom. As soon as she had the door closed, and her blue dress pulled over her body, she opened the door, shoving her hand through her tousled hair.

One glance at the girl's face and she held open her arms. "What's wrong, Kylie?"

"I couldn't sleep. The others don't know I left the room. I can't help it. I can't stop thinking about Melody."

Neither could Natalie and guilt wrapped around her heart. She'd been making love to a sexy man while her sister was being held in some godforsaken hell. Natalie hugged the girl to her chest, wishing she were Melody. Tears welled in her eyes. She blinked them back and vowed to work harder and smarter to come up with a plan to find and free her sister.

Kylie sniffed and looked up at Natalie. "Do you mind if I stay with you tonight? I don't know why, but I feel closer to Melody with you."

With a man in her bathroom, Natalie had to think fast. "You bet you can stay with me. But you'll need your own things. I'll walk you back to the others and let you gather what you'll need for the night." Natalie scooped her key card off the floor beside the door and followed Kylie out into the hallway.

By the time she and Kylie had returned to the room, Duff had cleared out, taking his clothes.

Though disappointed the night had ended the way it had, Natalie knew it was for the best. While Kylie ducked into the shower, Natalie inserted the earbud into her ear.

"About time you tuned in," Lance said.

"Sorry. I didn't take the communications equipment into the bar earlier. It's hard enough for me to think with all that's going on. I didn't need a man in my head talking to me."

"Understood," he said. "What have you got?"

She passed on the information about Rolf Schwimmer and the man she'd followed. "The man I followed might be a dead end, but I have to follow every lead."

"I'll check him out. You're right to suspect him if he was dancing with one of your sister's friends one minute and making a secret assignation the next. I'll let you know what I find."

"And you'll look into Rolf Schwimmer?"

"I'll run facial recognition software on the image I've pulled from the security cameras. I'll also run a background check on your secret lovers. Hopefully, I'll have something for you in the morning."

"Do you ever sleep?"

"Only when I don't have a case to help solve."

"Thanks, Lance," Natalie said. "You don't know how much it means to me to have your help on this case."

"If it were my sister, I'd want all the help I could get."

The shower shut off in the bathroom.

"Gotta go," Natalie whispered and turned off the headset, stashing it beneath her pillow.

A moment later Kylie entered the room, fresh-faced, with a towel wrapped around her head.

Not exactly the roommate Natalie would have preferred, but the right one to keep her on track.

DUFF LEFT THE hotel in search of his friends. He found them in Sawyer's bungalow, their voices a low murmur from outside the door. He knocked once and entered.

"Thought you were staying in the hotel tonight?" Sawyer slapped a cold beer into his hand and nodded toward an empty seat.

His body still humming from his encounter with Natalie, Duff popped the top off the bottle and downed half of the cool liquid before answering. "I am. I just wanted to give you a heads-up. If the women decide to go on an excursion tomorrow, we need to tag along to make sure they're okay."

Sawyer frowned. "What excursion?"

"Chichén Itzá. A Mayan ruin an hour away."

Quentin shook his head. "I thought we were here to enjoy the sun and sand. Not to go traipsing in the jungle. Been there, done that, could write the book."

"We might not need all of us, if Quentin wants to stay back and ogle bikini-clad women on the beach." Duff shot a glance at the other two members of his team. "What do you say?"

"I'm in," Sawyer said. "I wanted to see the ruins anyway."

"Count me in," Montana agreed. "This trip is getting more interesting by the second."

Quentin sighed. "I bet there won't be any bikinis at the ruins."

"Nope." Duff grinned. "But you'll go anyway, right?"

He nodded. "I'll go."

"We'll play it by ear in the morning. Natalie's sister's friends are only here for another day, they might decide to stay and hang out at the resort, given all that's happened."

Quentin brightened. "We can always hope. They were pretty cute in their bikinis."

"Rein it in, Romeo," Sawyer said. "They're on the young side for us."

"Each one of them is at least twenty-one, or pretty darned close, legal and single. That's only seven or eight years difference in age."

Sawyer frowned.

Quentin raised his hands, palms upward. "What?"

"They're still in college. Don't charm them into quitting." Sawyer nodded toward Duff. "We've got your six on this mission, Duff."

"Thanks. I'll be in the hotel should you need me."

"Yeah, closer to the women," Quentin grumbled.

"To sleep." Duff left the bungalow and glanced both ways along the path. A man stood outside a building near the beach, stretching his arms above his head. Since Duff had been there, he hadn't seen anyone coming or going from that particular bungalow. He turned toward the hotel and strolled along the path, glancing over his shoulder, keeping an eye on the stretching man. When the guy stepped back into the bungalow, Duff circled back. Moving silently, relying on his SEAL training, he worked his way back to the bungalow where the man had stepped inside.

In a resort environment, he found it hard to see the enemy in every person he met. Most of his targets had been pretty obvious. Here, anyone could be stalking young women. Human trafficking was a high-dollar business.

The guy he saw stretching could be the ringleader, or he could be a guy on his honeymoon, stretching after an active romp in bed with his new wife.

Duff eased up to the window of the bungalow. Only a sliver of light made it past the drawn shades. He could see the shadow of a figure moving around inside, but not much else. He circled the building to one of the other windows and found a little more of a sliver of light. Through it he noticed the bright glare of a screen. Not the blinking lights of a television screen playing different scenes. More the light of a computer monitor or a couple of monitors.

After studying the bit of an image he could see through the window, he concluded only one figure moved around. So he wasn't on his honeymoon. Perhaps he was a businessman, working remotely through a high-speed internet connection. That alone didn't make him a candidate for kidnapping.

Duff straightened, feeling a little foolish for suspecting every man he saw at the resort. For all they knew the culprit was a local making a quick buck selling females to a foreign market. Cancun was bigger than the resorts. On the other side of the resorts compound was an uglier reality of living where drug lords ran the government and the citizens answered to them. Hell, even at the resort, they were subject to the underpinnings of a corrupt government.

After leaving the bungalow, Duff stepped back onto the path, passing his bungalow and the one his friends were still inside, drinking beer and talking about women.

Duff passed the bungalow Natalie had been spying on earlier. A light still burned inside and he could hear voices. He walked on, refusing to look in another window. If the security patrol at the resort caught him, they'd throw him in jail. His commander would be livid, wanting to know what the hell he was doing.

With young women's lives on the line, he couldn't blame Natalie for following every lead. It just seemed as though they were taking shots in the dark. They needed some good, solid evidence or clues to lead them to the right party responsible.

Duff returned to the room beside Natalie's, showered and fell into bed. On the other side of the wall lay a woman who'd made him give up a perfectly good vacation to go chasing after clues that could either lead to nothing or to a huge can of worms with international implications.

And he'd come to Cancun for some much-needed rest and relaxation. He snorted in the dark. Why was it trouble found the Navy SEALs whether they were looking for it or not?

Which begged the question, why had he let himself get involved?

Hell, he couldn't picture it any other way. Natalie needed their help to find her sister and to keep her friends safe from whomever it was kidnapping young women. He couldn't ignore them.

Duff closed his eyes and willed himself to sleep. That itch he got prior to a mission made him restless. But like any other mission, he knew a well-rested body was his best defense. As he drifted to sleep, he dreamed of Natalie lying naked on the altar of a Mayan ruin. A faceless enemy dressed in ancient Mayan ceremonial garb raised a machete over her, ready to sacrifice her to a pagan god.

Duff woke with a start, shook himself, turned over and tried to go back to sleep, but he couldn't get that image out of his mind. No matter how hard he tried, he couldn't sleep.

In his gut he knew something was going to happen today, and it wasn't going to be a tour-guided picnic.

Chapter Ten

Natalie woke early the next morning. She'd been dreaming about Duff, lying naked with him in the sand, waves washing up over their bodies as they made love. The vibration of her cell phone on the nightstand beside her bed pulled her from the most glorious dream.

Natalie reached for the annoying sound and glanced at the screen. It was a text message from Lance: Got info on R and kissers, come see.

Natalie was awake immediately. She sat up and glanced across to where Kylie slept, her hand tucked beneath her cheek.

Dressing quickly, she plugged her headset into her ear and wrote a note to Kylie, saying she'd gone out for a run on the beach. The sun had yet to make its appearance, but the predawn gray light chasing the night away would make it easy to find her way to Lance's bungalow.

Dressed in shorts, a tank top and sneakers, she looked like any health-conscious runner out for a morning jog before the sun rose and heated the air.

Once outside the hotel, she jogged down the path that meandered through the bungalows until she reached Lance's. She stopped and pretended to tie her shoe, glancing around for signs of anyone watching. When she'd determined she was alone, she stepped up to the door. Lance opened it and waved her inside.

"What did you find?" she asked as soon as the door clicked closed.

"Well, actually, it's what I didn't find that had me wondering."

"Show me."

Lance sat at the computer and ran his fingers across the keyboard, then clicked the mouse, bringing up a passport image of the man Natalie followed to the bungalow the previous evening.

"Kissing guy is Frank 'Sly' Jones, former army ranger, now working in D.C. as a security consultant." He flipped to an image of a woman dressed in a skirt suit. "His girlfriend registered under the name Cassandra Teirney, real estate agent, also from D.C."

"Why was Sly dancing with one of our girls when he had a lover back in the bungalow?"

Lance shrugged. "Might be a player." He clicked the mouse and nodded toward the screen. "I'm more concerned about Rolf."

"Why?" Natalie leaned over his shoulder and stared at the monitor.

"I searched the hotel database for our friend Rolf and found Rolf Schwimmer. A quick lookup on the national passport database came up empty. None of the images matched the one you sent me via your cell phone nor of the images I was able to pull from security cameras located throughout the resort."

Natalie's belly tightened. "What *did* you find?"

"I had Royce run a facial recognition program starting with U.S. criminal databases. While he was doing that, I ran one against the U.S. military identification database and got a hit."

"He's one of our military?"

"Was." Lance brought up an image of Rolf dressed in the desert camouflage uniform of the U.S. Army Special Forces. "He left the service four years ago, after ten years and four deployments to the Middle East and two purple hearts. His legal name is Rex Masters. He was a sniper."

Natalie studied the image, recognizing the same man who called himself Rolf in Cancun. "What's he doing now?"

Lance shook his head. "That's just it. I can't find anything else on him from the past four years that he's been out of the military. No address, no tax records. Nothing."

Natalie's blood chilled in her veins. "Do you think he's hired on somewhere as a mercenary? Maybe for a foreign country or agency?"

Lance shrugged. "That's all I found. He actually arrived in this country a week ago."

"About the time the women started disappearing." Anger warmed her blood and made her want to march right out and confront the bastard. "If he's the one responsible for my sister's disappearance, I'll kill him and take great pleasure in doing so."

"We can't be certain he's involved with the missing women. However, he just left his room on the fourth floor of the hotel. If you want to get inside, I'll keep an eye on his movements and let you know when he gets close." Lance glanced at his watch. "People usually don't start stirring for another half hour."

"Then why is he?" Natalie asked.

"He's wearing running shoes, shorts and no shirt. I assume he's on his way out to run. Something I need to do."

"You got a way for me to get past his door lock?"

"I can unlock it from here." He grinned and pulled up a screen. "I'm tapped into the hotel security database. I can unlock any door anytime."

"Okay. It'll take me a couple minutes to get there. Can you block the security camera from following me to his room?"

"Got it covered. Hurry. I don't know how long the guy can run."

Natalie waited for Lance to give her the all-clear signal before she left his bungalow and jogged back to the hotel. If Rolf—Rex—got back before she was finished searching his room, she'd have a hard time justifying being in there. Given that he was a highly trained military man, he might take offense to having his privacy violated. And if he was involved in the kidnapping of the women, he'd have reason to want to insure her silence on whatever she might discover.

Her heart beating fast, Natalie entered the hotel and took the stairs to the fourth floor, running all the way up. Thankfully, she stayed in good shape and wasn't that winded by the time she emerged on Rex's floor.

Lance gave her the room number. As she reached it, she noted the Do No Disturb sign hung on the handle. The indicator light blinked green as she approached. Wrapping her hand in the hem of her tank top, she twisted the door handle and pushed it inward.

Inside she found a neatly kept room with clothes hung in the closet, the shirts all facing the same direction, the trousers neatly pressed.

A suitcase sat on the luggage rack zipped closed.

Natalie checked the drawers first, finding rolled socks, T-shirts and shorts. It looked like the inside of an army recruit's footlocker. Everything was placed precisely. A drill sergeant's ace cadet.

Careful not to disturb anything, Natalie checked beneath the clothing, pulled the drawers out and looked behind each. Hating to disturb the neatly made bed, she searched beneath the pillows, mattress and the bed itself. The lock box in the closet was locked.

"I don't suppose you could get me inside the lock box?" She spoke softly.

"Sorry. It's not on the security network."

Natalie turned to the suitcase. The lightweight, black, hard-plastic case appeared like any other. She unlatched the case and peered inside. It looked empty at first glance. But as she looked closer it appeared to be shallower than the exterior would indicate. Could it have a secret panel?

Running her fingers along the inside edges, Natalie couldn't feel anything out of the ordinary. She examined the exterior and couldn't see anything that looked like a button to be pushed to reveal an inner compartment.

She took the case into the bathroom and laid it on the counter in the bright lighting and opened it. Slowly, carefully, she looked again.

There. At the inside edge, there was a slight discoloration in the plastic rim. She slid her hand over it sideways and nothing happened. Bracing her thumb on it, she pushed it upward. Something clicked and the lining of the case rose on one side. "I found a secret compartment in his suitcase."

"Yeah, find out what's in it and get the hell out. He's on his way through the side entrance."

Her heart racing, Natalie tugged at the floor of the case, trying to open it. "Can't you stall his elevator or something? I need a little more time."

"I would, but he's headed for the stairwell."

"Damn." Natalie pulled harder, forcing the bottom of the case open. She gasped.

"What's in it?" Lance's voice echoed in her ear.

"A gun and an envelope."

"You don't have time. You have to get out."

"I need to know what's in the envelope." She pulled open the envelope and photographs fell out, landing on the floor of the bathroom. All of them were of beautiful blonde women. In the middle of the photos was one of Melody—one she'd posted on her profile page of her favorite social media site.

"He's in the stairwell," Lance said, his voice urgent. "Get out, Nat."

Natalie gathered the photographs and shoved them back into the envelope, tossed it into the secret compartment and secured it in place. It didn't quite fit right, but she didn't have time to return it to its original state. Slamming the case shut, she carried it back to the room, laid it on the luggage rack and slipped out the door. With no time to spare, she ran for the elevator and punched the button.

"You don't have time to wait for the elevator." Lance's voice sounded in her ear. "The room directly behind you is vacant. Go!"

Natalie spun, grabbed the door handle and pushed it open as the stairwell door opened at the other end of the hall. She dived inside and let the door close automatically. She could hear Masters's footsteps, but the door clicked shut before he reached her position.

Her heart thundering in her chest, Natalie waited for a few seconds.

"Masters is in his room," Lance's calm voice said softly. "The elevator is at the fourth floor and is about to open...now."

Natalie pulled open the room door as the elevator bell dinged. A quick glance toward Masters's closed door and Natalie scampered across the hall into the open elevator.

"Good morning, Natalie."

DUFF SHOOK HIS head at the red flush rising in Natalie's cheeks. "You're out and about early. I take it you found out something new."

She nodded. "Let's go to your room and I'll tell you all about it."

The elevator rose to the eighth floor and Natalie stepped out.

Duff could hear the women before he actually saw them. He strode into the hallway to find Melody's friends gathered at the elevator, wearing shorts, matching T-shirts and carrying light backpacks.

"What's going on?" Natalie asked.

"We're going down for breakfast. If you still want to come along, you need to hurry, the bus leaves at eight."

"We'll be right down," Natalie said. "Don't let the bus leave without us."

The girls stepped onto the elevator and Natalie hurried toward her room.

"Are you sure it's a good idea for them to go on that tour?" Duff followed Natalie into her room.

"No. But I'm going with them. Maybe there *is* safety in numbers."

"Do you mind telling me what you were doing on the fourth floor?"

When the door closed behind Duff, Natalie turned and wrapped her arms around his neck. "I may have found our kidnapper."

He held her for a brief moment. "Tell me."

She pushed away from him, her eyes suspiciously bright. "Look, I don't have time to explain everything, but I had reason to suspect our friend Rolf."

While she spoke, she slipped out of her tank top, pulled a light, short-sleeved blouse over her sports bra and tied it around her waist, leaving a significant amount of her midriff exposed.

Duff's groin tightened, but he resisted taking her back into his arms and kissing her all the way down to that tempting display of flesh.

"Rolf isn't Rolf. He's former army sniper Rex Masters."

Natalie slipped out of her running shorts and stood in front of her suitcase in a pair of sheer pink thong panties.

Duff dragged in a deep breath and let it out slowly. "You realize you're killing me."

She cast him a weak smile. "If we only had time…"

Duff willed his body to relax. As much as he wanted to make love to Natalie, they had bigger fish to fry. "What did you find in Masters's room?"

She reached for a pair of shorts and paused. "A secret compartment in his suitcase."

"I take it you got inside." When she nodded, he asked, "What did you find?"

Natalie glanced up at him. "A gun and an envelope filled with photos of blondes. One of which was my sister." She bit her lip, her eyes pooling with tears. One slipped down her cheek. She dashed her hand across, capturing it, and straightened her shoulders. Then she pulled on a pair of denim cutoffs, frayed at the hem. In the outfit, she appeared younger, the same age as her sister's friends.

Duff's brow knit. "If he's the one, why don't we confront him?"

"I can't afford to spook him. If he disappears, my sister's location disappears with him."

"So what now?"

"We go to Chichén Itzá with Melody's friends. I can't let them go alone."

"Talk them out of it."

"I can't. There have been what appear to be two attempts to nab blondes from the patrons of this resort. If Masters is the one responsible, he might try again on the trip to Chichén Itzá. I want to be the one he goes for. You can't be around when he makes his move. He has to think I'm alone and unprotected."

Duff's gut tightened and he grabbed her arms. "The man has a gun. How will you protect yourself against bullets?"

"If he's after me to sell me, he won't want to damage the goods." Natalie stared up into his face. "And I'm not completely alone here."

"What do you mean?"

She pulled the miniature earbud from her ear. "I have someone following my movements and helping me."

Duff frowned. "What are you talking about?"

She pointed to her foot. "I have a microchip embedded between my toes, and a highly trained man on the

YOUR PARTICIPATION IS REQUESTED!

Dear Reader,

Since you are a lover of our books – we would like to get to know you!

Inside you will find a short Reader's Survey. Sharing your answers with us will help our editorial staff understand who you are and what activities you enjoy.

To thank you for your participation, we would like to send you 2 books and 2 gifts – **ABSOLUTELY FREE!**

Enjoy your gifts with our appreciation,

Pam Powers

SEE INSIDE FOR READER'S SURVEY

For Your Reading Pleasure...

We'll send you 2 books and 2 gifts
ABSOLUTELY FREE
just for completing our Reader's Survey!

YOUR READER'S SURVEY
"THANK YOU" FREE GIFTS INCLUDE:
- ▶ 2 FREE books
- ▶ 2 lovely surprise gifts

PLEASE FILL IN THE CIRCLES COMPLETELY TO RESPOND

1) What type of fiction books do you enjoy reading? (Check all that apply)
- ○ Suspense/Thrillers
- ○ Action/Adventure
- ○ Modern-day Romances
- ○ Historical Romance
- ○ Humour
- ○ Paranormal Romance

2) What attracted you most to the last fiction book you purchased on impulse?
- ○ The Title
- ○ The Cover
- ○ The Author
- ○ The Story

3) What is usually the greatest influencer when you <u>plan</u> to buy a book?
- ○ Advertising
- ○ Referral
- ○ Book Review

4) How often do you access the internet?
- ○ Daily
- ○ Weekly
- ○ Monthly
- ○ Rarely or never.

5) How many NEW paperback fiction novels have you purchased in the past 3 months?
- ○ 0 - 2
- ○ 3 - 6
- ○ 7 or more

YES! I have completed the Reader's Survey. Please send me the 2 FREE books and 2 FREE gifts (gifts are worth about $10) for which I qualify. I understand that I am under no obligation to purchase any books, as explained on the back of this card.

❏ I prefer the regular-print edition
182 HDL GJ2F/382 HDL GJ2G

❏ I prefer the larger-print edition
199 HDL GJ2H/399 HDL GJ2J

FIRST NAME	LAST NAME

ADDRESS

APT.#	CITY

STATE/PROV.	ZIP/POSTAL CODE

I-216-SUR16

Accepting your 2 free Harlequin Intrigue® books and 2 free gifts (gifts valued at approximately $10.00) places you under no obligation to buy anything. You may keep the books and gifts and return the shipping statement marked "cancel." If you do not cancel, about a month later we'll send you 6 additional books and bill you just $4.74 each for the regular-print edition or $5.49 each for the larger-print edition in the U.S. or $5.49 each for the regular-print edition or $6.24 each for the larger-print edition in Canada. That is a savings of at least 11% off the cover price. It's quite a bargain! Shipping and handling is just 50¢ per book in the U.S. and 75¢ per book in Canada.* You may cancel at any time, but if you choose to continue, every month we'll send you 6 more books, which you may either purchase at the discount price or return to us and cancel your subscription. *Terms and prices subject to change without notice. Prices do not include applicable taxes. Sales tax applicable in N.Y. Canadian residents will be charged applicable taxes. Offer not valid in Quebec. Books received may not be as shown. All orders subject to approval. Credit or debit balances in a customer's account(s) may be offset by any other outstanding balance owed by or to the customer. Please allow 4 to 6 weeks for delivery. Offer available while quantities last.

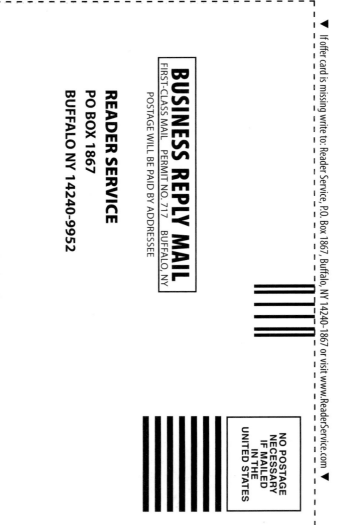

▼ If offer card is missing write to: Reader Service, P.O. Box 1867, Buffalo, NY 14240-1867 or visit www.ReaderService.com ▼

BUSINESS REPLY MAIL
FIRST-CLASS MAIL   PERMIT NO. 717   BUFFALO, NY

POSTAGE WILL BE PAID BY ADDRESSEE

READER SERVICE
PO BOX 1867
BUFFALO NY 14240-9952

NO POSTAGE
NECESSARY
IF MAILED
IN THE
UNITED STATES

other end of the tracking device who can locate me anywhere on earth."

"What good will that do if you're dead?"

Her lips tightened. "It's a chance I have to take to find my sister."

Duff stared at Natalie. "There seems to be a lot I don't know about you."

"And if, after this is all said and done, we are still interested in each other, I'll fill in the blanks. If anything happens to me on this excursion, my man will find you." She planted her hands on her hips. "Now, are you coming with us?"

Duff didn't like being kept in the dark, but he didn't have a choice. He couldn't let her go on her own. "I need to shower and change."

"I'll be downstairs with the others. When you get on the bus, sit with someone else."

"Won't the girls wonder why?"

"I'll sit with Kylie. I don't want whoever is abducting women to think we're together."

Duff brushes his finger across her shoulder. "I won't like it."

"Neither will I, but the longer my sister is missing, the greater the chance I won't find her. She's my only living relative. I won't let her go without a fight."

Duff circled that bare midriff and yanked Natalie close, her body pressing against his. "When we find your sister, you and I are going to have a little talk." He brushed his mouth across hers. "And then we'll talk some more." This time he claimed her lips, crushing her to him, in a desperate embrace. If his gut was right—and it always was—today would be hell.

This woman he'd only known for such a short time

had made an immediate impact on his thoughts and, he suspected, his heart.

Duff raised his head and brushed his lips across the tip of her nose "Don't do anything stupid."

"I'll do whatever it takes to free my sister," she said, her words warm against his lips.

"That's what I'm afraid of." He kissed her again and let go of her. "I'll be down before the bus leaves. Don't let it go without me on it."

Duff left her room and entered his. Dialing the number for Sawyer's bungalow, he waited while it rang.

"Yeah," Sawyer answered.

"We're going. Meet in front of the hotel at eight."

"Got it." Sawyer didn't wait for additional information, just hung up. Duff could rely on his friend to notify the other two members of his team.

Duff ducked into the shower, washing away the sweat from his run. In fewer than ten minutes he was dressed and downstairs. He met with his team at the breakfast table. They loaded up on protein and juice. Not knowing what to expect, they charged their bodies with what it took to run an extended mission.

"Keep an eye out for Rolf. He's not who he says he is and he might be armed," Duff told them, his voice low enough only they could hear.

Sawyer, Quentin and Montana nodded, finishing their meals in silence. Quentin and Montana would take the rental car and be on their way to the ruins before the bus left the hotel.

Sawyer and Duff met with the twenty-five people signed up for the tour. Natalie worked her way over to him without being too obvious. "Kylie gave the tour director your names. You're on the list in place of Lisa and Jodie."

Duff gave the slightest of nods and raised a hand when his name was called out.

Delayed several minutes by one late-riser, the bus left the hotel almost on schedule, the tour guide giving a running commentary on the rich history of the area and the Mayan culture dating back centuries earlier.

Duff sat near the back of the bus. Natalie sat toward the center with Kylie at her side. So far, he'd seen no sign of Masters. For that matter, he didn't see Loverboy from Natalie's Peeping Tom efforts the night before. Other than Sawyer, Duff and the missing Melody's young friends, the bus was filled with gray-haired senior citizens, excited to be on their way to completing items on their bucket lists.

Even if this turned out to be a nonevent, he'd be better off treating it as the most intense, focused mission he'd ever conducted. The trip seemed innocuous, but Duff had been on missions that, on the surface, should have been slam-dunks. Those had been the ones where he'd lost fellow teammates.

Chapter Eleven

Natalie sat beside Kylie, pretending to listen to what the tour guide was saying about the customs of the ancient Mayans and the importance of the temple they were about to see. All the while Natalie focused on everything around her, wishing she could have brought a gun. She felt naked and exposed in this foreign country, populated with drug lords vying for control and thugs looking for easy money.

A hundred questions roiled through her mind with each passing mile, leading them deeper into the jungle and away from the relative protection of the resort security.

Foremost in her mind was where they had hidden her sister and the other women. Who was in charge of the kidnapping ring? Was it Masters? Or was he a gun for hire? A mercenary who contracted out to the highest bidder no matter what the job entailed?

If he was a hired hand, who did he answer to?

As they rolled into the parking lot near the ruins, Natalie scanned the area. Hundreds of people came to see the ruins each day, and that day was no different. Other tour buses disgorged their passengers, the guides speaking a mix of Spanish, English, and even some Japanese or Chinese.

Natalie didn't care what language they spoke, her gaze panned the faces as she waited her turn to get off the bus. With so many people present, it was hard to pick out any one face in the crowd.

Kylie grabbed her hand and hurried her along to catch up to the other girls.

Natalie glanced back. Duff and Sawyer kept pace, staying several yards back, allowing others to come between them.

By the time they hiked from the parking area to the pyramid Castillo de Kukulcán, Natalie was perspiring in the humidity. Chelsea, Hanna, Briana, Kylie and Allison insisted on climbing to the top. "For Melody," Chelsea said.

Though not fond of heights, Natalie couldn't say no. She smiled and faked an excitement she didn't feel, hoping that from the top she might have a better chance of spotting Masters, if he was the one orchestrating the kidnappings.

Natalie brought up the rear on the long climb up the narrow steps. She didn't dare look down for fear she might freeze before she made it to the summit. No matter how much she wished she could go back, the long line of people following her wouldn't be too pleased if she made them move over to allow her to descend. So Natalie continued upward until they finally reached the top.

While the girls stood at the edge, taking pictures of the view and of themselves, Natalie hung back. She pressed a hand to her queasy stomach, petrified at the thought of going back down those narrow stairs when she couldn't even get close to the edge without hyper-ventilating.

"Are you okay?" Duff's deep voice said beside her.

Natalie shook her head.

"Afraid of heights?"

"Is it that obvious?" she said, her voice shaking more than she liked.

"You're as white as a sheet. Other than that, no, it's really not obvious." He chuckled. "Just wanted you to know my other two men are here, watching out for you and the girls."

"That's good to know." She dared a glance at the stairs leading downward and her vision blurred.

"The trick is to look at the back of the head of the person in front of you. Don't stare out at the view or look farther down than you have to. Take one step at a time."

"Thanks. But I'd prefer a rescue helicopter. I get dizzy looking down that long line of stairs. I'm not sure I can do this."

"I'll go down in front of you. If you slip and fall, I'll catch you."

"You're only making it a little better. I could have gone without the suggestion of slipping and falling."

"We're heading down." Kylie appeared in front of her. "Are you feeling okay? You look a little pale."

Natalie forced a smile. "I'm fine." *No, I'm not.* But she wasn't going to tell them that. They'd been through so much already, she didn't want to spoil their visit to the ruins by being a big baby about going down what she'd just come up.

Duff spoke to Sawyer, who managed to get in front of Chelsea before she started down.

Kylie followed the others, taking the stairs with ease.

Afraid they'd get too far ahead of her, Natalie gripped Duff's arm. "Okay, I'd like to take you up on catching me if I fall. Besides, you're tall. Even a step down from me you'll still be almost eye level."

Duff chuckled. "My pleasure." He stepped down and held out a hand to her. "Coming?"

As he made that step down, Natalie's heart stuttered, caught and held. When she placed her hand in his, her pulse raced ahead and her head spun. She stared down at the long flight of stairs to the bottom and swayed.

"Look at me," Duff commanded.

She glanced up, her gaze connecting with his. "I can't do this."

"You can, and you will," he said, his tone firm, confident.

"Easy for you to say," she quipped. "You're not the one terrified of heights."

"I was until the twentieth time I fast-roped out of a helicopter. By then I realized I was wasting a lot of energy better spent on the mission at hand." He stared into her eyes. "Your mission is to see those girls all get home safely to their parents and to find your sister. You can't do that from up here. So, are you going to stand there shaking, or are you going to follow me down off this temple?" The more he talked the stronger his voice.

Natalie straightened her shoulders and nodded. "I'm coming." Her hand in his, she took that first step down, only glancing at the steps long enough to place her foot, then focusing on the back of Duff's dark head. He really was a gorgeous man, and he was right. Her duty was to her sister and to the girls already halfway down the pyramid.

One step at a time, she placed her feet carefully, refusing to stumble, knowing she would take Duff down with her if she fell, and possibly everyone else in front of him. A domino effect of disaster.

Her breath caught in her throat and her pulse thundered in her ears.

"Breathe, Natalie," Duff said. "You've got this."

When she glanced up from the view of her feet on the stairs, she caught the intense green of Duff's eyes. "I've got this," she repeated, and took another step, then another until she settled into a rhythm that got her all the way to the bottom.

Once on the ground, her knees wobbled. She wanted to lie down spread-eagle and kiss the earth. And would have, except Duff's arm slipped around her waist and held her upright until she stopped shaking.

"Come on, Natalia," Kylie called out, fifty feet ahead of her and Duff, trailing Chelsea and her gang. "We're going to the Temple of Jaguars."

Natalie stared up into Duff's face and gave him a lopsided smile. "Thanks. I don't think I could have made it down without you."

"Glad to be of assistance." He stepped away, nodding toward the others. "You'd better get going."

Leaning up on her toes, she kissed his lips and then hurried after the young women, afraid if she stayed with him much longer, she'd make a complete fool of herself, throw her arms around his neck and promise him her firstborn child for getting her down off the sacred temple.

Natalie caught up with the others in front of the Upper Temple of the Jaguars. They spent the next thirty minutes wandering through the Ball Court where ancient Mayans had played some sort of sport with a large, heavy, rubber ball.

When they were standing in front of the Temple of the Bearded Man, Chelsea dug her hand into her small backpack. "Damn."

"What's wrong?" Natalie asked.

"I dropped my phone back on the playing field. I'll be right back."

"I'll go with you." Hanna turned around and followed Chelsea, who hadn't waited.

"My picture of the jaguar's head came out blurred. I'd like to go back and get another before we move on. I'll go with them." Allison dug her smartphone out of her pocket and hurried after them. "Wait up."

Natalie called out, "You should all stay together."

Chelsea spun, walking backward. "It's daylight and there are hundreds of people around. If something happens, we'll just yell. It will only take a few minutes."

Kylie shaded her eyes from the glare of the sun and stared after the three girls. "Should we wait here?"

"I'd rather not," Briana said. "There's no shade. We could at least wait in the Bearded Man Temple." She didn't wait for Kylie's response, moving into the shadows of the temple. Kylie followed.

Natalie paused, hoping to catch Duff's attention.

Pretending to admire one of the Ball Court's two stone rings, Duff and Sawyer stood near one of the high walls inside the Ball Court. Every so often Duff would glance in Natalie's direction, without being too noticeable.

On one such glance, Natalie caught Duff's eye and nodded toward the girls headed back to the center of Ball Court.

He gave her an imperceptible nod and nudged Sawyer. Sawyer shot a glance toward the girls.

Duff's other two friends were standing at the entrance to the Upper Temple of the Jaguar, on standby in case Duff and Sawyer needed their help.

Natalie felt better knowing the Navy SEALs were there, guarding her back.

When she turned back to Kylie and Briana, her stomach fell.

"Natalia." Briana hurried down the stone steps, her eyes wide, her hand pressed to her chest. "I don't know what happened. One minute I was staring at some drawings with Kylie. I turned my back and the next minute she's gone."

Natalia gripped Briana's arms. "What do you mean she's gone?"

Tears ran down her cheeks. "I searched all over the temple and I can't fine Kylie. I don't know where she disappeared to." Her damp eyes widened and she pressed her knuckles to her lips.

Natalie turned Briana toward Duff and Sawyer who, by now, were watching Natalie and Briana closely from the middle of the Ball Court. "See those two men who came with us on the bus?"

Briana nodded, wiped at the tears streaming down her face. "Yes."

"Go to them, tell them what you told me and do whatever they tell you to do."

"Why?"

"Just do it." Natalie gave her a shove toward Duff. Without waiting for Briana to get across the length of the field, Natalie ran up the steps into the Temple of the Bearded Man, cursing at her stupidity. She'd taken her gaze off the girls for a moment. Now one of them was gone. The one with the lightest blond hair.

The Temple of the Bearded Man sat closest to the jungle's edge. Over the centuries trees and bushes had crept closer, a perfect place for someone to lie in wait for that perfect moment to snatch an unsuspecting young woman away from her friends.

Her heart sick for Kylie, Natalie ran around the side of the temple toward the back where the jungle's shadows were darkest.

"Kylie?" she called out, praying the young lady had only stepped around the back to study the carvings on the wall.

Near the edge of the tree line, something pink lay on the ground.

Natalie ran toward it and scooped up the bright pink beaded necklace Kylie had worn that morning. The clasp had broken and beads had spilled across the ground. Natalie flung the necklace to the side and ran toward the trees. "You want a blonde, take me!" she shouted.

As she neared the dark, overhanging vines, a shadow shifted and a Hispanic man emerged, lunged for her and pulled her into the jungle.

Not until it was too late did Natalie realize he wasn't alone. Another man with wicked dragon tattoos twisting across the skin of his arms stood beneath the branches of a tree, holding a syringe in his hand.

Natalie started to scream. The man who held her clamped his hand over her mouth.

She bit his palm and struggled, twisting and writhing, trying to avoid the syringe.

The man who'd grabbed her slammed her to the

ground on her stomach and landed on her back. His partner jammed the needle into her arm and Natalie's body went limp.

She could hear and see what was going on, but she was powerless to fight back. The two men converged on her, one grabbing her beneath the arms, the other lifting her by the ankles. They carried her along a trail, half walking and half running.

Duff. Natalie tried to shout, her mouth as paralyzed as her arms and legs. Gray clouds gathered around the edges of her vision, creeping in until she was consumed by darkness.

As soon as Duff saw the girl running toward him and Natalie racing up the steps to the Temple of the Bearded Man, he knew something was wrong.

"We got a problem." Duff backhanded Sawyer and took off at a dead run.

"What?" Sawyer caught up to him before he'd gone five yards.

"See that girl running toward us?" Duff said without slowing.

"Yeah."

"Stay with her. Natalie just ran toward that temple."

"So?"

"Just stay with her," Duff called out.

When they came abreast of the crying young lady, Sawyer ground to a stop and pulled the girl into his arms. "Hey, everything's going to be okay."

"What happened?" Duff asked, pausing long enough to hear her story.

"Kylie disappeared..." The girl hiccupped and swallowed a sob. "Natalia is going after her."

Before the last words left the girl's mouth, Duff was already racing toward the temple. He took the stone steps two at a time, ran through the columns and slipped around the back of the ancient building. He stopped, willing the blood pumping through his veins to slow enough he could hear sounds past the pounding in his ears. Nothing stirred, no one moved and he found no sign of Natalie, just the darkness of the tree line teasing him, tempting him to enter. But where?

A bright flash of color lay at the edge of the jungle. He ran toward it and bent to study the remains of a pink beaded necklace like the one Kylie had worn that morning.

Duff entered the wooded area, pushing through the brush. He found several broken branches and the ground disturbed by footprints. He bent to study them and discovered an empty syringe almost hidden by the broad leaves of a plant.

His gut clenched and he straightened. What appeared to be a narrow path, possibly used by animals, stretched ahead of him. He ran through the jungle, realizing the path circled back. Eventually he emerged in a small clearing beside the road the tour buses came in on. Tire tracks led from the clearing to the road.

Duff ran out onto the road and stared both ways. A bus carrying a group of Japanese tourists rumbled past him, heading for the temples, stirring up a cloud of dust.

They were gone.

Whoever had taken Kylie and Natalie had gotten away. With no way of catching them on foot, Duff turned toward the ceremonial ruins of Chichén Itzá and jogged back.

He'd covered half a mile when a Jeep roared up to

him. Montana slammed on the brakes and Quentin leaned out. "Get in. Maybe we can catch them."

"What about the other women?" Duff said, climbing into the backseat.

"Sawyer is taking the bus back with them. We didn't have room in the Jeep to fit all of them."

Before Duff was fully in the Jeep, Montana shifted into gear and tore out, spitting gravel up behind them.

Duff was slammed back in his seat. He didn't care. He shouldn't have given Natalie so much space. Whoever had taken the women had used drugs to subdue them.

His chest tightened as he realized Natalie had gotten her wish. She'd wanted to be taken by the kidnappers to wherever they might be hiding her sister.

Despite how fast Montana drove they never caught up to the vehicle spiriting Kylie and Natalie away. As they rounded a bend in the road they came upon a grassy clearing, the grass bent and the branches on the nearby trees waved frenetically as a helicopter rose into the sky. Below, a battered white van stood with the doors opened wide. Empty.

Duff stared up at the helicopter. "Anyone catch the lettering on the tail?"

Montana and Quentin shook their heads.

"What are the chances of tracing that helicopter?"

"Better if we were in the States," Quentin answered.

"Nil here in Mexico," Montana agreed.

Duff's fists clenched. No way he'd let Natalie disappear. She was just the kind of woman who could handle a man like him. And he liked that she wasn't completely flawless. Her fear of heights only made her more adorably human.

Quentin turned to Duff. "Where to now?"

His jaw hardened with his resolve to find her and bring her back alive. "Go back to the hotel."

Montana shot a glance over his shoulder. "You don't think they took them back there, do you?"

"No," Duff said. "But someone there will know how to find them."

Chapter Twelve

Natalie faded in and out of consciousness, fighting to remain aware but unable to stay out of the deep, dark abyss that pulled her back each time. At one point she thought she heard the thumping of rotor blades. Wind whipped her hair across her face, the strands lashing her skin.

Fade out.

How long she'd been out, she didn't know. She bounced back to a semiconscious state when her body flopped over a bony shoulder and she was jostled and flung onto a pile of what felt like rags. Still, her eyes refused to open and she slipped away.

When she finally came to she thought she'd opened her eyes, only to find more darkness. Was she awake? Her body ached and something lumpy pressed into her hip.

The lump moved and a moan sounded close by.

Natalie tried to move her body, but it was too heavy, the drug having paralyzed her muscles. It would take time to wear off. Already she could feel tingling in the tips of her fingers. One by one, she wiggled her toes. Hopefully full control of her body would return before her captors came back.

In the meantime the gray fog began clearing from her

brain. Natalie forced air past her vocal chords. "Kylie?" she said, her voice gravelly, barely recognizable to her own ears.

Another moan and the lump beneath her hip twitched.

Taking in a deeper breath, Natalie tried again. "Kylie?"

This time the moan sounded vaguely like Kylie.

A brief feeling of relief stole over Natalie. At least she and Kylie were together. If Natalie could wake her body from the pall of death the drug had induced on it, she might have a fighting chance of getting the girl out of there.

She never wanted one of Melody's friends to be caught in the same human trafficking that had taken Melody from her vacation into this new hell.

Her pulse quickened at the thought of her sister. "Melody?" she called out, her voice getting stronger.

No other sound reached her but that of Kylie breathing and occasionally moaning.

"Where are we?" Kylie mumbled. "I can't move," she added, her tone tightening, her voice rising. "Why can't I move?" She sounded as if she was about to cry.

"Keep calm," Natalie said. "We've been given some kind of paralyzing drug. I'm sure it's temporary. I'm starting to get some movement in my toes and fingers."

Soft sobs echoed through the room.

While she waited for the drug to wear off, Natalie tried to see into the darkness to get an idea of where they were being held.

The lingering, pungent scent of oil and gasoline could mean a lot of different things. They could be in an abandoned auto-repair shop or in a warehouse where they used gasoline-powered forklifts to move pallets. They could be in a completely enclosed parking garage, but it, too, would have to have been abandoned or they would have heard more noise inside.

Natalie strained her ears to pick up any sound outside the building. A low rumbling reached her, then the deep clanking sound of metal hitting concrete. Were they in a warehouse? Maybe near a shipping yard?

"I'm scared," Kylie whimpered.

"It's okay to be scared. We're in a scary situation. But there are people who will find us and get us out of here."

"Who?"

"You know those guys that were hanging out at the bar? The ones that helped save Chelsea and Lisa when they almost drowned?"

"Uh-huh."

"They're Navy SEALs."

Kylie sniffed. "They are?"

"Yes. And they're going to help us get out of this mess."

"How? They don't know where we are." Her voice shook and more sobs followed.

"Trust me," Natalie said. "They'll find us."

"When?"

"I don't know. In the meantime we have to help ourselves."

"I can't even move. How can I help myself?"

"The drug is wearing off. We have to give it time."

"What if those men come back before it wears off?"

"We'll think of something." Natalie prayed the men wouldn't return before she came up with a plan. She'd told Kylie about the SEALs to give her hope. Natalie couldn't guarantee they'd come to the rescue. A lot depended on Lance's tracking device and how quickly they were able to locate her.

In a perfect world, Natalie would let her captors take her to their ultimate destination, after she got Kylie out of whatever warehouse they were in and back to the hotel. She could be on the plane back to the States tomorrow.

In a perfect world.

Hell, in a perfect world, Melody would never have been kidnapped. She and her friends would all have been on a plane back to the States tomorrow. Happy, sunburned and innocent of the ugly truths of the world they lived in.

"I want to go home." Kylie's voice shook and the sound of her sobs made Natalie wish she could pull the girl into her arms and comfort her.

"You will, sweetie," Natalie said softly. "You will."

The sound of voices speaking Spanish outside made her stiffen. "Shh, Kylie."

"Is it the men who took us?" the younger woman whispered.

"I don't know." Natalie listened. The men who'd attacked her had muttered curses in Spanish, but she couldn't tell if they were the same voices as those outside the walls of their prison. "Pretend that you're still unconscious."

Metal on metal clanked as if someone removed a padlock from a hasp. Then a large door swung open, spilling daylight into the interior of what appeared to be a warehouse.

Natalie closed her eyes, leaving them cracked open enough to peer through her lashes.

Four Hispanic men walked in speaking Spanish so fast, Natalie, with her limited grasp on the language, only caught a few words. Women. Night. Then she heard the

Spanish words for "four hundred thousand" followed by the English word "dollars."

Her heart pounded against her ribs. She'd figured this was a human trafficking ring, selling women for money, but hearing the negotiated amount made it terribly real.

Had they already sold Melody to some rich bastard who'd carried her off to some unknown location on the other side of the world?

Hopelessness threatened to overwhelm her. With her body out of commission and her mind going through every horrible scenario, she had to get a grip or lose it entirely. Even if she never found Melody, she could help Kylie escape this nightmare. She hadn't been trained as a special agent only to end up in some sick son of a bitch's harem or sex den.

The men moved toward Natalie and Kylie. Natalie had come to realize the lump beneath her hip was Kylie's foot. No matter how much it had twitched before, Kylie lay still, not moving anything.

Natalie was closest to the door.

One of the men nudged her with the tip of his boot and laughed. He nudged her again, this time a little harder.

Natalie played dead. She wanted them to think the drug was still working and she remained unconscious. Maybe it would buy her some time without them sticking another syringe full of the same drug into her.

A cell phone rang nearby and one of the men spoke in rapid Spanish. When he ended the call, he said something to the others. They turned and walked out of the building, closing and locking the door behind them.

Natalie watched through half-closed eyes as they left, making sure all four men went through the door. The voices faded away, leaving her and Kylie alone.

"What can you move?" Natalie whispered, stretching her fingers and toes.

"Nothing."

"Give it a try," Natalie insisted.

A quiet minute passed and then Kylie said, "I think I moved my fingers."

"Good girl," Natalie said. "Now your toes."

The foot under her hip wiggled.

"I think there's something on top of one of my feet." Kylie wiggled the foot again.

Natalie chuckled. "That's me. Wiggle it and make me feel it. Kick me, if you can. I dare you."

The twitching at her hip intensified until Natalie felt a definite nudge. "That's it. The more you move, the faster the drug wears off. Keep going."

Natalie flexed her hands, exercising her fingers until her arms tingled. Then she moved her arms and bent her knees. Soon she could fling her arm to the side, her body rolling with it, freeing Kylie's foot.

"Better?"

"Yes." Kylie gasped. "I can move my entire leg now."

Natalie could move her legs a little, and the more she tried the better she got until she rolled onto her stomach and pushed to a sitting position. A few more minutes and she might be on her feet and finding a way to get Kylie out of the warehouse.

Voices sounded again outside the building. By the escalating volume, the men were excited or anxious about something.

"Quick," Natalie urged. "If you don't want them to pump you full of drugs again, pretend you're completely unconscious. No matter what, don't let them know otherwise."

DUFF BURST THROUGH the doors of the hotel lobby. Natalie had said if something happened to her, the man behind her tracking device would contact him. He assumed the man would be at the hotel, near to where Natalie was staying.

In the lobby Duff ground to a halt and stared at every man wandering through. No one made eye contact with him.

"Are you sure Natalie said someone would get in touch with you if she disappeared?" Montana asked.

"Yes." Desperate to find Natalie and Kylie, he walked up to a man who appeared reasonably intelligent and demanded, "Do you know Natalie?"

The man backed a step, shaking his head. "No. I have no idea who you're talking about."

A woman stepped up beside the man and slipped her arm through his. "Who is this man, darling?"

The man covered the woman's hand and led her away. "I haven't a clue. I think he mistook me for someone else."

"Who's Natalie?" she asked, shooting a glare over her shoulder at Duff.

"If he's here, he'd have made contact," Sawyer reasoned.

"Damn it, where is he?" Duff pushed through the back door and strode past the pool to the path leading to his bungalow. Perhaps the man would be looking for him there. Or would he look in Natalie's room?

Duff stopped so fast, Montana and Quentin plowed into him. They were on the path to the bungalows. The sun was on its way down and Duff had no idea where to look for Natalie or who her contact was. He clenched his fists, wanting to punch something or someone.

"Dutton Calloway?" A man stepped out of the bungalow farther down from his—the one Duff had peered into when he'd been searching for potential kidnappers. He was the guy with the computer setup. Duff hurried toward him. "Are you Natalie's friend?"

"I am." He held out a hand. "Lance Johnson."

Duff took the hand and gave it a brief shake. "Natalie said you could find her."

"I can, as long as the tracking device is still working and on her."

"She said you embedded it in her."

"I did. It was the safest way to keep it on her. She wouldn't have a chance of losing it or having it removed from her possession."

Lance entered his bungalow and held the door for Duff. Once Duff was inside, the man hurried toward a desk set up with two computer monitors and a keyboard. "Close the door behind you," he called out to Montana and Quentin as he sat in a rolling desk chair.

Duff followed, leaning over Lance's shoulder.

"I knew something was up when she left Chichén Itzá sooner than the tour was scheduled to depart. And when she cut across areas with no roads, I figured whoever had Natalie airlifted her."

"In a civilian helicopter," Duff confirmed. "We didn't get any identification numbers off the tail."

Lance shrugged. "Might not have done any good unless the chopper was registered in the U.S. I tracked her until she came to a stop here." He pointed to one of the screens where a green dot blinked reassuringly.

"Where is it?" Duff asked. "Do you have a coordinate?"

Lance nodded. "I used the coordinate and overlaid

it with a local map. She's in a warehouse on the south side of Cancun."

"Address?" Duff barked.

Lance wrote the address on a piece of paper and handed it to Duff.

Duff spun toward the door.

"Wait," Lance said. "Do Navy SEALs travel with their own personal arsenal?"

Duff dragged in a deep breath. "Not on vacation."

"I packed my knife," Montana offered.

"Me, too," Quentin added. "But I'd rather have my M-4 or a submachine gun."

"Even a SIG P226 would be handy," Montana noted.

"We have to use our heads," Duff reminded them. "We're not on a mission. We aren't even authorized to perform this one."

"But we're going to, aren't we?" Montana asked. "We can't leave Natalie and Kylie to whatever those nutcases have in mind."

"We're going." Duff started for the door again.

Lance stepped in front of him. "You don't have to go unarmed."

Duff fought the urge to push the man out of his way. The longer they hung around, the more chance of the kidnappers moving Natalie and Kylie. "What do you mean?"

"If you'll give me a minute…" Lance stepped to the side and unlocked what looked like a large, ordinary suitcase. He flipped a hidden latch that opened a compartment and revealed several weapons. "I don't have the P226, but I have two SIG P239s and two H&K VP9s, several spare magazines and enough bullets to keep you in business for a short amount of time."

Duff hugged the man and then shoved him to the side. He grabbed the SIG P239, two magazines and four boxes of bullets.

Lance chuckled. "Never had quite that reaction over a couple of guns." He moved to another suitcase and threw it open. Inside was an array of electronic gadgets. He shuffled through them and pulled out two-way headsets. "You can stay in contact with each other." He also handed over a handheld two-way radio. "This is so you can keep in contact with me."

Duff fitted the headset earbud into his ear, tucked the pistol into the waistband of his khaki shorts and draped his T-shirt over the bulge.

Montana and Quentin did the same.

Grabbing the larger two-way radio from Lance, Duff nodded. "Thanks."

"Thank me by getting Nat out of this alive. We'd like to have her come back to work for us."

Duff didn't hang around to find out who "us" was. He had to get to the address Lance had indicated before the kidnappers moved the women. "We have one more man traveling back on the tour bus, Sawyer Houston. Could you fill him in on the operation?"

Lance nodded and tipped his head toward the weapons they carried. "Remember, if you get caught with those weapons, the Mexican government will throw you in jail and destroy the key. And you didn't get them from me."

Duff threw open the door and hurried out, followed by Montana and Quentin.

They returned to the rented Jeep and climbed in. Montana drove while Duff pulled up the map on his smartphone.

Five minutes from their destination, Lance's voice crackled through the radio. "Natalie is on the move. How close are you?"

Duff's fist clenched around the radio. "Five minutes based on my GPS and traffic."

"You don't have five minutes. Be on the lookout for a vehicle that could be carrying them. They appear to be heading northeast."

Montana shot through a stop sign and floored the accelerator.

Quentin leaned over the back of Montana's seat, peering through the windshield.

"Turn left at the next corner," Duff said.

Montana took the corner too fast and the Jeep slid on loose gravel.

Duff hung on to the door handle and prayed they'd get there on time. "At the next street, turn right."

"Natalie is moving fast," Lance said into the handheld radio.

His heart racing, Duff leaned forward, his gaze swinging left and right.

As they neared the next corner, a black van flew threw the intersection.

Montana stomped on the brakes. The Jeep slid toward the van, stopping in time to avoid hitting another open-topped Jeep following the van.

Four men rode in the trailing vehicle, armed with rifles. They aimed them at Montana, Duff and Quentin.

Montana swerved to the right, away from the armed men.

The rapid fire of automatic weapons screamed through the air.

Duff, Montana and Quentin ducked as bullets blasted

through the windshield of their Jeep. Montana jerked the steering wheel in time to keep from ramming into the corner of a building.

The vehicle trailing the van spun in a one-hundred-eighty-degree turn and raced back toward the SEALs.

"Get out and get down!" Duff yelled.

Montana slammed on the brakes, shoved the Jeep into park and all three men dived to the ground. Duff rolled beneath the Jeep, pulled his weapon from the waistband of his pants and opened fire on the oncoming vehicle.

The man carrying the automatic weapon ducked but let loose a stream of bullets, hitting the rented Jeep.

Montana, SEAL Boat Team's sniper, cursed and opened fire with the loaned weapon. "Need my damned rifle. This toy doesn't have the range."

Quentin waited until the vehicle was in range and opened fire.

Duff took careful aim and hit one of the men holding an automatic rifle. The man collapsed against one of the others, knocking his aim off, his bullets sailing wide of their target.

Montana took out another one of the men. The driver spun the SUV around and raced away.

Duff rolled to his feet. The van had disappeared. He ran for the Jeep and jumped in. "Let's go!"

Montana leaped into the Jeep, shifted gears and gunned the accelerator as Quentin threw himself into the back.

The Jeep leaped forward, pulling hard to the left.

"What's wrong?"

Montana leaned out the window as he struggled to keep the vehicle headed straight down the road. "We took a hit to the left front tire." Montana shook his head, slowing to a stop. "We won't catch them on a flat tire."

"Damn!" Duff shoved open his door and leaped out.

Between the three of them they changed the flat tire almost as fast as a pit crew in a race. But by the time they climbed into the vehicle the other two were long gone. The sound of a police siren wailing in the distance made their decision for them.

"We have to get out of here. We don't have the time to answer questions that will only lead to one or all of us landing in jail."

Montana slammed the shift into drive and raced in the opposite direction of the sirens. With Duff telling him which way to turn, they managed to elude the Mexican authorities and eventually parked in a dingy alley behind a deserted building.

Duff grabbed the two-way radio. "They got away and we had to hide to avoid the Mexican authorities. Where is Natalie now?"

"You're not going to like this," Lance said.

"I don't care if I'll like it or not. Where is she?"

"So far, she's still moving. I'm working on an exact location. From what I can tell, she's somewhere off the Mexican coast headed in the direction of Cozumel."

Chapter Thirteen

The men had returned to the warehouse just when Natalie and Kylie had gotten most of the movement back in their muscles. This time eight men entered. Two women against eight men didn't stand a chance, especially when all eight of the men carried weapons.

Natalie forced her body to remain limp, her eyes almost all the way shut. She could see through her eyelashes, but not well enough to make an escape. Even if she could, she wouldn't try to make a run for it. She couldn't leave Kylie behind.

Four of the men moved toward them. One turned her onto her back and reached for her arms while another grabbed her legs. They swung her up and carried her toward the open doorway and the glaring Mexican sunlight. Though she faked being unconscious, her ears were actively listening to ensure they weren't separating her and Kylie.

A loud scream rent the air. Through the crack of her eyelids, Natalie saw Kylie struggle as two men fought to subdue her. Another man ran toward them and jabbed a needle into Kylie's arm.

Natalie's heart sank. While she might have immediate use of her arms and legs, it would be hours before Kylie regained the use of hers. She'd have to bide her time and come up with a plan to free the girl. She hoped wherever they were taking them, she'd have that opportunity.

The man carrying her tossed her into a waiting van. Natalie flopped onto the hard metal floor and lay still. Kylie's limp form landed on top of her, knocking the wind from her lungs. She refused to budge in case one of the two men who climbed into the back of the van with them noticed she wasn't actually unconscious. The driver climbed in, another man with a gun took the front passenger seat and the van lurched forward.

They hadn't gone far when the driver swerved sharply then straightened.

The man riding shotgun cursed and urged the driver to go faster. The two men in the rear of the van moved to the back window, their weapons held at the ready position.

Natalie heard the squeal of another vehicle's tires. The two men watching through the rear windows of the van cursed and shouted to the men up front. The muffled rumble of automatic weapons loosing a round of bullets reached her through the open front windows of the van.

Natalie's pulse raced. Had her Navy SEAL already caught up with them?

The driver gunned the accelerator, taking corners dangerously fast. The van slid sideways at one point, throwing her two armed guards into the side wall of the vehicle. They leaped to their feet and resumed their positions staring out the rear windows.

If the SEALs had found them, were they prepared to defend themselves against automatic weapons? She prayed they were okay and that the driver of the van they were in didn't crash into a building trying to get away from the firefight.

Soon the van slowed, entered a darkened tunnel or building and came to a stop. The driver cut off the motor. He and the other three men climbed out of the van and spoke to someone else. They sounded angry, their Spanish coming too fast for Natalie to translate.

She faced the open sliding door of the van. Through the narrow crack of her eyelids, she saw two men carrying another man. They dropped him onto the ground and straightened, their faces angry and blood-spattered.

Two more men carried another and laid him next to the first.

Natalie figured there were now six men where there had been eight. Still, six heavily armed men were overwhelming odds when it was just her and an unconscious college coed.

The loud rumble of an engine roaring to life echoed through the dark building. By the sound of it, a marine engine like one used on a high-speed jet boat. Natalie cringed. The farther away from Cancun they went, the harder it would be for Lance to track her and for anyone to come to her and Kylie's rescue. Lance would have to call in the big guns and Royce would have to mobilize more resources to free them. Natalie's Navy SEALs were on vacation. They wouldn't have the firepower to take on this elaborate human trafficking operation.

Natalie fought an overwhelming bout of dread and hopelessness. She couldn't give up. Kylie and Melody depended on her to keep a level head and to think through all her options.

The men returned to the van and one scooped Kylie off Natalie, threw her over his shoulder in a fireman's hold and carried her away.

Another man grabbed Natalie's arm and yanked her up and over his shoulder. With the man's hands holding her thigh clamped to his chest, he carried her toward a waiting boat and dumped her into the arms of another man on deck.

It took total concentration to pretend to be unconscious when the man could as easily have missed and let her crash to the deck. But he caught her, carried her down some steps into a cabin and dumped her onto a bunk. Kylie lay on the other bunk, her eyes closed.

The man left the cabin, shutting and locking the door behind him.

Natalie studied the room before moving, searching for any hidden cameras. When she determined there were none, she sat up and left her bunk to check on Kylie. She pressed her fingers to the base of the young woman's neck and felt the reassuring beat of Kylie's pulse. She lay motionless, but her chest rose and fell with each breath. She was drugged but alive.

The engines throbbed beneath Natalie's feet and the vessel jerked forward as the boat left its mooring.

Natalie rubbed the spot between her toes where Lance had injected her with the tracking device. Locked in a boat's cabin, headed out to sea, their options for escape had considerably narrowed. But, hell, they eventually had to stop somewhere to fuel up, if nothing else. She'd make her escape then. In the meantime she had to find out as much as possible about this boat, the human trafficking operation and where they were taking the women.

Natalie closed her eyes and prayed—something she hadn't done much of since her parents died.

Please let me find Melody and get her and Kylie out of this mess.

DUFF, MONTANA AND Quentin headed for the nearest marina. Ditching the bullet-pocked Jeep behind a building two blocks from their destination, they continued on foot. They stopped at a shop and purchased a straw beach bag and colorful beach towels. Wrapping their pistols in the towels, they stuffed them into the bag, along with the handheld radio. Quentin carried the bag as they approached a dive shop at the marina.

Lance had informed them Sawyer had returned with the tour bus. He'd been full of questions, wanting to know where they were and what the hell had happened. Lance had filled him in and then given Duff the location of the marina. He and Sawyer would be at the marina's dive shop before them.

Duff entered the shop at the marina, not sure what to expect.

Sawyer stood beside Lance who spoke in fluent Spanish with the owner.

Four tanks and four buoyancy control devices lay across the floor at Lance's feet and it appeared he was negotiating with the owner for more items.

Duff edged up to Sawyer. "I take it we're going on a diving excursion."

Sawyer grinned. "Yup."

"Won't we need a boat?" Duff asked.

"Lance's boss has arranged for one."

Apparently, Lance's boss had connections. "Any idea who his boss is?"

Sawyer shook his head and glanced down at Duff's skinned knees. "Looks like you took a beating."

Duff shrugged. "I've been through worse."

Lance completed his negotiations and handed the

man a wad of American bills. The owner shoved it into his pocket.

Transaction complete, Lance turned toward Duff and his team. "Let's get this gear on board and test it out before we leave."

Duff didn't ask Lance where they were going. He grabbed a mask, fins, snorkel, tank and buoyancy control vest, heavy with weights, and carried them outside the building.

Lance led the way along the dock to a beautiful forty-foot luxury yacht.

"This belongs to your boss?" Montana asked.

"No. He has friends in high places. This boat is on loan." Lance's lips twisted. "We're under orders to treat it nicely."

Quentin nodded, a smile spreading across his face. "Now this is what I call traveling in style."

They loaded the gear into the yacht and tested all the diving equipment before going any farther.

Once all the devices passed muster, Lance stepped up to the helm. "I could drive this boat, but I'll bet one of you would do a better job while I man the tracking device."

"I'll drive," Duff said. As a member of SEAL Boat Team 22, he'd been trained to operate a variety of military watercraft. Growing up near Port Aransas, he'd had the opportunity to operate a variety of fishing boats, as well. Duff knew his way around small seafaring vessels, but never anything as luxurious as this. He sat in the cushioned seat and fired up the engine. "Has Natalie's motion stopped?"

"Not yet. She appears to be heading in the general direction of Cozumel. There aren't a lot of private islands between here and there, so it might be where they're heading." Lance pulled a tracking device from a bag he'd carried on board and switched the power on.

The green blinking dot was only slightly reassuring to Duff. Not until he had Natalie alive and safe in his arms would he feel any sense of relief.

Carefully maneuvering the luxury yacht out of the port, Duff set it on course for Cozumel, following Lance's directions.

"The boss mentioned there's a safe below," Lance informed them. "He said we could find everything we might need in it. The combination is nine, one, one, two, zero, zero, one."

"I'll check it out." Montana started down the steps to the cabin below.

"I'll go with you," Quentin said. "The idea of a safe on board intrigues me." He followed Montana.

Duff, intent on navigating, didn't look away from the water in front of him. The busy port required all of his attention until he cleared the majority of the cruise ships and small touring watercraft. When he heard a whoop of excitement, he couldn't help but shoot a glance toward the cabin below.

"The last information I gave Natalie was about the identities of the kissing couple from the night before and Rolf. Did you see any of them at the ruins?"

"No. But tell me what you learned." Duff's fingers tightened on the wheel as Lance filled him in on Rex Masters and the couple Duff and Natalie saw kissing outside the bungalow, Frank "Sly" Jones and Cassandra Teirney.

When Lance finished, Duff asked, "Do you think Rex is responsible for the missing women?"

"I don't know. Why would Jones dance with other women when he had a girlfriend stashed in one of the bungalows?"

"You're not going to believe what I found." Quentin emerged carrying a submachine gun. Montana ascended carrying a black wetsuit and mask, an array of dive knives, scabbards and more.

"This isn't all of it," Quentin said. "There's also C4 and detonators."

"You're kidding," Duff said.

Montana grinned. "I'm happy to report he's not."

Sawyer lifted one of the cushioned seats at the back of the yacht and whistled. "You're not going to believe this."

"What?" Montana hurried to where Sawyer stood staring down into a large storage compartment.

Quentin joined them. "I'll be damned."

Duff, tied to his duties as helmsman, twisted in his seat. "What did you find?"

Sawyer didn't answer, but glanced at Montana. "You grab one end, I'll get the other." Together, they lifted out a long, sleek, metal device almost the length of one of the men.

Duff shot a glance toward Lance. "Who *is* your boss's friend?"

Lance chuckled. "I never know. But that's a state-of-the-art, military-grade diver propulsion device capable of propelling three or four divers at a time."

"I know what it is," Duff said. "What private citizen owns one of those?"

Looking away, Lance answered, "My boss has amazing connections all over the world."

Duff's eyes narrowed. "Who is your boss?"

Lance gave Duff a twisted grin. "Sorry. I'm not at liberty to say. I'd have to get clearance from him."

Duff snorted. "At least tell me he's not a drug lord or someone on the wrong side of the law."

Natalie's friend stared across at Duff, all humor wiped from his face. "He's one of the good guys. Our organization fights *for* justice and *against* corruption."

"Good to know." Duff accepted Lance's word at face value. He appeared to mean what he said with a passion of conviction Duff had only seen in members of the military, in particular, members of the SEALs. "From what I've seen so far, you take care of your own."

"Damn right we do. Natalie would do the same for me or anyone else on the team, even though she hasn't been an active member for the past two years. She left her mark, and it was a good one."

Duff didn't doubt that in the least. She'd been hell-bent on rescuing her sister, but when her sister's friends were in equal danger, she'd looked out for them, as well. And she wasn't afraid of anything.

His lips twitched.

Except heights.

"How much of a lead do they have on us?" Duff asked.

Lance pulled a laptop out of his satchel and fired it up. Within seconds he had the tracking blip overlaid with a satellite map. "They have a forty-five-minute lead. And they're in a fast boat equal to the speed of this one. Until they stop, we won't catch up."

"Then we'll have to hope they stop soon."

"We won't be able to overtake them in daylight," Lance commented. "They could be heavily armed."

"That's just as well. We do our best work in the dark.

And with this equipment and arsenal at our disposal, we can make a go of almost any situation."

"Even if they have an army of guards?" Lance asked.

"We won't borrow trouble." Duff stared at the ocean in front of him. "Let's get to where we're going and put eyes on the situation."

In the distance Duff could make out the thirty-mile-long island of Cozumel.

"They're slowing," Lance glanced up, his eyes wide, energy rippling off him.

"Around Cozumel?" Duff asked.

"Off the northern coastline of Cozumel."

"Isn't most of the development on the east coast?" Duff asked.

"The resorts and tourist areas are. But there are some million-dollar mansions on some of the less accessible areas. People can only reach some of these by boat."

"Will you be able to tell if she goes ashore?"

"Yes. The tracking device can track the exact location to within mere inches." Lance adjusted the screen display to enlarge the image of the island. "It appears as though they are anchoring in a private cove."

"Good. And we'll need to know if we're going to make a ship-to-ship breach or if we'll be going ashore. Either way, we'll get Natalie and Kylie out of there." Duff stared at the map. "We'll stop out of sight of the cove and go in using the diver propulsion device to recon what we can in daylight."

As they neared the island Duff aimed the yacht toward the northern tip of Cozumel, stopping short of rounding the point.

"So what's the plan?" Lance asked.

"We're going fishing." Duff hit the switch to lower the anchor, letting it fall to the ocean floor.

Lance's brows dipped. "Fishing?"

"Well, you are. Three of you will stay with the yacht and pretend to fish. Hell, if you catch anything, we can cook it for supper." Duff shut off the engine and moved toward his team. "Sawyer, you're with me."

"What do you want us to do besides fish?" Montana asked.

"Get the gear together for a night raid. We need to be prepared for climbing onto a boat or going ashore. All the while, you'll be pretending to fish, in case the people holding Natalie have a more elaborate security system that includes this side of the point."

Montana popped a salute. "Gotcha." He turned to Quentin. "Hear that? We're gonna get to do that fishing you wanted to do, after all."

Quentin grinned. "If you thought the armory was impressive, you should see the fishing gear this guy has."

The men checked serviceability and fuel levels on the diver propulsion device. Using a small boom system, they hooked up the DPD and lowered it into the water. Duff and Sawyer geared up in black wetsuits, hoods and scuba gear.

Duff stepped off the back of the boat into the water and sank several feet. The water cooled him in the thick wetsuit. Kicking his fins, he surfaced, adjusted his mask and climbed aboard the propulsion device. The engine started immediately. Duff thanked God for a fastidious yacht owner who knew his military-grade equipment and kept it in great shape.

Sawyer dropped into the water and swam over to him. "Ready?"

"Climb on." Duff stretched into the prone position, holding on to the handles. Sawyer piggybacked Duff, holding on to the side handles of the craft.

They set off. The DPD submerged and left only their heads above the water long enough for them to get around the northern tip of the island. Once around the tip, Duff weaved in and out of the rocky shoreline until they approached a cove. He slowed the craft and let it drift in the waves as they studied the water and the island terrain. Three yachts were anchored in the small bay. A white mansion dominated the hill, overlooking the white crescent of a sandy beach.

The mansion was surrounded by stucco walls, the structure rising three stories, massive windows facing the ocean. A dream house for the rich. A nightmare for anyone unlucky enough to be imprisoned within the walls. The hill surrounding the mansion was thick with short, scrubby vegetation. Not the kind they could easily push their way through in a hurry. If they wanted to gain access to the mansion, it would have to be by sea.

As Duff and Sawyer bobbed in the water, movement on one of the yachts closest to shore captured Duff's attention. Two men climbed into a dinghy at the rear of the yacht and turned to face the boat. Another man emerged on deck, carrying something large over his shoulder. A flash of hot pink made Duff's pulse ratchet up. Based on size and shape, Duff had a good idea what it was the man was carrying. Or rather who.

Kylie had been wearing a pink shirt when she'd been touring Chichén Itzá. The man carrying her dropped her into the arms of one of the men on the dinghy. He caught her and laid her out on one of the seats. Then he turned to face the yacht again.

Another man emerged from a cabin, another body thrown over his shoulder. The woman in the white blouse and cut-off shorts could be none other than Natalie.

His hand on the throttle of the DPD, Duff hesitated. As much as he wanted to rush in and rescue Natalie and Kylie, racing up to the yacht or dinghy would only get him and Sawyer killed.

As if to prove his own point, a shadow moved on the deck and a man holding a submachine gun appeared, his weapon pointing outward toward the other boats in the cove. Another thug dressed in black pants, a black shirt, a black cap and sunglasses, also carrying a submachine gun, stood against the upper railing and stared down at the operation. He lifted his head and stared out at the other yachts in the cove, his head turning as if to take in all movement.

"Going deep," Duff said. He and Sawyer sank to the bottom, directly beneath the yacht.

When he'd been down a good two minutes, he surfaced.

The man in black no longer stood on the top deck. The dinghy pulled away from the back of the yacht and motored toward the shore, with the man in the black cap sitting at the bow, facing the mansion. It didn't take long for the dinghy to run up on the sand. The women were lifted out and carried up the hill toward the mansion.

"At least we know where the women are," Duff said, his jaw hard, his gut clenched.

"I take it we'll be back after dark," Sawyer said behind him.

"Damn right we will." Once the men carrying the women disappeared behind the wall of the estate, Duff turned his attention to the other yachts in the harbor. A man stood on the deck of one, his gaze having followed the progress of the women.

He wore white slacks and a sky-blue polo shirt. He had blond hair and broad shoulders. Duff squinted against the bright sunshine. If he wasn't mistaken, the man in the blue shirt was Rex Masters, the former Army Special Forces sniper. As he stood staring out at the progress of the women being transferred to the mansion, he was joined on deck by a man wearing tailored khaki slacks, a long-sleeved, white, button-up shirt and a light-colored fedora. His facial features were indiscernible beneath the hat and mirrored sunglasses. Considerably shorter than Rex, he appeared thin and somewhat frail in comparison to the former army ranger. He spoke to Rex, waving toward the shore.

Rex nodded several times.

The man in the fedora stared toward the shore for a moment longer, then returned to the cabin.

Rex lifted a pair of binoculars and stared through them toward the mansion.

From what Duff could tell, Rex worked for the man in the fedora. Perhaps he was the scout to find the women his boss desired. Or he was security to his wealthy employer.

Duff's fists tightened around the handles of the DPD. What kind of sick bastard employed former American military to run interference for him?

If Rex was involved in trafficking those women, Duff would make certain the man paid dearly for forsaking his pledge to duty, honor and protecting the freedom of the people in his country.

"Come on, we need to get back and come up with a plan."

"I spotted a number of gunmen on each of the yachts," Sawyer said. "And that doesn't count the ones in the mansion compound itself. I might have caught glimpses of them, but not much more. I couldn't give you an accurate count."

"We'll figure it out when we get there. We'll just have to be loaded for bear." Duff swung the DPD and headed back around the point to the yacht on the other side. The sun lay low in the sky on its path toward the horizon.

Ahead, the yacht cut a long shadow across the water. Three men stood on deck, fishing poles in hand.

When Duff and Sawyer pulled up alongside the yacht, Montana and Quentin were there to tie the DPD to the back. They'd need it again later when darkness settled over the island.

"Stow your fishing gear," Duff said. "We're going hunting tonight."

Chapter Fourteen

Natalie had no idea where they'd been taken. All she knew was they were being transported from the boat to land. At least on land she might have more of a chance of escaping her captors. While waiting in the cabin belowdecks, she'd tried to wake Kylie several times. Unfortunately the dosage they'd given the girl, on top of the last dosage, had knocked her out. Natalie took comfort in the fact she was still breathing.

If Kylie had been awake and able to swim, Natalie would have attempted a get away as soon as the yacht stopped and they'd been carried out on deck and loaded into a dinghy. She could have easily overturned the dinghy with the three men on board. While they scrambled to save their own lives, Natalie would have led Kylie to shore and hidden in the vegetation.

Then again, the vegetation was thick but short. She'd have to find her way through it. To what, she didn't know. If they were on the mainland, she might be hiking a very long time before finding anyone to help them. If they were on an island, it might be a private island with nowhere to go. She'd have to stay hidden until Lance notified Royce and her old boss sent in the cavalry to rescue her.

She didn't think the Navy SEALs would have access to what they'd need to stage a rescue. They weren't on a mission. They were on vacation. Unless Royce armed them and sent them in. If that was the case, she hoped the SEALs wouldn't get in trouble for participating in an unsanctioned mission.

She mustered every ounce of self-control to give the appearance of being semiconscious as opposed to fully aware. When the men came to get her and Kylie, she'd pretended to be drugged to the point she couldn't fight back as one of the men threw her over his shoulder. Kylie didn't have to pretend; she was out.

They were loaded into a dinghy and transported to shore where they were carried up the beach to a walled compound. A white-stucco mansion towered above the walls. A gate opened as they approached and they entered the compound, passing by men with serious-looking machine guns.

"Took you long enough," a man said in English. In Spanish he told the men to follow him.

The voice sounded familiar to Natalie, but she couldn't see the man's face. With her head hanging down behind her henchman's back she could only see what they passed.

They climbed a long, wide staircase leading up to the mansion. The sun slid low in the sky. It would be dark soon. Natalie had to get her, Kylie and anyone else trapped in the mansion out. She prayed this was the place she'd find Melody. And when she did, she'd get them all out. Alive. She also prayed she'd come up with a way to do that.

Once inside the mansion they were carried down long corridors, twisting and turning into the back of the structure. They descended another set of stairs, the hall-way narrower and darker and lined with what appeared to be metal doors on both sides. Each was equipped with a heavy-duty lock requiring a key to open it from the outside.

The sound of metal scraping metal indicated their host was unlocking one of the doors.

Natalie wanted to lean around her captor to see the man with the familiar voice, but she couldn't give herself away. Natalie and Kylie's freedom depended on her faking the extent of the drug's effect.

As she passed through the open door, she glanced up through her lashes.

The man had turned to speak to one of the other guards in Spanish. All Natalie could make out through the gaps between her eyelashes was that he had dark hair.

The man carrying Natalie let her slide off his shoulder, landing hard on her side on a concrete floor. Kylie was dropped beside her. The henchmen backed out of the room, closed the door behind them and the lock clicked in place.

The tiny room was much like a jail cell with nothing other than a sink and a toilet on one side.

Natalie stared at each corner, searching for cameras. Nothing indicated the room was tapped for sound or images. She could move around without worrying someone would figure out she no longer was drugged.

She rolled over to where Kylie lay sprawled on the concrete, her blond hair tangled around her face. Natalie pushed the hair out of her eyes and tapped the young woman's face. "Kylie. Wake up."

The girl's eyes fluttered and opened briefly, revealing that they were glassy and bloodshot with dilated pupils.

"Hey, sweetie," Natalie said softly. "You need to shake it off."

"Can't move," she said.

"Start with your fingers and toes."

"Tired," she muttered, her eyelids closing. "Sleep."

"No, sweetie." Natalie shook her. "You have to wake up. We have to find a way out of here." Natalie grabbed one of her hands and slapped her palm. "Please, Kylie. I can't carry you out, and I won't leave you behind."

Kylie's eyes remained closed but her fingers moved.

"That's it. You moved them. Now, move your toes." Natalie's chest squeezed. How was she going to get them out of there when she had no way to unlock the door? And she couldn't carry Kylie. She'd never move fast enough to escape.

She rolled to her feet and stood in front of the door. Damn. There was no doorknob on the inside. Even if she had a hairpin or file, she couldn't pick the lock. She'd have to wait for someone to open the door and then make her move.

A soft sobbing sound made Natalie stop and hold her breath. It hadn't been from Kylie. It had come from outside the room they were trapped in.

Natalie pressed her ear to the door and listened.

More sobbing and a hiccup.

"Hello?" Natalie called out.

The sobbing stopped.

Natalie tried again, her heart pounding against her ribs. "Hello? Can you hear me?"

"*Ja,*" the voice sounded. *"Vem är där?"*

It was a woman's voice, but she wasn't speaking English. "My name is Natalie. Do you speak English?"

She didn't answer immediately, then she said softly, "A little."

"What's your name?" Natalie asked.

"Sigrid."

"Are you from Sweden?" Natalie asked, her breathing ragged, her eyes stinging.

"Ja."

Natalie closed her eyes to keep tears from falling. She had to swallow several times before she could speak past the knot in her throat. "Are there any other women here?"

"Ja." Sigrid sniffed. *"Två*—how you say?—two."

"Do you know their names?" Natalie braced her palm on the door, her ear pressed hard to the metal surface, straining for what she wanted to hear.

An answer came from farther down the hall. "I'm Katherine Stanton."

Her accent was decidedly Australian, if somewhat slurred.

"Is there another woman?" A tear slipped down Natalie's face.

"There was," Katherine said. "She was taken out of here just before you arrived. They said something about she was up first for sale."

"Did she tell you her name?" Natalie couldn't bear another moment.

"Melody, I think," Katherine said. "Yes, she said her name was Melody."

Natalie sank to her knees, the tears spilling down her cheek. Her sister was alive. Deep in her heart, she'd known. But hearing the other woman say she'd been there moments before filled Natalie's heart with a great joy and a profound terror.

Brushing her tears away, she rose to her feet. "Do you know why they brought you here?" Natalie asked.

Sigrid's sobs started and an answering whimper came from down the hall.

"They're going to sell us." Katherine's voice caught on the last word.

"Not if I can help it." Natalie's tone was firm and determined. "We're going to get out of here."

"How? They have guns. We're on an island. Nobody knows we're here."

Sigrid's sobs grew louder.

Katherine had already lost hope, as had Sigrid.

"Are they still drugging you?" Natalie asked. "Do you know?"

"They haven't injected anything into us since we came, but I don't feel right. I'm dizzy and tired all the time."

"Are they feeding you?" Natalie persisted.

"Yes. They usually bring food twice a day. Once in the morning and again at sunset."

"The drug might be in the food or water." Natalie leaned close to the door. "Don't eat or drink again until we get out of here."

"What are you going to do?" Katherine asked.

"I don't know yet, but you need to be ready when I figure it out."

Her opportunity came knocking with the clomping footsteps in the hallway. A key scraped in the lock.

Natalie dropped to the floor and waited as the door swung open.

THE DIVER PROPULSION device was taxed to its maximum capabilities taking all four SEALs around the point. The men hung on, knowing the DPD would get them there faster and conserve their energy for the fight ahead.

Since Duff and Sawyer had performed their reconnaissance, more yachts had arrived. Now, instead of the three that had been there before, there were eight yachts of various sizes anchored in the cove, their dinghies deployed and resting on the beach, guarded by one of their crew.

Sawyer dropped Duff near one of the larger yachts and then angled the DPD toward the shore where he and the others would wait for him. They would slip from the water, haul the DPD up on the beach and bury it in sand or hide it in the shadows of the underbrush rimming the white sandy beach. They'd wait for Duff before moving forward, needing every man to make this operation viable.

Duff dived beneath the surface and swam up to a fifty-foot luxury yacht, careful not to bump his tank against the hull. He couldn't afford to make a sound that would attract the attention of one the armed guards standing watch on the deck.

Pulling a packet of Semtex plastic explosives from inside his vest, he pressed it against the hull and jammed a detonator into the claylike mass. The charge would be a backup in case they needed a distraction. Once the charge was in place, he swam for shore and the designated landing zone where his team waited.

Sawyer, Montana and Quentin had their gear off but were still dressed in the black wetsuits and masks. They'd piled their fins, tanks and buoyancy control devices on the beach near the vegetation. For any casual observer glancing at the shoreline from a distance, the pile appeared to be just another big bush. Duff shucked his gear and added it to the pile.

"Whatever they have planned is happening tonight," Duff said, fitting the earbuds of the two-way radio headset into his ears. Lance had wrapped them carefully in a waterproof bag along with the two-way radio they would use if they needed Lance to pull a Hail Mary and drive the yacht into the cove to extract them.

Lance had passed on to his boss back in the States the location of the women and the potential of them being sold at auction that night. His boss had promised backup as soon as he could mobilize a team. In the meantime it would be up to the SEALs to stage a rescue operation to free Natalie, Kylie and any other captives.

As well as the communication equipment, they had brought along a larger waterproof bag with the submachine guns, pistols and knives.

Duff took point, followed by Sawyer, Quentin and Montana. Montana would provide cover fire if they were unable to make a silent entry.

As they neared the stuccoed eight-foot wall, Duff told himself getting into the compound would be just like scaling the mud walls of Afghan villages. They were a good seventy-five feet away from the entry gate. Unfortunately all of the visitors were apparently inside and there would be no one to distract the guards while the men slipped over the fence.

Duff glanced at the sky, eyeing a drifting cloud, heading toward the bright moon. As bright white as the walls of the compound were, their black wet suits would stand out when they breached it. Timing would be everything.

Clouds passed over the moon. Sawyer cupped his

hand. Duff stepped into it and pulled himself up to the top of the wall.

The gate guards were smoking cigarettes, their guns slung over their shoulders.

Duff dropped to the ground and rolled into the nearby shrubs. He aimed his submachine gun at the guards, ready to provide cover should they turn toward his position.

Sawyer dropped down next. Quentin stayed atop the wall long enough to haul Montana up, then the two of them landed on the ground and rolled into the brush.

The cloud cover floated away, leaving the grounds exposed to the moonlight.

One of the guards dropped his cigarette and ground it out with his foot, then turned toward where Duff and his team hid in the brush.

After a tense moment he turned back to the other guard and spoke in Spanish. They laughed and pulled out another cigarette.

Hunkered low to the ground, Duff moved toward the mansion, hugging the shadows of the bushes and palm trees. As he neared the house he paused in the shadow of a palm and studied the wide porches. Entering through the front door wasn't an option. There had to be other entrances, including a servant's entrance. He eased around the side and stepped up onto a wide porch. Hugging the shadows of the deep overhang, he slipped up to a French door that appeared to open into a study or library with shelves of books lining the walls. He tried the door handle. It was locked.

Keeping that entrance in mind, he worked his way along the porch to the rear of the building where several utility carts were parked. A door opened and two guards exited the building laughing and speaking in Spanish. Each carried rifles that appeared to be similar to the M-4s used by the American military. They split and headed in opposite directions—one away from Duff, the other toward him.

Duff shrank back against the wall of the building, pulled his knife from the scabbard on his thigh and waited for the guard to pass.

The guard didn't know what hit him. As soon as he passed the shadowed area where Duff stood, Duff slipped up behind him and dispatched him. No fuss, no cries of pain. The man slipped to the ground in a silent heap. Duff dragged him behind a bush and wiped the blood from the knife on the man's shirt.

The other guard had gone around the other end of the mansion, out of sight. Duff moved swiftly toward the back entrance the guards had come through. The door was locked.

Duff jammed his knife between the door and the frame and forced the lock. The door swung open and he slipped inside.

The room he entered appeared to be the laundry room and storage area for pantry staples and cleaning supplies.

Duff leaned out and waved the others in.

He didn't wait for them, but moved toward what smelled like the kitchen. He hovered near the half-open door and peered through the crack.

Servants hurried in and out of the room, carrying trays of drinks and hors d'oeuvres.

Duff waited until the wait staff left the room. He slipped up behind the one who appeared to be the chef and pressed his knife to the man's throat.

The spoon he'd been using to stir something on the gas stove clattered to the floor.

Duff backed him to the storage room and left him with Sawyer who, armed with a roll of duct tape, made quick work of silencing the chef.

Making his way through a swinging door, Duff entered a hallway that split in opposite directions. He could hear the sounds of voices from the left. Footsteps came from that direction. Duff slipped back into the kitchen and waited for the persons owning the feet to either pass the door or enter for more appetizers and drinks for the invited guests.

The footsteps paused on the other side of the door and then moved on.

Duff pushed the door open a crack. Two guards hurried away from the noise, speaking in Spanish. Duff understood the words *llevar las mujeres*. Bring the women. Duff motioned for the team to follow. If these guards were going to get the women to be auctioned that night, they could lead them to Natalie and Kylie.

Duff waited until the men turned a corner then he ran down the hall, careful not to make a noise. His team had his back with Sawyer following close behind, Quentin behind Sawyer, then Montana, who would back down the hallway, weapon raised.

As he neared the corner, Duff slowed. Ducking low, he peered around. The guards had disappeared but there was a staircase leading to a lower level, possibly a basement.

Pushing forward, he eased down the steps. The sounds of Spanish-speaking voices echoed off the walls at the lower level. A woman's scream made Duff abandon caution and take the rest of the stairs two at time.

He arrived at the bottom to find the guards struggling with a blonde woman Duff didn't recognize. She kicked the guard nearest to her in the shin.

He yelped and let go of her.

The woman made a run for it, but the other guard grabbed her hair and yanked her so hard she fell backward, landing on the ground, forcing the guard holding her hair to hunch over.

Duff pointed his weapon. "Let go of her." He didn't care that the guards might not know English. He didn't plan on letting them live long enough to translate.

The guards' heads jerked up at the same time as Duff fired. First one then the other slumped to the floor. The woman between them scrambled to her feet and stared at him wide-eyed.

"Please tell me you're one of the good guys Natalie was alluding to." Her voice had a pleasant Australian accent, similar but different from the one Natalie had tried to use as a disguise.

Duff nodded. "Where is Natalie?"

"She was taken away a few minutes ago." The woman bent to one of the men on the floor and dug in his pockets, unearthing a set of keys. Her hands shook so hard she couldn't push the key into the lock on the door beside her.

Quentin stepped forward. "Let me." He took the key from her. "What's your name, sweetheart?"

"Katherine Stanton." She wrapped her arms around her middle, her entire body shaking. "Are you going to get us out of here?"

"We're sure as hell gonna try." Quentin twisted the key in the door and pushed it open. "Found Kylie." He knelt on the floor and checked her pulse. "She's alive but appears to be drugged."

Duff turned to Katherine. "Do you know where they took Natalie?"

"Probably where they took Melody." Katherine bit her bottom lip, tears rushing to her eyes. "To be auctioned off like cattle."

Duff had to get to Natalie and her sister before that happened. "Sawyer, Montana, you're with me. Quentin, see to the safety of the women. Get them outside if possible. Meet at the rally point."

"How are we going to get them off the island?" Quentin asked.

"That's where Lance comes in. And if all else fails, we'll take one of the yachts anchored in the cove." Duff turned back the way they'd come. He didn't know how many more guards to expect, and being down to three men on his team didn't give him the level of confidence he preferred to have going into a mission. He had no choice. Failure wasn't an option. Natalie's and her sister's lives depended on the SEALs coming through for them. As he neared the room where the voices were getting louder, he fished in his pocket for the detonator and pressed the button.

Chapter Fifteen

The guards had dragged Natalie out of the room she'd shared with Kylie. She didn't like being split up, but then Kylie wasn't going anywhere soon. The drugs they'd given her had incapacitated her to the point she couldn't stand on her own.

Until she found Melody, Natalie couldn't fight back. She needed to save that element of surprise for when they led her into the same room with her sister. If that was their plan. She hoped the buyers weren't taking possession of their women and leaving the island immediately upon payment. The guards led her up the staircase to the main level of the mansion and turned her toward the rear of the building and a large wooden doorway.

The door opened and she was shoved into what appeared to be a large entertainment area with plush leather sofas, modern artwork and men standing, sitting and drinking. Some wore suits, others were more casual in tailored slacks and polo shirts.

All of them turned their attention from the woman at the far end of the room, positioned on a raised dais, her long blond hair brushed smooth, her body barely covered in a sexy pink corset and negligee. She crossed her arms over her breasts, her cheeks pink, her chin tilted up, her blue eyes flashing.

Melody.

Her sister's eyes were glazed and she swayed where she was standing. If not for the armed guards on either side of her, she would have fallen from her perch.

Natalie's heart pinched hard in her chest. She wanted to charge forward and stand in front of her sister, to protect her and take out every one of the sick bastards who'd come to purchase women for their own disgusting desires.

Holding back her gut instinct to barge in kicking butt, Natalie took in the occupants of the room. Eight men who appeared to be buyers. They looked as if they hailed from all over the world. When one of them turned, Natalie swallowed her gasp.

Rolf Schwimmer—or Rex Masters. By either name the man was lower than the worst form of life. He'd fooled them into thinking he was one of the good guys. She'd take him out first.

A man entered through a door at the far end of the room and walked directly across the floor to the side of the dais where a wing-backed chair sat half-facing the stage.

Frank "Sly" Jones, yet another man Natalie was determined to take down when this show got going. The only other woman in the room besides Natalie and Melody sat in a chair near the dais, her face in profile, her hand curled around the stem of a wineglass. When she turned to face Natalie, her lip curled up in a sneer.

Natalie's breath caught in her throat. The woman in front of her was Cassandra Teirney, the real-estate agent from Washington, D.C. How could Royce's data be so wrong? Real-estate agent, ha!

The woman stood without spilling a drop of the red wine. She wore a long black dress that hugged her figure and flowed with every step she took toward Natalie. "Gentlemen, let me present our second offering." She waved her hand at Natalie's figure. "We didn't have time to package her for the occasion, but you can see she is fit, beautiful and should bring top dollar. Do I hear fifty thousand?"

A man held up his hand, his gaze on Natalie's naked midriff, practically salivating.

"Perfect. Notice her long, supple legs and perky, generous breasts. Who will give me one hundred thousand for this prime specimen?"

Natalie's fingers clenched into fists, her nails digging into her palms to keep her from taking a swing at Cassandra and her sneering lip and attitude. She had to let them believe she was as drugged as her sister.

She counted the number of men she presumed were guards, some of them obviously armed, others who could be hiding a weapon beneath their jackets. In all, she counted ten. How the hell she was going to fight ten guards was beyond her. But she wouldn't let Melody leave the room without her. And she refused to let someone hurt her while she was there.

The guards led her toward the dais and pushed her to stand beside Melody.

Melody's head lolled and she glanced up at Natalie. "Nat?" she whispered.

"Shh," Natalie urged. "Don't talk."

"As you gentlemen can plainly see, these two women

are worth every penny and will bring many hours of pleasure," Cassandra continued.

Able to stand on her own, Natalie shook off the hands of the guards and stood in front of the men, trying not to glare and call every last one of them arrogant sons of bitches. These were the kinds of men who gave men of their countries bad reputations.

One of the men walked up to Melody and reached for one of her breasts.

That move broke the camel's back. Without a plan, acting on pure instinct, she cocked her leg and threw a sidekick, catching the buyer in the jaw. He stumbled backward, hit his legs against a side table and fell on his back.

The guards holding up Melody let go and lunged for Natalie. She dodged their hands, swung her leg around and caught the closest one in the nose. A loud snap sounded and blood rushed down his face. He clapped a hand to his broken nose and staggered sideways. His foot caught on the edge of the dais and he tipped over the edge, falling to the floor, landing hard.

The other guard grabbed her arm and yanked it up behind her.

"Wait." Rolf raised his hand. "Don't hurt her or the other woman. I want both of them." He turned to Cassandra. "Three hundred thousand for both."

Cassandra nodded to Frank, who scurried across to the man Natalie had first kicked. He helped him to his feet.

"She's a feisty one, which will translate to much enjoyment in bed." Cassandra turned to the others. "Do I hear a bid of four hundred thousand for the pair?"

The buyer who'd been kicked straightened and held up his hand. "Four hundred thousand."

With her hand pushed up between her shoulder blades, Natalie could barely breathe past the pain.

Rolf raised his hand. "Five hundred thousand dollars."

Natalie wanted to spit in the man's face.

"My, my, she really has your attention, doesn't she?" Cassandra crossed to Rolf and ran her fingers down his chest. "I'll bet you're pretty hot in bed, too." She stared up into his eyes. "Two women might slake your desire." Cassandra snorted softly. "But I doubt it."

Frank stood on the other side of a buyer, his face a ruddy red, his nostrils flaring. He had to be jealous of Cassandra paying too much attention to Rolf.

"Five hundred thousand dollars going once." She paused. "Going twice." Cassandra stared around the room, giving the buyers a chance to bid again. "Sold to this young man who needs two women to make him happy."

The guards shoved Natalie and Melody toward Rolf. He grabbed Natalie and pulled her against him, his hand reaching down to squeeze her bottom. "Don't say anything. I'm here to help," he whispered into her ear. Louder he said, "Nice firm bottom." He reached down and hefted a gray suitcase up onto the table. "Your money." He took Natalie's hand and turned toward the door. "Thank you for setting up this little shindig. My boss will be highly satisfied with his purchases."

Natalie hooked Melody's arm and led her along with them toward the exit. Before they could make it outside, a loud boom shook the crystal chandelier hanging from the ceiling and a shout rang out.

Everyone moved at once. The buyers ran for the exit

and the guards pulled their weapons and turned in circles, searching for the source of the sound. They didn't have long to wait.

Three men charged into the room. Dressed completely in black from the tops of their heads to the tips of their toes, they carried submachine guns. As soon as they entered the room, they dived to the sides of the door, rolled to their feet and fired at the guards holding weapons.

At first confused, Natalie didn't know whether to run for the door or to join the fight. When she caught the flash of green eyes, her heart fluttered and she warmed inside. The cavalry had arrived in the shape of three Navy SEALs.

Grabbing Melody's hand, she pulled her to the ground and shoved her behind a sofa. "Stay!" she said and rolled to her feet to assess how best to help.

DUFF REALIZED NATALIE and Melody would be in danger if they stormed the room. The explosion outside would breed chaos and hopefully Natalie would get down. First through, Duff threw himself to the side, rolled and came up on his haunches. He fired at the nearest gunman, took him down and aimed for the next.

Sawyer and Montana breached the door and performed the same maneuver, taking up positions on the other sides of sofas, dodging the bullets of the guards and returning fire.

Duff scanned the room for Natalie and her sister. His throat closed and his breathing tightened in his chest until he caught a glimpse of Natalie hiding behind a white leather couch on the other side of the room. Though her clothes were wrinkled and her hair was a mess, she appeared relatively unharmed and just as beautiful as when she'd worn the black swimsuit that first caught his attention. Behind Natalie a guard reached for her.

Duff aimed, fired and eliminated that threat. The man fell forward, landing on Natalie's back. She went down on her knees, taking the weight of the heavy man. Then she turned sideways, dumping him to the floor. Glancing across the room, she made eye contact with Duff and mouthed the words *thank you*. Her eyes widened and she yelled, "Duff, behind you!"

Duff rolled to his back. A man stood over him aiming a 9 mm pistol at his chest.

A shot rang out and the man dropped where he stood, his body landing on Duff's legs.

Duff looked around to see Rex Masters retracting his handgun. He turned and fired at a guard about to shoot Sawyer. People ran and yelled. Chaos reigned in the big room.

Kicking his feet free, Duff lurched to a standing position holding his submachine gun at the ready.

The unarmed men ran for the exit. A woman Duff recognized as the one Lance had identified as Cassandra the real-estate agent lifted her dress and raced after the men in suits.

The guards still alive were either wounded or had run out the door with the others.

Sawyer and Montana rose from their positions behind the sofa. They aimed their weapons at the wounded guards on the floor. "Throw your guns to the side."

Those who could, did.

Former army ranger, Frank "Sly" Jones, cut off from the door by Rex and Montana, ran toward Natalie where she remained hunkered down in a squatting position. He pulled a gun from the inside of his jacket and aimed it at her head. "Stop! Or I'll shoot her."

Duff stood, refusing to lower his weapon. For all he knew, Frank would kill Natalie anyway. Duff had a small chance of pulling the trigger first. God, he didn't like playing with the woman's life. But the look on Frank's face didn't bode well for Natalie.

"Throw down your weapon," Frank said. "I will not hesitate to pull the trigger and kill your girlfriend. Do it!"

"Like hell you will." Natalie rolled into the man, hitting him hard in the knees.

Frank's hand went up in the air to balance him. He squeezed the trigger as he teetered and fell backward. The shot hit the ceiling. As soon as he landed, Natalie sprang to her feet, kicked the gun from his fingers and stepped out of reach, holding out her hand. "Give me a gun. I'll kill him for what he did to my sister and the others."

Frank sneered. "You don't have the guts."

"And you are an animal." Natalie's voice shook with her anger.

Duff crossed the room and pulled her into the curve of his arm, his submachine gun aimed at Frank's chest. "It's over, Jones."

Rex Masters stepped up beside Duff. "I'll take care of him."

"Keep him alive," Duff said. "We need to find out who he's working for."

Masters jerked Jones up by the collar, spun him around and tied his wrists with zip-ties.

Duff frowned. "And when you have time, I want to

hear how you got involved in this, and why you were here as a buyer."

"I promise I'll have your answers for you. But for now, I'd like to take this man for interrogation."

Duff's eyes narrowed. "Save it for when we can all be there."

"You bet." Masters shoved Jones toward the exit.

Duff nodded toward Montana. "Stay with him. He might have saved mine and Sawyer's lives, but I still don't know that I trust him."

"You got it." Montana took off after Masters while Sawyer slipped outside to check the surrounding area for the group's escape.

Natalie pressed her face into Duff's chest. "Thank you for coming to the rescue."

Duff chuckled. "I have no doubt you would have gotten yourself out of this mess."

"I could have, but getting the others out alive was more important, and I couldn't have done it without your help." She pushed away from him and ducked behind the white leather couch. When she rose, she helped another blonde to her feet who had a slight resemblance to Natalie.

Natalie glanced up at him and beamed. "Dutton Calloway, I'd like you to meet my sister, Melody."

Melody shoved her hair out of her face and stuck out a hand. "Nice to meet you." She frowned at Natalie. "Who is this man? Are you dating and you haven't told me about it?"

Natalie hugged her sister. "Baby, I'm just glad you're going to be okay. We can catch up when we get back to civilization."

Melody pressed fingers to her temple. "What the

heck did they give me? I feel like I have a heck of a hangover and didn't have the pleasure of the buzz."

Natalie laughed.

Melody's brows puckered. "And where did you learn to kick like that. You've got to teach me that move. I might not be in this situation had I known it."

"There's a lot we need to talk about." Natalie hugged her sister.

"For now, unless we want to spend time in a Mexican jail, we need to get back to Cancun." Duff waved his weapon toward the exit.

Quentin appeared with the three blondes who'd been incarcerated in the basement. "I put in the call for our taxi service."

"Good," Duff said.

Kylie smiled at Natalie, tears trickling down her cheeks. "You were right. You got us out of there."

Natalie shook her head. "I believe our own Navy SEALs saw to that."

The Australian woman, Katherine, flung her arms around Duff's neck and laid a big kiss on both his cheeks. "Thank you so very much for coming to our rescue. Me mum will likely ask you to come visit us in Australia. You're more than welcome to stay with us."

Duff chuckled. "Thank Quentin. He kept you safe while all hell broke loose."

Katherine hugged Quentin's neck. "Already did. He promised me a date when we get back to Cancun. He also promised not to let me out of his sight." She winked at him.

"I wish we could round up the buyers and throw them in jail," Natalie said.

As they walked through the spacious marble-tiled hallway, Duff slipped an arm around Natalie's waist.

"We'd have a hard time explaining our weapons to the authorities. My bet is those men are hightailing it back to whatever country they belong to."

"What about Cassandra? We should at least take her back to the States and have her hit up with charges." They stepped outside into the clear night air.

The thumping sound of helicopter rotors sounded overhead.

Sawyer ran up to them. "The female got away. Do you want me to shoot the helicopter out of the sky?"

Duff shook his head. "No, we need to get away from here before half of the Mexican government finds us."

Already, the yachts in the cove were either backing out or turning, leaving as quickly as possible.

Rex Masters shoved Frank Jones into a dinghy and stepped in behind him. Montana climbed in, too. "I'm under orders to go with you and our interrogation subject."

Duff chuckled, certain Montana would keep anything from happening to their prize captive.

The big SEAL dwarfed the boat as they puttered out to the waiting yacht. The thin, little man with the fedora stood at the bow, watching the activity in the cove.

Lance maneuvered the yacht into the cove. Sawyer took the DPD out to the yacht and returned with a dinghy. They ferried the women to the yacht and went back to collect their gear. Duff was one of the last to leave the island, glancing back at the mansion. So much more could have gone wrong. But didn't.

He would be more than happy to return to Cancun to finish his vacation in peace. It was hard to believe he still had almost a week and a half to relax on the beach. He hoped Natalie would spend that week and a half with him. After all that had happened in just a few days, he felt he knew her better than any other woman, but he wanted to know everything about her.

He and Sawyer climbed into the dinghy and headed to the yacht.

"I have to say this has been one of the least relaxing vacations I've ever been on. And that includes the time we all went to the dude ranch with Montana and herded cattle."

"It has to get better from here. We got the women back. What else could go wrong?"

Sawyer smacked his palm to his forehead. "You had to ask."

Chapter Sixteen

"I could get used to this lifestyle very easily." Natalie stretched out in a lounge on the *Take Me Away* yacht owned by Mica Brantley, the woman Duff had mistaken for a man. As soon as they'd met up in Cancun, Mica had removed the fedora and shaken out her long, dark hair, surprising the SEALs.

She was Rex Masters's boss.

Duff, Natalie, Lance, Mica and Rex had spent the better part of the previous night interrogating Frank Jones.

Since his girlfriend had left him without batting an eyelash, Frank had been more than willing to share everything he knew about her. That wasn't much.

Cassandra Teirney wasn't even her name. She'd grown up on the streets, becoming adept at conning people. Her forte was stolen identities. One day she'd been caught stealing from someone who'd given her a choice. She either went to work for him or went to jail.

Of course she'd opted out of the jail scenario and had gone to work for the man who would become her benefactor.

Frank had snorted. "I thought she and I were a thing. I should have known better."

"Who is her benefactor?" Mica asked.

Frank shrugged. "Hell if I know. She never mentioned his name. Money showed up when we needed it along with helicopters, vehicles, vans…whatever our operation called for. The man had an entire network of drug runners at his fingertips here in Mexico."

"Why human trafficking?" Natalie asked, her voice hard, her gaze boring a hole into Frank. She still wanted to kill him, but the information he provided might help her find the people at the crux of the operation.

Frank glanced around at the people surrounding him. "You heard how much those men were willing to pay. It's insane. I never made that much in the army. Not even when I was selling guns to the enemy."

"Bastard," Rex said, between clenched teeth.

"Yeah, and you were so high and mighty?" Frank glared at Rex. "How many babies did you kill? How many innocent civilians died because you shot them or blew up their homes with them inside? What's the difference?"

Mica Brantley had stepped in. "Were there more women before these?"

Frank nodded. "They raised money on a regular basis. I came in on this operation when I met Cass in D.C. We hit it off and scored some identity theft jobs together. Being members of the real-estate community made it easy. Then she turned me on to the more high-dollar games."

Mica slapped her palm on the table in front of Frank. "The other women…where did they go?"

"I don't know. I didn't get involved until this round. You'll have to ask Cass." He smirked. "Good luck finding her. She's a master of disguises."

"We'll find her," Lance said. He'd already been on the satellite phone with Royce. If anyone could find the woman, Royce could.

Natalie wanted to be in on the raid that brought Cassandra to justice.

But she was quickly realizing it wasn't just Cassandra. Her benefactor funded her gigs. He was the one they needed to find. The sooner the better.

Frank couldn't tell them anything more about Cassandra or her benefactor. But he wasn't getting away with the part he'd played in their human-trafficking venture.

Royce had sent two of his SOS agents and the SOS plane to collect Frank late in the night. The Mexican authorities never knew and couldn't interfere in justice being served to the former army ranger who'd betrayed his country.

Lance then had turned to Mica Brantley. "Why were you here and how did you get an invitation to the auction?"

"You might have heard of my husband, Trevor Brantley."

Natalie had heard his name mentioned in the news. "Wasn't he the multimillionaire who was found dead in his mansion?"

Mica nodded and looked away, her eyes shiny with unshed tears. "My husband had connections. And enemies. The connections got me into the auction, the enemies cost my husband his life. Those same enemies took my stepdaughter. I fear she was sold at a similar auction." Mica glanced at Rex. "Rex has been helping in my effort to find her and bring her home."

Natalie had fallen silent. If she could help this woman

recover her stepdaughter, she would. If Royce would have her back, she'd ask if that could be her first assignment.

They'd split up, going their separate ways, each heading for a shower and bed. Natalie hadn't gotten the opportunity to say a proper good-night to Duff as they'd piled into taxis and returned to the resort in the early hours of the morning.

Natalie yawned in the bright light of day. None of them had had much sleep the night before. She'd been happy to sit up the rest of the night talking with Melody, bringing her up to speed on what had happened while she'd been imprisoned on Cozumel. Natalie told her sister about her former life as an agent for SOS and the role the organization had played in her rescue.

Mica Brantley had sent the invitation to join them that morning and they had been too curious to refuse, despite their lack of sleep.

"Would you like a Pain Killer?" Melody handed Natalie one of the fruity drinks packed with enough alcohol to make Natalie not care for a little while.

"I prefer beer, but thanks." Natalie took the drink and downed half of it before she laid back and smiled. "So, are you going to stay with me for the next week and have that vacation you came here to enjoy?"

Melody shook her head. "I'm going back in the morning. I've had enough of Cancun. I don't feel safe here and I need to get back to school."

Natalie sat up and leaned across, resting her hand on her sister's knee. "Do you want me to come back with you?"

Melody smiled. "No. I'll go with Kylie. We'll stick together like glue. She's as shaken as I am." She tossed back her golden-blond hair and sighed. "But you don't have to leave so soon." Her gaze shifted to the SEALs standing at the rail, staring out at the ocean, talking softly and drinking beer. "I know one person who would like you to stay."

Natalie's cheeks heated. "I have to admit, I think I could get used to him, as well."

"You know, it's about time you started living your life for yourself. In a year, I'll graduate college and move to some city where I'll live on my own. You can't always be there for me. I have to learn to live by myself."

Natalie frowned. "But you're my only living relative. I care about you and want you to be safe."

Melody crossed her arms over her chest. "And your job is all that safe?"

Natalie glanced away. "I won't go back to work for SOS if you don't want me to."

Melody leaned toward her sister. "See? You're doing it again. I want you to do what *you* want to do. Not what you think *I* need. Before you know it, life will pass you by and you'll only have regrets. If working for SOS makes you happy, do it. I'm just sorry you didn't tell me about it sooner."

Natalie stared at her sister for a long time, then nodded. "I'm glad you feel that way. I've missed the work. I like making a difference."

Melody sat straighter and gave Natalie a direct look. "Then you won't be upset when I tell you I'm applying to the FBI. I hope to get accepted and start as soon as I graduate."

Natalie's gut clenched but then she relaxed. "If it makes you happy, I say do it." They hugged and laughed.

Melody glanced toward Duff's back. "You know, if

things work out between you and Dutton, I wouldn't mind having another relative in the family."

Natalie shook her head. "We've only just met."

"Uh-huh. And I can feel the chemistry between you already." Melody held up her hands. "Just saying, you shouldn't rule out the possibilities."

Natalie's lips quirked. "Oh, I haven't." She rose from the lounge. "I just have to find a way to get him alone."

Duff turned at that moment and held out his hand.

Natalie placed her hand in his bigger one, liking the way he made her feel all soft and feminine.

He lifted her fingers to his lips and pressed a kiss to the tips. "Ready to head back? I'd like to take you out to dinner and dancing."

She let him pull her into his arms. They swayed to the rhythm of the ocean. Natalie laid her head on his chest, loving the contrast of his smooth skin and hard muscles. "I'm ready."

Ready for the infinite possibilities of what the night held in store. Ready to grab each day and live it as though it might be her last. And more than ready to let a man have a chance at stealing her heart.

"By the way, what are you doing when we get back Stateside?" Duff asked. "Two weeks with you just doesn't seem to be nearly enough. Hell, a lifetime might be too short."

Natalie's heart swelled and she wrapped her arms around his neck. "You're willing to take the risk? You know what I'll be doing for a living."

"It goes both ways, sweetheart. Until I can't do it anymore, I belong to the Navy SEALs. If you're up for the challenge of dating a SEAL, you're up for practically anything."

"Oh, I'm up for it."

Duff swung her off her feet and planted a kiss on her lips. Then he stared around. "Where's that dinghy? We have a date to get to."

* * * * *

WHAT HAPPENS ON THE RANCH

USA TODAY Bestselling Author

DELORES FOSSEN

CHAPTER ONE

ANNA MCCORD FIGURED she had committed a couple of sins, maybe even broken a few laws, just by looking at the guy in the bed. He was naked, so it was hard not to have dirty thoughts about him.

Drool, too.

Mercy, he was hot.

Thick blond hair all tousled and bedroomy. Lean and muscled. At least what she could see of him was muscled anyway. He was sprawled out on his stomach, his face cocooned in the fluffy feather pillows of the guest bed. He reminded her of a Viking just back from a good pillaging, minus the bed and feather pillows, of course.

But who was he?

Even though she should have bolted out of there the moment she opened the guest room door and saw a partially exposed butt cheek, Anna stayed put. Someone had obviously glued her feet to the floor. Glued her eyeballs to the hot guy, too.

She glanced around the room and spotted a clue as to who he was. There was a military uniform draped over the back of a chair and a duffel bag on the floor near the bed.

Anna didn't actually need more clues to know he was an Air Force officer and likely a friend that her brother Riley had brought home. But she also saw the dog tags. The ball chain holding them was still around the hot guy's neck, but the tags themselves were lying askew on the bed like smashed nickels.

Maybe he sensed she was there, because he opened an eye, and the seconds trickled by before it must have registered in his mind that he had a woman ogling him.

He made a grunting sound mixed with some profanity and rolled over, no doubt because that was the fastest way he could reach the sheet to cover himself. However, the rolling over gave her a view of his front side.

Definitely more dirty thoughts.

"Sorry, I didn't know anyone was in here," Anna said, as if that explained the gawking. The drool. The long, heated look that she was giving him.

But both the heated stuff and the drool came to a quick halt when Anna got a better look at his face. "Heath?"

He blinked. "Anna?"

Good gravy. It was Heath Moore, all right. Well, a grown-up Heath anyway. The last time she'd seen him had been nine and a half years ago when he was barely eighteen, but he had filled out a lot since then.

Oh, the memories she had of him came flooding back.

He'd been naked then, too—for part of those memories anyway, since she'd lost her virginity to him. Though she certainly hadn't seen as much of him during that encounter in the hayloft as she'd just witnessed. He had filled out *everywhere*.

He sat up, dragging the sheet over his filled-out parts, and still blinking, he yawned and scrubbed his hand over his face. More memories came. Of his memorable mouth. The equally memorable way he'd kissed her.

She fanned herself like a menopausal woman with hot flashes.

"Why are you here?" she asked at the same moment that Heath asked, "Why are you here?"

Anna figured he was going to have a lot better explanation than she did. "I thought I might have left a book in here," she told him.

A total lie. She had been in search of a book that the housekeeper, Della, had said she'd left in her room on the nightstand. But when Anna had seen the guest room door slightly ajar, she'd opened it and had a look.

She made a show of glancing around for a book that had zero chance of being there since it was all the way at the end of the hall.

"This is your room now?" Heath asked.

"No. But I come in here sometimes. For the view." Anna motioned to the massive bay window. She wouldn't mention that every bedroom on the second floor had similar windows, similar views. As did her own room on the first floor.

Heath glanced in the direction of the bay window as if he might get up to sample that view, but his next glance was at his body. Considering he was naked under the sheet, he probably didn't want to get up until she'd left, and that was her cue to leave. First though, she wanted an answer to her question.

"Why are you here?" she repeated.

"Riley. He saw me at the base in San Antonio and said I needed some…R & R before I left on assignment. He was headed back here to the ranch to finish out his leave, and he asked me to come."

All of that made sense because Riley, too, was an Air Force officer and had indeed been at the base the day before. Yes, it made sense except for Heath's hesitation before R & R.

"You weren't here last night when I went to bed." She would have noticed Heath, that's for sure.

"We stopped for a bite to eat, then to visit some mutual friends, and we didn't get in until late. We didn't want to wake anyone up so Riley just sent me here to the guest room." Heath paused. "Riley's my boss."

Uh-oh. That wouldn't play well with Riley if he found out about her lustful thoughts over his subordinate. It wouldn't play well with Heath, either, since he probably didn't want to do or think anything—or have *her* do or think anything—that would cause his boss to hit him upside the head with a shovel.

A threat that Riley had first rattled off nine and a half years ago when he thought a romance was brewing between Heath and her.

If Riley had known what had gone on in the hayloft, he might not have actually carried through on the shovel threat, but Anna would have never heard the end of it.

And there was that whole underage-sex thing.

When Heath had first started working at the ranch, he'd been eighteen. But she'd been only seventeen. Riley and her other brothers had made a big deal about the attraction they'd sensed going on between Heath and her.

The term *jail bait* had been thrown around.

Since Heath had been making a big deal of his own about going into the military, it was an issue. Heath wanted to go into special ops, which would have required a lengthy background check for a top-secret clearance, and Riley had brought up her age for the sole purpose of scaring Heath into keeping his jeans zipped.

It had worked. Until the day Anna turned eighteen, that is. After that, she'd made the trip to the hayloft with Heath, and she had the memories of the orgasm to prove it.

Heath smiled at her, but it felt as if he'd had to rummage it up just to be polite. Again, the nudity was probably driving that. But the nudity didn't stop him from looking at her with those sizzling blue eyes. Also bedroomy like his hair. He slid his gaze from her head to her toes, lingering in the middle. Lingering especially on her breasts. Perhaps because she was wearing a T-shirt and no bra.

"Riley didn't mention you'd be here at the ranch," Heath said.

"Oh? Well, usually I leave the day after Thanksgiving, but I decided to stay a little longer." Since it was already two days after Thanksgiving, she probably hadn't needed to add that last part. "I'm in law school at University of Texas, but I finished my courses early this semester. I'm also planning a transfer. I need a change of scenery...or something."

And a life.

And perhaps sex, but she'd only gotten that idea when she'd seen Heath naked.

"Yeah, a change of scenery," he repeated, as if he were aware of what she meant by the *or something*.

"So, how long will you be here?" Anna tried to keep her eyes directed just at his face, but her gaze kept drifting a bit to that incredibly toned chest. Either he'd gotten very good with contouring body paints or the man had a six-pack.

"Until the cows come home," he said.

That's when she realized both her eyes and her mind had seriously drifted off, and she didn't have a clue what he'd been talking about before that.

The corner of his mouth lifted. A dreamy smile, and he hadn't had to rummage up this one. It was the real deal.

"I'll be here about two weeks," he said. Probably repeated information. "How about you?"

"Two weeks. More or less. I was going to stay until the final exams were over and the campus was less busy. Then, the plan was to talk to my advisor about the transfer."

"For that change of scenery or something?" Heath made it sound like a question.

Anna pretended not to hear it. No need to get into all that. Instead, she glanced at his left hand, the one part of his body she'd failed to look at during her gawking. No ring.

"I'm not married," Heath volunteered. "Never have been." He looked at her left hand, too, where she was still wearing the opal ring her Granny Ethel had left her.

Anna shook her head. "No I-do's for me, either." Close, though, but best not to get into that after her change-of-scenery slip. "So, catch me up on what you've been doing."

"Maybe I can do that after I've put on some clothes? Or we can talk like this?" Another smile.

He was flirting with her, a ploy she knew all too well since she'd been on the receiving end of his flirting that summer. Well, she could flirt, too.

"I guess I can restrain myself for a quick catch-up," she joked. "A *quick catch-up*," she emphasized. "What are you doing these days? I mean, other than sleeping naked, that is. How's the job going?"

The smile faded, and she was sorry she'd taken the conversation in that direction. Of course, it was something a normal nondrooling woman would have asked the man who had been her first.

Even though it was a dumb-as-dirt thing to do, she went closer. Much closer. And she sat down on the bed. Not right next to him, though, because she didn't want to move into the dumber-than-dirt category, but it was still too near him. Six miles would have been too near.

"Sorry," she added. "Didn't mean to hit a nerve. And I should have known better because Riley doesn't like to talk about his assignments, either. I think he believes it'll worry me, but whether he talks about it or not, I still worry."

"You shouldn't. Riley's been on plenty of deployments and hasn't gotten a scratch. Some guys are just bullet-proof, and Riley's one of them."

Maybe. But Anna had a bad feeling about this deployment coming up. A bad feeling she definitely didn't want to discuss with Heath. Or Riley. If she didn't mention it aloud, maybe the feeling would go away. Maybe the danger would as well, and her brother would come back with his bulletproof label intact.

"You okay?" Heath asked.

That was a reminder to push aside her fears and get on with this catch-up conversation. "Riley always says if he tells me about his job, he'll have to hit me with a shovel afterwards. Riley really likes that shovel threat."

"I remember." Heath took a deep breath, causing the muscles in his chest and that six-pack to respond. "Well, shovels aside, I can tell you that I just finished up a deployment in a classified location where there was a lot of sand, followed by eight months in Germany where there was a lot of paperwork. That's where Riley became my boss. Small world, huh?"

Yes. Too small, maybe. "Riley and you are in the same career field?"

"For now." The short answer came out so fast. As did his hand. He brushed his fingers over the ends of her hair. Even though he didn't actually touch skin or anything, it was enough of a distraction. "Your hair is longer," he said.

"Yours is shorter." And yes, she achieved dumber-than-dirt status by touching his hair, as well. Since it was on the short side, she also touched some skin.

She felt everything go still, and even though Anna was pulling back her hand, it seemed to be in slow motion. The only thing that was in the revving-up mode was this flamethrower attraction that had always been between Heath and her.

"Yeah," he drawled. No other words were necessary. They were on the same proverbial page along with being on the same actual bed. The flamethrower had had a go at him, too.

"I, uh…" Anna stuttered around with a few more words and syllables before she managed to say something coherent. "This could be trouble."

"Already is." He drawled that, too. Hitched up another smile.

The past nine and a half years just vanished. Suddenly, Anna was eighteen again and was thinking about kissing him. Of course, she hadn't needed vanishing years for that to happen, but it was as if they were back in that hayloft. On all that warm, soft hay. Heath had taken things so slow. Long kisses. His hand skimming over various parts of her body.

Then, into her jeans.

That had been the best part, and it'd all started with a heated look like the one he was giving her now.

Even though they didn't move, the foreplay was in full swing. His gaze lingered on her mouth. She picked up the rhythm of his breathing—which was too fast. Ditto for her heartbeat. Everything was moving in sync.

"Anna, we're playing with fire," he whispered. It was a drawl, too.

She was near enough to him now that his breath hit against her mouth like a kiss. "Yes," she admitted, but she was in the "fire pretty" mindset right now, and she inched closer, her drifting gaze sliding from his mouth to his abs.

"Is it real?" she asked, but was in the wrong mindset to wait for an answer. She touched that six-pack.

Oh, yes. Definitely real.

It probably would have been a good time to snatch back her hand and be outraged that she'd done something so bold, but she kept it there a moment and saw and heard Heath's reaction. He cursed under his breath, and beneath the sheet his filled-out part reacted, as well.

He cursed some more, but it was all aimed at himself. "I really do need you to leave now so I can get dressed. Once I can walk, that is. Maybe you can shut the door behind you, too."

That caused the past nine and a half years to unvanish. Heath was putting a stop to this. As he should.

Anna was about to help with that stopping by getting to her feet and doing something that Heath clearly would have trouble doing right now—walking. But before she could budge an inch, she saw the movement in the doorway.

And saw the source of that movement.

Riley.

His eyes were so narrowed that it looked as if his eyelashes were stuck together.

"What the hell's going on here?" Riley growled. He opened his eyes enough to look at her. Then at Heath. Then at the other *thing* that was going on. "And what are you doing with my sister?"

No way was Heath going to be able to explain with the bulge of his filled-out part beneath the sheet. And neither could Anna.

CHAPTER TWO

WELL, HELL IN a big-assed handbasket. This visit was off to a good start.

Heath had known it wasn't a smart idea to come to the McCord Ranch, and he was getting a full reminder of why it'd been bad, what with Riley glaring at him.

"Get dressed," Riley ordered, and yeah, it was an order all right. "And we'll talk." Then he turned that ordering glare on his sister.

But Anna obviously wasn't as affected by it as Heath was, even though Riley was in uniform and looked thirty steps past the intimidation stage. Still, Anna matched Riley's glare with a scowl and waltzed out.

Thankfully, Riley did some waltzing as well and left, shutting the door behind him. Though it was more of a slam than a shut. Still, he was gone, and that gave Heath some time to take a very uncomfortable walk to the adjoining bathroom for a shower. Cold. Just the way he hated his showers. And if he stayed on the ranch, there'd be more of them in his near future.

It was time for a change of plans.

Not that he actually had plans other than passing time and moping. Yeah, moping was a definite possibility. At least it had been until Anna had shown up in the doorway. Difficult to mope in his current state.

Regardless, Anna was off-limits, of course.

He repeated that while the cold shower cooled down his body. Repeated it some more while he dressed. Kept repeating it when he went down the stairs to apologize to Riley and tell him that he'd remembered some place he needed to be. Riley would see right through the lie, but after what he had witnessed in the guest room, he'd be glad to get Heath off the ranch.

Heath made his way downstairs, meandering through the sprawling house. Since he was hoping for some coffee to go along with the butt-chewing he would get from Riley, he headed toward the kitchen.

He heard women's voices but not Anna's. He was pretty sure they belonged to Della and Stella, sisters and the McCords' longtime housekeeper and cook. Yep. And Heath got a glimpse of them and the coffeepot, too, before Riley stepped into the archway, blocking his path.

"I know," Heath volunteered. "You want to hit me on the head with a shovel."

"Hit who with a shovel?" Della asked, and when she spotted Heath, she flung the dish towel she was holding. Actually, she popped Riley on the butt with it and went to Heath to gather him into her arms for a hug. "It's good to see you, boy."

Heath hadn't even been sure the woman would remember him after all this time, but clearly she did. Or else she thought he was someone else.

"Nobody's gonna get hit with a shovel in this house," Della warned Riley, and then she added to Heath, "Have you seen Anna yet?"

"Earlier," Heath settled for saying.

"Well, I hope you'll be seeing a lot more of her while

you're here. Never could understand why you two didn't just sneak up to the hayloft or somewhere."

Heath choked on his own breath. Not a very manly reaction, but neither was the way Riley screwed up his face. Della didn't seem to notice or she might have used the dish towel on him again.

"Have a seat at the table, and I'll fix you some breakfast," Della offered.

"Heath and I have to talk first," Riley insisted.

"Pshaw. A man's gotta have at least some coffee before he carries on a conversation. Where are your manners, Riley?"

"I think I left them upstairs."

Della laughed as if it were a joke and, God bless her, she poured Heath a cup of coffee. He had a couple of long sips, figuring he was going to need them.

"Thanks. I'll be right back," Heath said to Della, and he followed Riley out of the kitchen and into the sunroom.

No shovels in sight, but Riley had gone back to glaring again, and he got right in Heath's face. "Keep your hands off Anna, or I'll make your life a living hell."

Heath had no doubts about that. He didn't mind the living hell for himself so much, but he didn't want any more of Riley's anger aimed at Anna. "I'll get my things together and head out."

Riley's glare turned to a snarl. "And then Anna, Della and Stella will think I've run you off."

Heath had some more coffee, cocked his head to the side in an "if the shoe fits" kind of way. Because in a manner of speaking, Riley was indeed running him off. Except that Heath had already decided it was a good idea, too. Still, he didn't acknowledge that. He was getting some perverse pleasure out of watching Riley squirm a little.

"I'm guessing Anna, Della and Stella will make your life a living hell if they think you've run me off?" Heath asked. And he said it with a straight face.

Riley opened his mouth. Closed it. Then he did a wash, rinse, repeat of that a couple more times before he finally cursed. "Stay. For now. And we'll discuss it later. I've got to do some more paperwork at the base. Just keep your hands off Anna while I'm gone. Afterwards, too."

His hands were the least of Riley's worries, but Heath kept that to himself. Besides, Riley didn't give him a chance to say anything else. He lit out of there while growling out another "Stay" order.

Heath would stay. For the morning anyway. But it was best if he put some distance between Anna and all those parts of him that could get him in trouble.

He went back into the kitchen, got a hug and warm greeting from Stella this time, and the woman practically put him in one of the chairs at the table.

"How do you like your eggs?" Della asked.

"Any way you fix them." Heath added a wink because he figured it would make her smile. It did.

"Tell us what you've been doing with yourself for the past nine years or so," Della said as she got to work at the stove. "I seem to recall when you left here that summer you were headed to boot camp."

Heath nodded, took a bite of the toast that Stella set in front of him. "I enlisted in the Air Force, became a pararescuer and took college classes online. When I finished my degree, I got my commission and became a combat rescue officer."

"Like Riley," Stella said.

"Yeah, but he outranks me."

"How is that? Didn't you go in the Air Force before Riley did?"

Heath nodded again. "Only a couple months earlier, though. We've been in the service about the same amount of time, but for most of that I was enlisted. I've only been an officer for three and a half years now. And Riley's my boss. Well, until the rest of my paperwork has cleared. That should be about the time Riley leaves for his assignment in two weeks."

Della stopped scrambling the eggs to look at him. "You won't be going with him?"

There it was. That twist to the gut. Heath tried to ease it with some more toast and coffee, but that was asking a lot of mere food products. And Della and Stella noticed all right. He'd gotten their full attention.

"No, I won't be going with Riley this time," Heath said.

He still had their attention, and judging from their stares, the women wanted more. Heath gave them the sanitized version. "The Air Force feels it's time for me to have a stateside assignment. It's standard procedure. A way of making sure I don't burn out."

His mouth was still moving and words were coming out, but Heath could no longer hear what he was saying. That's because Anna walked in. Or maybe it was just a Mack Truck that looked like Anna because he suddenly felt as if someone had knocked him senseless.

She'd changed out of her sweats and T-shirt. Had put on a bra, too. And was now wearing jeans and a red sweater. Heath tried not to notice the way the clothes hugged her body. Tried not to notice her curves. Her face.

Hell, he gave up and noticed.

Not that he could have done otherwise. Especially when Anna poured herself a cup of coffee, sat down next to him and glanced at his crotch.

"Back to normal?" she whispered. Then she gave him a smile that could have dissolved multiple layers of rust on old patio furniture. Dissolved a few of his brain cells, too. "So, did Riley try to give you your marching orders?"

Since Della and Stella got very, very quiet, Heath figured they were hanging on every word, so he chose his own words carefully and spoke loud enough for the women to hear. "Something came up—"

Anna glanced at his crotch again and laughed. Obviously, a reaction she hadn't planned because she clamped her teeth onto her bottom lip after adding "I'm sorry." Too late, though. Because Della and Stella weren't just hanging on every word but every ill-timed giggle, too.

"Well, I'm sure whatever came up—" Della paused "—you can work it out so you can stay here for at least a couple of days. That way, Anna and you have time to visit."

"Especially since Anna needs some cheering up," Stella added.

Anna certainly didn't laugh that time. She got a deer-about-to-be-smashed-by-a-car look. "I'm fine, really," Anna mumbled.

Which only confirmed to Heath that she did indeed need some cheering up. Maybe this had to do with the "change of scenery or something" she'd mentioned upstairs.

Well, hell.

There went his fast exit, and no, that wasn't the wrong part of his body talking, either. If Anna was down, he wanted to help lift her up.

Stella dished up two plates of eggs for Anna and him, and she smiled at them when she set them on the table. "You two were as thick as thieves back in the day." She snapped her fingers as if recalling something. "Anna, Heath even gave you that heart necklace you used to wear all the time. It had your and his pictures in it."

Hard to forget that. Heath referred to it as the great engraved debacle. He'd spent all his money buying Anna that silver heart locket as a going-away gift. Something to remember him by after he left Spring Hill and the McCord Ranch. It was supposed to be engraved with the words *Be Mine*.

The engraver had screwed up and had put *Be My* instead.

Since Heath hadn't had the time to get it fixed, he'd given it to Anna anyway, but he hadn't figured she would actually wear it. Not with that confusing, incomplete *sentiment*.

"Where is that necklace?" Della asked.

"I'm not sure," Anna answered, and she got serious about eating her breakfast. Fast. Like someone who'd just entered a breakfast-eating contest with a reprieve from a death sentence waiting for the winner.

Della made a sound that could have meant anything, but it had a sneaky edge to it. "I think Heath needs some cheering up, too," Della went on. "And not because Riley was going on about that shovel. That boy needs to get a new threat, by the way," she added to her sister before looking at Anna again. "I get the feeling Heath could use somebody to talk to."

Heath suddenly got very serious about eating his breakfast, as well. Either Della had ESP, or Heath sucked at covering up what was going on in his head.

Anna finished gulping down her breakfast just a bite ahead of him, gulped down some coffee, too, and she probably would have headed out if Stella hadn't taken her empty breakfast plate and given her a plate of cookies instead.

"I need you to take these cookies over to Claire Davidson at her grandmother's house."

"Claire's back in town?" Anna asked, sounding concerned.

Heath knew Claire. She'd been around a lot that summer he'd worked at the McCord Ranch, and if he wasn't mistaken Claire had a thing for Riley. And vice versa.

"Her grandmother's sickly again. Thought they could use some cheering up, too." Della shifted her attention to Heath. "And you can go with Anna. Then maybe she could show you around town."

"Spring Hill hasn't changed in nine and a half years," Anna quickly pointed out.

"Pshaw. That's not true. The bakery closed for one thing. And Logan bought that building and turned it into a fancy-schmancy office. It has a fancy-schmancy sign that says McCord Cattle Brokers. You can't miss it."

Logan—one of Anna's other brothers who ran the family business and probably also owned a shovel. Ditto for Logan's twin, Lucky. At least the two of them didn't stay at the ranch very often, so Heath might not even run into them. Well, he wouldn't as long as he avoided the fancy-schmancy office and any of the local rodeos since Lucky was a bull rider.

"I thought I'd go out and see if the ranch hands needed any help," Heath suggested.

That earned him a blank stare from the women. "You don't have to work for your keep while you're here," Stella said. "You're a guest."

"I know, but I like working with my hands. I miss it." He did. Not as much as he'd miss other things—like having the job he really wanted—but grading on a curve here, ranch work was missable.

"All right, then," Della finally conceded. "At least walk Anna to the truck. There might be some ice on the steps. We had a cold spell move in."

"Now, go," Stella said, shooing them out. "Della and I need to clean up, and we can't do that with y'all in here."

This wasn't about cleaning. This was about matchmaking. Still, Heath grabbed his coat so he could make sure Anna didn't slip on any ice. He only hoped Anna didn't ask why he needed cheering up, and he would return the favor and not ask her the same thing.

"So, why do you need cheering up?" Anna asked the moment they were outside.

He groaned, not just at the question but also because it was at least fifty degrees with zero chance of ice.

"Is it personal or business?" she added.

"Is yours personal or business?" he countered.

She stayed quiet a moment and instead of heading toward one of the trucks parked on the side of the house, she sat down in the porch swing. "Both. You?"

"Both," he repeated. But then he stopped and thought about her answer. "Yours is personal, as in guy troubles?"

For some reason that made him feel as if he'd been hit by the Anna-truck again. Which was stupid. Because of course she had men in her life. Heath just wasn't sure he wanted to hear about them.

She nodded to verify that it was indeed guy trouble.

No, he didn't want to hear this, so he blurted out the first thing that popped into his head. He probably should have waited for the second or third thing, though.

"I had a girl break up with me once because I kept calling her your name," he said.

"*My* name?" She didn't seem to know how to react to that.

"Uh, no. I kept saying *your name* because I couldn't remember her name." And he added a wink that usually charmed women.

But, of course, it'd been Anna's name. The way stuff about her often popped into his head, her name had a way of just popping out of his mouth.

"Any other confessions you want to get off your chest and/or six-pack?" she asked. And she winked at him.

Man, that's what he'd always liked about Anna. She gave as good as she got. "Let me see. I don't wear boxers or briefs. I like mayo and pepper on my French fries. And my mother's in jail again."

All right, so that last one just sort of fell from his brain into his mouth.

Anna didn't question the *again* part. Maybe because she remembered the reason he'd ended up at the McCord Ranch all those years ago was that his mother had been in jail then, as well.

In jail only after she'd stolen and spent every penny of the money that Heath had scrimped and saved for college. She'd also burned down their rental house with all his clothes and stuff still in it.

Heath had snapped up Riley's offer of a job and a

place to stay—since at the time Heath had had neither. His father hadn't been in his life since he was in kindergarten, and what with him being broke and homeless, he'd had few places to turn.

If it hadn't been for his jailbird mom, he would have never met Anna. So, in a way he owed her.

In a very roundabout way.

"Want to talk about why your mom's in jail?" Anna asked.

Well, since he'd opened this box, Heath emptied the contents for her. "Shoplifting Victoria's Secret panties. She'd stuffed about fifty pairs in her purse—guess they don't take up much room—and when the security guard tried to stop her, she kicked him where it hurts. Then she did the same to the manager of the store next door. Then to the off-duty cop who tried to stop her. My mom can be a real butt-kicker when it comes to high-end underwear."

Anna smiled, a quiet kind of smile. "I do that, too, sometimes."

"What?" And Heath hoped this wasn't about butt-kicking or stealing panties.

"Diffuse the pain with humor. I'm not very good at it, either. Pain sucks."

Yeah, it did, and he thought he knew exactly what she was talking about. "You lost your parents when you were a teenager."

"Yes, they were killed in a car accident before you and I met. I was fourteen, and I thought my world was over. That was still the worst of the *world's over* moments, but I've had others since."

"Is that why you need cheering up?" he asked.

She didn't answer. Anna stood. "I should deliver these cookies before the ice gets to them."

Heath put his hands in his pockets so he wouldn't touch her as she walked away. Not that he would have had a chance to do any touching. Because someone pulled up in a truck. Not a work truck, either. This was a silver one that Della would have labeled as fancy schmancy. It went well with the cowboy who stepped from it.

Logan McCord.

The top dog at the McCord Ranch and the CEO of McCord Cattle Brokers. He made a beeline for the porch, passing Anna along the way. She said something to him, something Heath couldn't hear, but it put a deep scowl on Logan's face.

"Smart-ass," he grumbled. "She threatened to hit me with Riley's shovel if I didn't make you feel welcome. So—welcome."

Warm and fuzzy it wasn't, but at least it wasn't a threat. Not yet anyway.

"Riley called," Logan continued. "He said I was to come over here and convince you to stay."

"Because of Anna, Della and Stella."

Logan certainly didn't deny that, and his gaze drifted to Anna as she drove away before his attention turned back to Heath. "You're only going to be here two weeks at most, and then you'll leave, right?"

Since that pretty much summed it up, Heath nodded.

"Well, the last time you did that, it took Anna a long time to get over you. *Months*," Logan emphasized. "We all had to watch her cry her eyes out."

Hell. Crying? Months? This was the first Heath was hearing about this, but then he hadn't been around to see those tears. He'd been off at basic training at Lackland Air Force Base. He'd written her, of course. In the beginning at least. She'd written back to him, too, but she damn sure hadn't mentioned tears.

Logan took a step closer, got in his face. So close that Heath was able to determine that he used mint mouthwash and flossed regularly. "You won't hurt my kid sister like that again."

"The shovel threat?" Heath asked, aiming to make this sound as light as a confrontation with Logan could be. Heath wasn't sure friendly bones in a person's body actually existed, but if they did, Logan didn't have any.

"Worse. I'll tell Della and Stella what you've done and let them have a go at you. If you piss them off, the shovel will be the least of your worries."

Heath didn't doubt that. In fact, the whole McCord clan would come after him if he left Anna crying again. And that meant Anna was way off-limits.

He'd survived months in hostile territory. But Heath thought that might be a picnic compared to the next two weeks with Anna and the McCord brothers.

CHAPTER THREE

HEATH HAD BEEN avoiding her for the past three days. Anna was certain of it. And she was fed up with it, partly because if Heath avoided her, it was like letting her knot-headed brothers win.

The other *partly* was that she couldn't get him off her mind, and she didn't know what riled her more—her brothers' winning or her own body whining and begging for something it shouldn't get.

Shouldn't.

Because another fling with Heath would only complicate her life and possibly get her heart stomped on again. That was the logical, big-girl panties argument, but the illogical, no-underwear girl wanted Heath in the hayloft again.

And the hayloft was exactly where she spotted him.

He was standing in the loft, tossing down bales of hay onto a flatbed truck that was parked just beneath. He was all cowboy today: jeans, a blue work shirt, Stetson, boots. Oh, and he was sweaty despite the chillier temps.

She wasn't sure why the sweat appealed to her, but then she didn't see a single thing about him that didn't fall into the appeal category.

Anna stood there ogling him, as she'd done in the bedroom, and she kept on doing it until his attention landed on her. Since she should at least make an attempt at not throwing herself at him, she went to the nearby corral and looked at the horses that'd been delivered earlier. It wasn't exactly the right day for horse ogling, though, because the wind had a bite to it.

An eternity later, which was possibly only a couple of minutes, the ranch hands drove off with the hay, and Heath made his way down the loft ladder. Then he made his way toward her.

"You've been avoiding me," she said. All right, she should have rehearsed this or something. For a soon-to-be lawyer, she was seriously lacking in verbal finesse when it came to Heath.

"Yeah," he admitted in that hot drawl of his. And he admitted the reason, too. "Your brothers are right. I'm not here for long, and they said you cried a lot the last time I left."

Her mouth dropped open, and the outrage didn't allow her to snap out a comeback. But her brothers were dead meat. Dead. Meat.

"They told you that?" She didn't wait for an answer. "I didn't cry. That much," Anna added.

Heath lifted his eyebrow, went to her side and put his forearms on the corral fence. "The fact that you cried at all tells me that I should keep avoiding you."

"Should?" she challenged.

He cursed, looked away from her. "You know I'm attracted to you. You saw proof of that in the bedroom."

She had, indeed. "And you know I'm attracted to you."

There, she'd thrown down the sexual gauntlet. But it caused him to curse again.

"I don't want to hurt you," he said.

"And I don't want to get hurt—"

A commotion in the corral nipped off the rest of what she was about to say. And it wasn't a very timely commotion.

Sex.

Specifically horse sex.

It went on a lot at the ranch. So often in fact that Anna rarely noticed, but because Heath was right next to her, she noticed it now. And he noticed that she noticed.

With all that noticing going on, it was amazing that she remembered how to turn around, but she finally managed it. She took hold of Heath's arm and got him moving away from the corral and toward the pasture.

Where she immediately saw cow-and-bull sex.

Dang it. Was everything going at it today?

Heath chuckled. "The Angus bull was getting restless, trying to break fence, so the hands brought in some company for him."

The ranch's version of Match.com. And the icy wind definitely didn't put a damper on things. Not for the bull anyway, but it did for Anna. She shivered and wished she'd opted for a warmer coat instead of the one that she thought looked better on her. It was hard to look your best with chattering teeth and a red nose.

"In here," Heath said. He put his hand on her back and maneuvered her into the barn.

"The scene of the crime," Anna mumbled. She'd fantasized about getting Heath back in here, but not like this. Not when she needed a tissue.

He glanced up at the hayloft, his attention lingering there a moment before coming back to her. The lingering lasted more than a moment though, and he took out a handkerchief and handed it to her.

"I should probably take you back to the house so you can warm up," he offered.

She considered it just so she could blow her nose. It was tempting, but Riley was inside. Della and Stella, too. So Anna touched the handkerchief to her nose and hoped that did the trick. In case it didn't, she went for what Riley would have called a tactical diversion.

"I'm surprised you're not off somewhere enjoying some *company* like that bull before you leave for your deployment," she said.

Anna figured that would get Heath to smile. It didn't. And she saw it again—the look on his face to remind her that he needed to be cheered up about something. Apparently, it had something to do with his assignment.

"Unless a miracle happens, I won't be deploying," he finally answered. The strewn hay on the floor was suddenly riveting because he stared at it. "The Air Force wants me to take an instructor job in Florida."

With the hay-staring and the gloomy look, Anna had braced herself for something a lot worse. "You make it sound as if you're being banished to Pluto."

"In a way, it is like that for me. I trained to be a combat rescue officer, like Riley. I didn't go through all of that to work behind a desk."

Anna wasn't sure how far she should push this so she just waited him out. Waited out the profanity he muttered under his breath. Waited out more hay-staring.

"I feel washed up," he added.

Ah, she got it then. "But the instructor job is temporary, right? You'll go back to being a combat rescue officer?"

"In three years."

She got that, too. It was an eternity for someone like Heath or Riley.

Anna touched his arm, rubbed gently. "The three years will fly by. Look how fast the past nine and a half years went."

The hay finally lost its allure for him, and he looked at her. "Yeah." Not so much of a sexy drawl this time. The hurt was still there. Time to pull out the big guns and do a little soul-baring.

"Remember when I told you I needed a change of scenery? Well, what I really need is to get away from my ex-boyfriend," Anna confessed. "We had a bad breakup."

Evidently, Heath didn't like this soul-baring so much because he frowned. "Are you telling me this is rebound flirting you've been doing with me?"

"No. The breakup happened two years ago, but he's getting married to one of my classmates. And they're having a baby. Twins, actually. The classmate is a former Miss Texas beauty pageant winner."

He nodded, made an "I got it" sound. "You're still in love with him."

"No!" And she couldn't say that fast or loud enough. "He's a lying, cheating weasel. My need for a change of scenery isn't because I still care for him but because I'm sick and tired of everybody walking on eggshells around me."

Her voice had gotten louder with each word, and she couldn't stop the confessions now that the floodgates were open.

"Poor pitiful Anna McCord got dumped for the beauty queen," she blathered on. "It reminds me of the stuff my brothers pull on me, and I'm tired of it. Tired of being treated like someone who needs to be handled with kid gloves."

She probably would have just kept on blathering, too, if Heath hadn't slid his hand around the back of her neck, hauled her to him and kissed her.

All in all, it was the perfect way to shut her up, and Anna didn't object one bit. In fact, she would have cheered, but her mouth was otherwise occupied, and besides, cheering would have put an end to this kiss.

She didn't want it to end.

Apparently, neither did Heath, because he put that clever mouth to good use and made the kiss French. And deep. And long.

All the makings of a good kiss even if Anna's lungs started to ache for air.

Heath broke the kiss just long enough for them to take in some much needed oxygen, and he went in for another assault. Anna was no longer shivering, could no longer feel her nose, but the rest of her was hyper-aware of what was happening. The heat zoomed from her mouth to her toes, but it especially fired up in her orgasm-zone.

Soon, very soon, the kiss just wasn't enough, and they started to grapple for position. Trying to get closer and closer to each other. Heath was a lot better at grappling than she was because he dropped his hands to her butt and gave her a push against the front of his jeans.

Anna saw stars. Maybe the moon, too. And she darn near had an orgasm right then, right there while they were fully clothed.

Her heart was pounding now. Her breath, thin. She was melting. And there was a roaring sound in her head. That roaring sound was probably the reason she hadn't heard the other sounds until it was too late. Not horse or bull sex this time.

Footsteps.

"Interrupting anything?" someone asked.

Not Riley or Logan. Her brother Lucky.

And he was standing in the barn doorway with a shovel gripped in his hand.

ONCE AGAIN HEATH was facing a McCord brother when he was aroused. Hardly the right bargaining tool for dealing with Anna's older siblings who were hell-bent on protecting their sister.

Anna stepped in front of him as if she were his protector, but Heath remedied that. He stepped in front of her. But that only prompted her to attempt another stepping in front of him, and Heath put a stop to it. He dropped a kiss on her mouth, a chaste one this time hoping it would get her to cooperate.

"I need to talk to your brother alone," Heath told her.

"No way. He's here to browbeat you, and he's got a shovel."

Lucky shrugged. Propped the shovel against the wall. "Riley said I should bring it and do my part to remind Heath that he should keep his jeans zipped around you." He shrugged again when he glanced at the front of Heath's jeans. "The zipper's still up, so my work here is done."

Lucky turned to walk away.

"That's really all you've got to say?" Anna asked.

Her brother stopped, smiled in that lazy way that Lucky had about him. Heath knew Lucky loved his sister, but he'd never been as Attila the Hun as Riley and Logan. Heath suspected that's because Lucky got out all his restless energy by riding rodeo bulls. And having lots of sex.

"Should I ask you two to stay away from each other?" Lucky didn't wait for an answer though. "Wouldn't work. You two have the hots for each other, and there's only one way to cool that down." His gaze drifted to the hayloft before he turned again to leave.

Was Lucky really giving them his approval?

No.

This had to be some kind of trick.

Heath went after Lucky. Anna, too, and they caught up with him by the porch steps. However, before Heath could say anything else, the door opened, and Della stuck her head out.

"Anna, you got a call on the house phone. It's Claire."

Anna volleyed glances between Heath and her brother and then huffed. "Don't you dare say anything important before I get back."

She hurried inside. So did Lucky and Heath, but they stopped in the sunroom.

"Zippers and haylofts aside," Lucky said. "I don't want Anna hurt again. She sort of fell apart the last time you left."

"Yes. I heard about the crying from Logan." Heath paused. "Define *fell apart*."

"It wasn't just the crying." Lucky paused, too. "It was the pregnancy scare."

Heath felt as if all the air had just been sucked out of his lungs. Out of the entire planet. And if there was air on Pluto, it was also gone.

"Anna doesn't know that I know," Lucky went on. "No one does, and I'd like to keep it from my brothers. If Riley and Logan find out, they'd want to kick your ass. And mine since I didn't tell them. Then I'd have to kick theirs. If you don't mind, I'd rather not have to go through an ass-kicking free-for-all."

"Pregnancy?" Heath managed to ask. Considering there was still no air, he was doing good to get out that one word.

Lucky nodded. "A couple of weeks after you left, I went into Anna's bathroom to get some eye drops, and I saw the box for the pregnancy test in her trash can. She'd torn up the box, but I was able to piece it together to figure out what it was."

Heath managed another word. "Damn."

"Yeah. Two words for you—safe sex."

"I used a condom."

Lucky shrugged again. "Then, it must have worked because when I found the pee stick—it was in the way bottom of the trash can, by the way—it had a negative sign on it."

Heath heard the words. Felt the relief at that negative sign. Then managed another word.

"Hell."

Anna had gone through a scare like that, and she hadn't even told him.

"The only reason I dragged this up now was so that you'd understand why I'm protective of her," Lucky went on. "Now, go find her. Confront her about all of this. Then use a condom when you have makeup sex."

There'd be no makeup sex. Because Heath wasn't touching her again. Hell. She could have had his kid.

Heath went looking for Anna, and when he didn't find her in the kitchen or any of the living areas, he went to her bedroom. Of course she was there. The one room in the house where he shouldn't be alone with her. The door was open, and she was still on the phone, but she motioned for him to come in. He did, but only because he wanted answers and didn't want to wait for them.

But he had to wait anyway.

He listened to Anna talk niceties with Claire. Several "you're welcomes" later, she finally ended the call and looked at him. The smile that was forming froze on her mouth though when she saw his expression.

Heath shut the door just as he blurted out, "You had a pee stick in the bottom of your trash can."

Anna gave him a blank look.

"The pregnancy test from nine and a half years ago," he clarified. "Lucky found it and just told me about it. I'm wondering why I had to hear it from him."

She laughed. Hardly the reaction he'd expected. "It wasn't my pee on that stick. It belonged to Kristy Welker. I bought it for her so her folks wouldn't find out, and she did the test here."

Heath had vague memories of this Kristy. Anna and she had been friends, and Kristy had come over a couple of times that summer.

Anna's laughter quickly stopped. "What the heck was Lucky doing in my bathroom?"

She was using her sister voice now, and it wouldn't have surprised Heath if she'd gone running out of there to confront her brother about it. She might have done that if Heath hadn't done something so unmanly as having to catch on to the wall to steady himself.

"Whoa. Are you all right?" She slipped her arm around his waist, led him to the bed.

Heath didn't even try to say he didn't need to sit down. He did. "I thought… Well, I thought…"

"Trust me, if you had knocked me up, I would have told you about it."

Of course she would have. But it might take a year or two for his heart rate to settle down.

She gave his arm another rub like the one she had in the barn. "Relax. You were my first, but I wasn't totally clueless." She stopped, paused. "I wasn't your first though, and that's why you knew to bring a condom to the hayloft."

Even though Heath was still coming down from the shock-relief whammy, he heard her loud and clear. She'd given him something that a girl could only give once. Her virginity. That upped the encounter a significant notch, and maybe she was looking for some kind of assurance that she'd given it to the right guy.

"You were the first one that mattered," he said. "I risked being hit by a shovel to be with you. That should have told you something."

No smile. No more arm rub, either. "And yet you left."

He nodded, tried to ignore the sting of that reminder. "I was leaving for basic training, and you were barely eighteen."

Anna waved that off. "I know where this is going. We were too young for it to have been real love."

"No, we weren't too young."

Okay, he hadn't meant to say that, and it was another opened box with contents that Anna was clearly waiting to be spilled.

"What I felt for you was real," Heath said. And strong.

He hadn't cried as Anna had done, but leaving her had left a hole in his heart. Best not to mention that, especially since he would be leaving again soon.

"I knew I couldn't give you a good life," he added. "Not when I was still trying to figure out my own life."

She stayed quiet a couple of seconds. "Fair enough. And if you'd stayed, you would have resented me because you gave up your dream of being in the military. Your wanderlust and need for an adrenaline fix would have come into play. We would have fought, broken up, and all these years later we would have cursed the mere mention of each other's names."

Heath frowned. He didn't like that version of what could have been, but she was probably right. Probably. Now he was cursing her name for a different reason. Because it reminded him of how much he wanted her.

"I still have the need for that adrenaline fix," he admitted. "The need to be…something. Somewhere. It's easier if I stay on the move."

"I get it." She motioned around the room. "That's why it's hard for me to be at the ranch sometimes."

He was pretty sure they were talking about her parents now, about the hole in her heart that their deaths had no doubt left. "Are the memories of your folks harder to deal with while you're here?"

"Every now and then. But sometimes it's hard no matter where I am. Sometimes, I wake up, and I can't remember what they looked like. That sends me into a panic. So I run to grab one of the photo albums just to remember their faces."

"It's your way of keeping them in your life," Heath said around the lump in his throat.

"Yes. The past has a way of staying with you like that." Anna took a deep breath, then sighed. "And you can't run away from your past. I know, I've tried. It's like that little mole I have on my right butt cheek. It just goes with me everywhere." She looked at him. "I know what you're thinking."

Because he thought they could use some levity, Heath asked, "You have a little mole on your butt cheek?"

"All right, I didn't know what you were thinking after all. I thought you might be wondering if I was trying to outrun my past by transferring colleges."

That hadn't even crossed his mind, mainly because he wondered why he hadn't noticed that mole on her butt cheek. He was also wanting to see that mole. Clearly, he had a one-track mind here.

He shook his head. "I didn't think the transfer was about running, more like ulcer prevention. No need for you to have to face a daily dose of Mr. Wrong and his new family."

"Exactly." She smiled in a triumphant *I didn't think you'd get that* kind of way.

Heath got it all right. He got a lot of things when it came to Anna. A lot of things because of her, too. Like that tug below his belly that nudged him to kiss her again. That was his red-flag warning to get moving, and he would have done just that if he hadn't spotted the silver heart locket on her nightstand.

When she saw that he'd spotted it, she tried to put it in the drawer, but Heath took hold of her hand to stop her.

Yes, it was the locket he'd given her all right.

"After Della asked about it, I found it in my old jewelry box," she said. Then, she frowned. "All right, I wear it sometimes. Okay?"

She didn't sound especially happy about that, but it pleased Heath that she still had it. Pleased him even more than she occasionally wore it. What didn't please him was the reminder of the two words engraved on it.

"Be my." Anna ran her fingertips over it. "I wasn't sure what you were saying—be my heart, be my locket. Be my lay in the hay." She chuckled, poked him with her elbow.

"It was a fill-in-the-blank kind of thing," he joked, poking her back with his elbow.

"It sounds to me as if you didn't know what you wanted to say." No elbow poke that time.

"I was eighteen. I didn't know."

"And now?" she asked.

For two little words, it was a mighty big question. One that he didn't have to answer because there was a knock at the door, and the knocker didn't wait for an invitation to come in. The door opened.

Riley.

Well, at least Anna and he weren't in a butt-grabbing lip-lock as they'd been in the barn when Lucky had found them.

"I need to talk to you," Riley said, looking at Heath. Then his gaze swung to his sister. "And no, this isn't about you. It's business."

Damn it. That didn't sound good.

Anna must have thought so, too, because she gave Heath a sympathetic look as Riley and he headed out. They didn't go far, just into the foyer.

"I just found out that you're still trying to get out of your instructor assignment, that you put in a request to go on another deployment," Riley threw out there.

Heath cursed. He wasn't exactly keeping it from Riley. Okay, he was, but he didn't want to justify what he was trying to do.

"You've already had two back-to-back deployments

as an officer," Riley reminded him. "Before that, you had back-to-back-to-backs as a pararescuer."

"You're going on another one," Heath reminded him just as fast.

"I've had breaks in between. In the past ten years, the only time you've been stateside is for leave and training." He put his hand on Heath's shoulder. "You don't have anything to prove."

"No disrespect, *sir*, but I have everything to prove. To myself anyway."

Riley huffed. "You can prove it by being the best Air Force instructor you can be."

"That sounds like a recruitment pitch."

"It is." Riley took his hand from Heath's shoulder, and his index finger landed against Heath's chest. "And here's some more advice—sometimes life gives you crap, and you just have to make crappy lemonade out of it."

Heath frowned, thinking he might never again want another glass of lemonade. Or another lecture from Riley. Of course, there wouldn't be any more Riley lectures if Heath got stuck with that instructor job he didn't want. Then Riley would no longer be his boss.

Frowning, too, possibly over that bad lemonade analogy, Riley walked away. Heath would have, as well. He would have headed back to the pasture to do something, anything, to burn off some of this restless energy inside him.

Yeah, he needed an adrenaline fix *bad*.

He figured in that moment that his thought must have tempted fate, because his phone dinged with a text message. There was that old saying about when the gods wanted to punish you, they gave you what you wanted. Well, it wasn't from the gods.

It was from Anna.

And the text flashed like neon on his phone screen.
A sort of warning from the gods out to punish him.

Meet me in the hayloft in one hour.

CHAPTER FOUR

ANNA FIGURED SHE wasn't just going to be able to sneak out of the house without anyone seeing her.

And she was right.

As she was cutting through the sunroom, Della spotted her. Anna smiled, tried to look as if she weren't up to something, but that was sort of hard to do considering she had a six-pack of beer in a plastic grocery bag. A six-pack Anna had just scrounged from the fridge.

Della glanced at the bag and its distinctive shape. Then gave Anna no more than a mere glance.

"What are you up to?" Della asked.

Anna shrugged. "I'm considering playing with some fire. Running with scissors. Taking candy from some guy I don't know."

Falling hard for an old flame she shouldn't fall hard for was something Anna could add to that list of no-no's.

"So, you're going to the barn again with Heath," Della said. It wasn't a question.

"No. Yes," she admitted when Della gave her that liar-liar-pants-on-fire look. Anna huffed. "Don't give me a hard time about this. I'm tired of everyone babying me."

"They do that because you're the baby."

"Was the baby," Anna corrected. "I'm a grown woman now, but none of them can seem to accept it."

"They love you," Della pointed out.

"And I love them, but I want the key to my own chastity belt."

Della smiled that sly little smile of hers which meant she could be up to something. But she only kissed Anna on the cheek. "Honey, you've had that key for a long time now. Might be time to see if it works the way you want it to work."

Anna opened her mouth to respond, but she had nothing to say. Not a word. Instead, she returned the cheek kiss, tucked the beer under her arm so the bottles wouldn't jiggle and clang, and headed out the back.

No brothers in sight. No ranch hands, either.

But she also didn't see Heath.

Since it was—Anna checked the time on her phone— three minutes to rendezvous, she'd hoped she would see him waiting for her. He better not have blown her off. Except Heath wouldn't do that. Well, he might have done it with a text, call or chat, but he wouldn't do an unannounced blowing-off.

And he hadn't.

The moment she stepped in the barn, she saw him. Not in the hayloft, but standing by the steps that led up to the loft.

"You came," she said.

"Of course I came. I'm a guy and I'm not stupid. All right, maybe I am stupid, but the guy part's still true, and I've got the junk to prove it."

She smiled, chuckled. All nerves, and she hated the nerves because they didn't go well with this blistering attraction. "Yes, I got a glimpse of your junk. You're definitely a guy."

He smiled, too. "Beer?" he asked, tipping his head to the bag.

"I thought you might be thirsty. It was either this, milk or a questionable green smoothie."

"You made the right choice. I've already had my quota of milk and questionable green smoothies for a while."

He reached out, took her by the fingertips. That was it. The only part of her he touched. It was like being hit by a really big dose of pure, undiluted lust.

"You may have made the right choice with the beer," he added a heartbeat later. "But asking me to meet you here might fall into the stupid category."

"Might?" she repeated. Well, it was better than an out-and-out "this ain't gonna happen."

"Is this going to happen?" Anna came out and asked.

With only that teeny grip on her fingertips, he inched her closer. So close that when she breathed, she drew in his scent. Mixed with the hay and the crisp November air, it gave her another dose of lust.

"It shouldn't happen," Heath said. "I've tried to talk myself out of it."

"And?" She was still breathing, through her mouth now. Still taking in that scent. Still feeling him play with her fingers. "I hope you're really lousy at talking yourself out of things."

He closed his eyes a moment. Groaned. And, as if he were fighting—and losing—a fierce battle, he brought her another inch closer. She figured if the lust doses kept coming that she was going to launch herself into his arms.

"I'm leaving soon," he reminded her. "And I'm trying to do the right thing here."

She wanted to point out that unless he was leaving within the hour, then this could indeed happen, but that would just make her sound needy. Which she was. So very, very needy.

He let go of her fingertips, and she figured this was it. Heath would send her on her way. But he took the beer from her, and as if he had all the time in the world, he set the bag next to a hay bale.

"So, what now?" she asked.

Heath didn't answer her. Not with words. He reached out, and just when she thought she was going to get more fingertip foreplay, he took hold of her, snapped her to him and kissed the living daylights out of her.

Anna forgot all about the stupid argument that he was leaving soon. She forgot how to breathe. But other feelings took over, too. Probably because Heath didn't just kiss.

He touched.

He slipped his hand between them and ran his fingers over her right breast. Nice, but he double-whammied it with a neck kiss, and Anna felt herself moving. At first she thought it was just her body melting, but nope, she and Heath were walking.

"What are we doing?" she asked.

"Complicating the hell out of things."

"Good. I like complications." At the moment she would have agreed to a lobotomy.

Heath kept kissing her, kept moving. Not up the steps of the hayloft but rather toward the tack room. Maybe because it had a door. Maybe because it didn't require the coordination of step climbing with an erection. Maybe because it was just closer.

It was the erection thing, she decided, and since she

could feel it against her stomach, Anna added some touching of her own. She worked her hand over his zipper and would have gotten that zipper down if Heath hadn't stopped her.

She heard herself make a whiny sound of protest, but then he put her against the back of the door that he'd just shut, and he lifted her. Until his hard junk was against her soft junk. Everything lined up just right to create a mind-blowing sensation.

"Let's play a game," he said. And yeah, he drawled.

Anna nodded. She would have agreed to a second lobotomy.

"On a scale of one to ten, rate the kisses, and then I'll know which parts to concentrate on."

She wasn't sure she could count to ten, much less rate kisses, but Heath jumped right into the game. He kissed her mouth.

"A ten," she said after he left her gasping for air and reaching for his zipper again.

He put his hand over hers to stop her, but Anna just used the pressure of his hand to add pressure to his erection.

"We'll play that particular game later," he promised.

Heath moved on to the next kiss. He placed one in the little area just below her ear, and he must have remembered that was a hot spot for her because it didn't seem like a lucky guess.

"Fifty," she blurted out. If Heath hadn't held her in place with his body, she would have dropped like a rock. There were no muscles in her legs, and her feet had perhaps disappeared.

"I'll definitely put that on my playlist," he said and

added a flick of his tongue in that very hot spot that needed no such licking to further arouse it.

She went after his zipper for a third time, and the only reason she failed, again, was because he pushed up her sweater, pushed down her bra and did that tongue-flicking thing over her nipples.

"A seventy," she managed to say.

"Scale of one to ten," he corrected.

"Ten plus sixty."

He chuckled, which made for some very interesting sensations since he still had his mouth on her nipple.

"And this one?" he asked. He went lower, kissed her stomach.

"Ten," she admitted, and she was about to pull him back to her to breast and neck.

Then he went down a few more inches.

Heath clearly had some experience in zipper lowering. *Fast* zipper lowering. He slid down, unzipping her and dragging her jeans just low enough so that he could plant the next kiss on her panties.

Anna threw back her head, hitting it against the door and perhaps giving herself a concussion. She didn't care if she did. That's because the only thing that mattered now was the pleasure. Such a puny word for the incredible things Heath was doing with his mouth.

"Your rating?" he asked, and mercy, he added some breath with that question.

"Six million," she managed to say.

He laughed.

"One more kiss," he said. "Then it'll be your turn."

Oh, she wanted a turn all right. Wanted it badly. Until he shimmied down her panties, put her knee on his shoulder and kissed her again. A special kiss.

Tongue flicks included.

After a couple of those flicks, Anna went into forget mode again. The thought of taking her turn went right out of her head. Everything vanished. Except for the feeling that she was about to shatter. And fall. And shatter some more.

Heath made sure he gave her the *more* she needed for shattering. One last well-placed kiss. An equally well-placed tongue flick. And all she could do was fist her hand in his hair and let him shatter her.

She had to take a moment to gather her breath. Another moment to keep gathering it. But even with the ripples of the climax tingling through her, she wanted to get started on her turn. And she was going to torture the hell out of Heath and his junk.

"Damn," Heath growled.

It took her a moment to realize that he was reacting to something he heard.

A knock at the tack room door.

"Heath?" Riley called out.

Hell.

"Uh, Heath, I need to talk to you," Riley added. "It's important."

Unless the world was about to end and Heath could stop it, then it wasn't that important, but Anna conceded that was the lust talking.

"How important?" Heath asked.

"Very."

Heath and she both cursed.

"Anna's in here with me," Heath volunteered.

It took Riley several snail-crawling seconds to respond to that. "Yes, I figured that out. Didn't think you'd go into the tack room alone and close the door. But this isn't about Anna. It's about your assignment."

Heath groaned, stood back up, helping her fix her jeans and panties. "You can wait in here if you want," he offered.

"Not a chance," Anna argued. "Riley knows what we've been doing. Or rather what we started doing, and the assignment thing could be a ruse to draw us out so he can ambush you with a shovel."

He brushed a kiss on her mouth. "You've got a very active imagination." Though she knew there might be a grain of truth in her theory.

Heath went out ahead of her, and Riley was indeed right there. He was sitting on a hay bale, drinking one of the beers. She braced herself for him to say something snarky like had she been trying to get Heath drunk or why did she have this thing for barn sex?

He didn't.

Riley did give her a look that only a big brother could have managed, but it had some, well, sympathy mixed in with the brotherly snark. A strange combination.

"I just came from the base," Riley said to Heath. "They want to see you about your deployment request."

"Deployment request?" Anna repeated. "I thought Heath was going to Florida."

Riley remained quiet, clearly waiting for Heath to explain.

"I asked to be diverted from the instructor job to another deployment," Heath said.

Riley's arrival had been a killjoy in the sexual-pleasure department, but hearing about Heath's request was a different kind of killjoy. Although obviously not for Heath since this was something he wanted.

Very much.

After all, he'd told her that the instructor job made him feel washed up, and maybe now he wouldn't have to feel that way because he could go back to one of those classified sandy locations. Where people shot at him and where he could be hurt or killed.

Mercy.

That felt as if she'd been slammed with a truckload of bricks. And there was no reason for it, because this was Heath's job. No logical reason anyway. But Anna wasn't feeling very logical at the moment.

"They want to see you out at the base right away," Riley added.

Heath nodded, looked at her as if he needed to say something, but Anna let him off the hook. She smiled, brushed a kiss on his cheek.

"Go," she insisted, trying to keep that smile in place. "We can talk when you get back."

Heath hesitated, gave another nod and then walked toward the house. Anna managed to keep her smile in place until he was out of sight. Riley opened a bottle of beer and handed it to her.

"Will he get to come back here to the ranch if the deployment is approved?" Anna asked, though she was afraid to hear the answer. "Or will they send him out right away?"

"Hard to say."

Or maybe not. The next thing Anna saw was Heath leaving the house, carrying his gear. He put it in his rental car and drove off. Obviously, he was prepared to go.

Anna took a long swig of that beer and wished it was something a whole lot stronger.

"Best to forget him," Riley said as they watched Heath drive away. "Heath isn't the settling-down type."

If only that weren't true.

"It's just a fling," Riley added. "That's what it was nine and a half years ago, and that's what it is now."

If only that were true.

CHAPTER FIVE

THE MCCORD BROTHERS were waiting for Heath when he got back from the base, and they didn't even try to make it look like a friendly, casual meeting. They were in the living room just off the foyer, and the moment Heath stepped inside, they stood.

No shovels. Not physical ones anyway.

"Where's Anna?" Heath asked. "You didn't lock her in her room, did you?"

The joke didn't go over so well, but Heath didn't care. He was tired, frustrated and wanted to talk to Anna, not the kid-sister police.

"Anna's Christmas shopping in San Antonio," Logan answered. "She'll be back any minute now."

Good. Well, sort of good. Heath definitely wanted to see her even if she probably hadn't liked his news. Hell, he hadn't liked it much, either.

"My request for deployment was denied," Heath explained. "The Air Force wants me to report to the base in Florida day after tomorrow so I'll have to cut my visit here short."

He expected them to jump for joy. Or at least smile. They didn't.

Riley immediately shook his head. "I didn't have anything to do with that."

Heath nearly snapped out "Right," but he knew in his gut that Riley was telling the truth. He wouldn't do anything like that even if it meant saving his sister from having sex with a guy Riley didn't think was right for her.

And Riley was spot-on.

Heath wasn't right for her. End of subject.

"I'll leave tomorrow," Heath added. "I just want a chance to say goodbye to Anna first."

None of the brothers objected, and Heath wouldn't have cared if they did. Yeah, it was the pissed-off mood again, but he had to get something off his chest.

"I know you think I'm a jerk, that I'm here only to try to seduce Anna, but I do care about her. Always have. If I hadn't cared, I would have never had sex in the hayloft with her nine and a half years ago."

There. He'd said it. But they weren't saying anything back to him. Maybe because Riley and Logan hadn't known about the sex. Lucky had, of course, because of the pee stick discovery, but even Lucky might have been stunned to silence to hear the de-virgining had taken place in the barn.

"Anna cares about you, too," Lucky finally said.

"She'll cry a lot again when you leave," Logan added.

"She'll be hurt," Riley piped in.

Maybe. Probably, Heath silently amended. Yeah, he was a jerk all right, but he was a jerk on orders, and that meant leaving whether he wanted to or not.

And he did want to leave, Heath assured himself.

He did.

Silently repeating that, Heath went to the guest room so he could finish packing.

HER BROTHERS WERE waiting for Anna when she got home. Hard to miss them since they were on the sofa in the living room.

She so didn't have the energy to deal with them now.

"You're all grounded," Anna said, going on the offensive. "Now, go to your rooms."

Of course, they didn't budge. Well, except to stand, and judging from the somber looks on their faces they had something serious to tell her. But she had something to say, too.

"I already know about Heath's deployment being denied. He texted me right after he got the news. He was at the base and couldn't talk, but he wanted to let me know that he's leaving tomorrow."

They stared at her as if expecting her to sprout an extra nose or something. Then Riley's hawkeyed gaze moved to the Victoria's Secret bag she was holding.

"Yes, I bought it for Heath," Anna admitted. "For me to wear for Heath," she amended when their stares turned blank. "It's red and slutty, and if you don't quit staring at me like that, I'll give you lots of details about what I want Heath to do to me while I'm wearing it."

Logan's eyes narrowed. Riley's jaw tightened. Lucky shrugged and went to her. He pulled her into his arms despite the fact she was as stiff as a statue from the mini hissy fit she'd just thrown.

"I've got two words for you," Lucky whispered to her. "Condom."

She pulled back, looked at him. "That's one word."

"If you wear what's in that bag, you'll need two condoms. Three if you skip what's in the bag all together and just show up in your birthday suit. Either way, condoms."

In that moment he was her favorite brother. Lucky had always been her champion and not judgmental. Most of the time anyway. Plus, he was the only brother who talked safe sex with her. Or any kind of sex for that matter. He wasn't just her brother, he was her friend.

Anna kissed his cheek. "Thanks."

He shrugged in that lazy but cool way that only Lucky or a Greek god could manage. It was as if he drawled his shrugs. And his life.

Lucky returned the cheek kiss and apparently considered his brotherly/friendly duties done because he strolled toward the door and headed out. Logan went to her next.

"I love you," Logan said. "And no matter what happens, I'll be here for you. You can cry on my shoulder all you need. Or if you prefer, I can kick Heath's ass for you. Your choice."

She had to fight a smile, but she didn't have to fight it too hard because the nonsmiling emotions were just below the surface. "I don't want his ass kicked, but I might need the shoulder."

Logan tapped first one shoulder, then the other. "Any time. They're reserved just for you, and I swear *I told you so* will never cross my lips or my mind. You're a grown woman, and if you want to wear what's in that bag, then you have my blessing."

In that moment she loved Logan best. Logan had been her father more than her brother, mainly because he'd been the one to step up after their folks died. He'd been the one to bust her chops when she needed it and had been a whiz helping with her math homework.

Logan would walk through fire for her and not once complain. Well, maybe he would complain, but he'd still do it.

He kissed her forehead and headed off, not out the door but to his old room. Since he lived in town and no longer spent many nights at the ranch, Logan must have wanted his shoulders to be nearby in the event of an impending crying spell.

Uh-oh.

It was Riley's turn.

"If Heath makes you cry again, I'm hitting him with the shovel," Riley growled. "And wear a robe with whatever's in that bag."

Anna sighed. The support of two out of three wasn't bad.

Riley sighed as well, and he pulled her into his arms. "FYI, Heath did some crying, too, after he left here that summer."

Anna wiggled out of his grip so she could see if he was serious or not. He was.

"I don't mean he actually shed tears," Riley went on, "but he cried in his own man kind of way."

"How do you know that?" she asked.

"Because I'm the one who drove him to his basic training." A muscle flickered in his jaw. A sign that he was remembering that day as unfondly as she was. Some of the anger returned. "Heath asked me to make sure you were okay. Can you believe it?"

"The bastard," Anna joked.

"He said it as if I needed to be reminded of it. I didn't. Not then, not now. If you need someone to make sure you're okay, I'll do it. As long as I don't have to hear any sex details. Or see what's in that bag. And I'll do that—minus the exceptions—because you're my sister."

Anna blinked back tears. In that moment, she loved Riley best. Yes, he was hardheaded, and they had a history of sibling squabbles. Plus, there was the time when he'd ruined all her dolls with camo paint and duct-tape combat boots, but still she loved every stubborn, camo-painting ounce of him.

Riley wasn't her father or her friend. He was her brother.

And sometimes, like now, that was exactly what a sister needed.

CHAPTER SIX

HEATH PACED. CURSED. He figured this much debate hadn't gone into some battle plans, but a battle plan would have been easier than trying to figure out what to do about Anna.

Or better yet what to do *with* Anna.

If he went to her room, sex would happen. Then tomorrow he would leave—just as he'd done nine and a half years ago. That hadn't turned out so well, what with all the crying and her brothers wanting to shovel him.

If he didn't go to her room, sex wouldn't happen. But then he would have to leave things unsettled between them—again—as he'd apparently done before.

He was screwed either way, so Heath decided he might as well go for it. He threw open the door and nearly smacked right into some idiot wearing a hoodie and an army-green vinyl poncho.

Except this was no idiot. It was Anna, and in addition to the garb, she was also carrying a blue sock.

She practically pushed him back into his room and shut the door. "Shhh," she said. "Della and Stella's book club is meeting tonight."

He was still wrapping his mind around the fact that Anna was there, that she had come to him, and maybe that's why Heath couldn't quite wrap his mind around the book club or the poncho.

"There are six of them in the living room, and I had to sneak past them," Anna added when he gave her a blank look.

When Heath kept that blank look, Anna pulled off the poncho, and he saw the hoodie. No pants. No shoes. Just a pair of really tiny devil-red panties.

He was sure his blank look disappeared because his mouth dropped open. This was the best kind of surprise.

"I didn't have a robe here at the ranch, and the plastic poncho felt sticky against my skin so I put on the hoodie," she explained. Then she unzipped it.

No top. No bra. Just the Be My heart locket dangling between her breasts. Heath thought maybe his tongue was doing some dangling, too.

"And the sock?" he asked.

She smiled and emptied the contents onto the bed. Condoms. At least a dozen of them.

"I took them from Lucky's bathroom," Anna explained. She was still whispering, but it had a giddiness to it. "The poncho and hoodie didn't have pockets so I put them in the sock. I only brought the normal-looking ones. Some had pictures on them and some were glow in the dark." Anna looked at him. "Why would a man need that?"

Heath didn't have a clue. He didn't need any illumination to find anything on Anna's body. His most vital organ agreed. In fact, it wanted to go on that particular search mission right now.

But there was a problem.

"You got my text saying I was leaving, right?" he asked.

She nodded. "Tomorrow. That's why I didn't want to wait until after the book club left. Sometimes they hang around until midnight if Della breaks out the tequila, and we don't have much time."

Not if they were planning on using all those condoms, they didn't, but Heath had to make sure that Anna was sure. She stripped off the hoodie, and he was sure she was sure.

At least he wanted her to be.

He wanted that even more when she slipped into his arms and kissed him. Heath was stupid and weak so it took him a moment to break the kiss.

"Anna, I don't want you hurt," he said.

She frowned. "I think that ship's sailed. I'll be hurt, but I'll get over it. And tonight you'll give me some really good memories to help me get over it, right?"

Yeah.

Whether they had sex or not, Anna would be hurt. Or at least she would be sad to see him go. Ditto for him being sad to leave her. But at least this way they'd have new memories, and they didn't need glow-in-the-dark condoms to do it.

Now that he had a clearly defined mission, Heath pulled her back to him to kiss her. One of those kisses that reached scorch level pretty darn fast. But Anna was aiming for fast, too, and not with just the kisses. She was already going after his zipper.

"We're going to play that scale-of-one-to-ten game," she insisted.

Maybe. But the way she was tugging at his zipper, it was possible she was also trying to finish this all way too fast. Tonight, he didn't want the kissing game, and he didn't want fast.

Heath stopped what she was doing by catching on

to her wrists and putting her against the wall. He liked walls because it gave him some control...

Damn.

He had no control. Anna ground herself against him, sliding her leg up the outside of his so that the millimeter of red lace was right against his crotch. Apparently, the orgasm she'd had earlier in the barn hadn't done anything to take the edge off because she was going for another one very quickly.

Again, Heath tried to slow things down. With her leg still cradling his, he turned her, intending to put her against the dresser, but he tripped over the poncho and fell onto the bed.

With Anna on top of him.

"Let's play a game," she said. Definitely not a virginal tone or look. "I'll use just my tongue to find all your special spots. You don't have to give it a number rating. Just a grunt for pleasure. A groan for find another special spot that's more special."

"Men only have one special spot," he told her. Heath took her hand and put it over his sex.

She laughed. Not a humor kind of laugh but the sound of a woman who'd come to play. Or maybe give a little payback for the things he'd done to her in the tack room. Well, Heath wanted to play, too. After all, he had a nearly naked Anna straddling him, and her breasts were making his mouth water.

He managed a quick sample of her left nipple before she moved away. Anna didn't waste any time. With her hand still on his special spot, she went in search of others. His earlobe.

He grunted, but Heath didn't know if that was because, at the same time, she started lowering his zipper.

"That wasn't a loud enough grunt," she said and went after his neck.

Heath grunted. Again, mainly because she lowered the zipper, and when she did that, her breasts got closer to his mouth again. She didn't grunt when he kissed her there, but she did make that silky sound of pleasure that Heath would never tire of hearing.

He would have kept on kissing her breasts, but apparently it was special-spot search time again because she scooted lower and ran her tongue over his own left nipple.

Oh, yeah. He grunted.

Grunted some more when she circled his navel with her tongue. All that tonguing and circling though didn't stop her from getting his zipper all the way down, and as he had done to her earlier, she shimmied his jeans lower.

"You really do go commando," she said.

"Yep—"

He might have added more. Something clever or at least coherent, but her hands were on him. The condom, too. Heath wasn't sure when she'd opened one of the packets. Nor did he care. The woman had clever hands after all—

Hell.

He grunted loud enough to trigger an earthquake when she dropped down onto him. That's when he figured out really, really fast that the panties were crotchless and that he was in her warm and tight special place all the way to the hilt.

"That's not your tongue," he said through the grunts.

"So, I cheated."

The woman was evil. And damn good. Heath usually liked to be the alpha when it came to sex, but even more than that, he liked taking turns with Anna. Apparently, she was going to make the most of her turn, too. She had the whole *ride 'em, cowgirl* motion going on. So fast that Heath knew this would all end too soon.

Of course, sixteen hours was going to be too soon.

As if she'd read his mind, she slowed. Anna put her palm on his chest and, still moving against his erection, leaned down and kissed him.

"After this," she said, "I want you all the way naked."

Heath thought that was a stellar idea. He wanted those panties off her, too, even though they fell into the *why bother* category of women's undergarments.

The locket whacked him in the face, but even that didn't put a damper on the moment. Heath just pushed the locket aside, gathered her close and let his cowgirl screw his brains out.

CHAPTER SEVEN

ANNA WISHED THERE were some kind of anticry shot she could take. Even one that worked for just an hour or so would do. She figured she'd do plenty of crying after Heath had left, but she didn't want any tears shed in front of him.

Or in front of her brothers.

She wanted Heath to remember her smiling. Or maybe naked, since that's how he'd seen her for a good portion of the night. It was certainly how she wanted to remember him.

With that reminder/pep talk still fresh in her mind, Anna left her bedroom and went in search of Heath so she could give him that smiling goodbye she'd practiced in the mirror. But he wasn't in his bedroom. Or the living room. Or the kitchen. In fact no one was, and she figured they'd all cleared out to give her a chance to have a private goodbye with Heath.

Or maybe they'd cleared out because Heath was already gone. She had several moments of panic when she sprinted to the back porch to make sure his rental car was still there.

It was.

And so was Heath.

He was at the fence pasture, looking at some cows that'd been delivered that morning. He made a picture standing there with his foot on the bottom rung of the fence, his cream-colored cowboy hat slung low on his face.

He must have heard her approaching because he turned, smiling. It looked about as genuine as the one she was trying to keep on her face. Until he reached out, pulled her to him and kissed her.

Then the smiles were real.

"How soon before you leave?" she asked.

"Soon."

That reminder made her smile waver. Anna wasn't sure how far to push this part of the conversation, but there was something she had to know. "Are you feeling any better about the instructor job?"

"I've accepted it. Sometimes, that's the best you can do with crappy lemonade. Sorry," Heath added when she frowned. "It was just something Riley said. An analogy of sorts."

Riley not only needed a new threat, he needed new analogies, as well.

Since their time together was about to end, Anna reached into her pocket and took out the "gift" she'd gotten him on her shopping trip the day before. She hadn't wanted it to be a big gift because that would have made this goodbye seem, well, big.

Which it was.

But she didn't want it to feel big to him.

She took his hand and dropped the smashed penny in it. "It reminded me of your dog tags, and it's supposed to be good luck."

He stared at it, gave a slight smile. "Thanks."

"I was going to give you the red panties," she added, "but I thought it would look strange if the TSA went through your luggage."

Now she got the reaction she wanted. A bigger smile. A bigger kiss, too.

"I have something for you," he said. He took out a silver heart locket. It was similar to the other one he'd given her nine and a half years ago. Very similar.

Right down to the Be My engraving.

Anna checked to make sure she had on the original one. She did. And she was shaking her head until Heath opened it, and she saw what was inside. Not pictures of him and her.

But of her parents. Her dad on one side of the heart. Her mother on the other.

"Della got the pictures for me," he explained. "You said sometimes you forget their faces, and this way you won't forget."

Oh, God.

She was going to cry.

No matter how hard she blinked, the tears came, and they just kept coming.

"I'm sorry." Heath pulled her back in his arms. "I didn't know it would upset you."

"It doesn't," she said, sobbing. "It's a good kind of upset." Still sobbing. "Thank you, Heath, thank you."

He held her while she sobbed, and it took Anna several long moments to stop.

"I got you something else," he added.

Anna couldn't imagine getting anything better than the second locket. It was even more precious to her than the first one. But Heath must have thought "the more the better" because he took out a wad of lockets from his coat pocket.

"I went to the jewelry store this morning and bought every locket they had."

She had no doubts about that—none. There was another silver one, one gold and another in the shape of a cat's head.

"They're, uh, beautiful." Though she couldn't imagine needing that many lockets. Or the ugly one with the cat's head.

"I had them engraved," he added, "and this time I watched to make sure they did it right. You can choose which one you want."

It took her a second to realize he'd finished his sentence. Not "which one you want *to wear.*" Not "which one you want *to keep.*" Not "which one you want *to remember me by.*"

Heath turned over one of the silver ones, and she saw the engraving there. One word.

Lover.

He put the Be My locket next to it, and she got the message then. Be my lover.

She laughed. "Does this mean you want to see more of me?"

"Well, I've already seen more, but I'd like to see more of you more often."

That dried any remnants of her tears, and she blurted out an idea she'd been toying with for days. "I could look into transferring to a law school in Florida." And she held her breath.

No smile from him. "I don't want you to sacrifice going to a school that maybe doesn't have as good of a reputation as the one you're in now."

"No sacrifice. There are a couple of really good ones. And besides, I was transferring anyway. Might as well transfer so you can—" she held up the two lockets to finish that thought "—Be My Lover."

Anna tested his neck again with a kiss. And her tongue.

"Keep that up, and you'll be my lover again right now," he grumbled.

"If that's supposed to make me behave, then it won't work. Not with the hayloft so close. How much time do you have before you need to leave for your flight?"

"Not enough time for the hayloft."

She kissed him again, and he seemed to change his mind about that. He started leading her in that direction.

"Not enough time for the hayloft unless we hurry," Heath amended.

Good. The kisses were working.

Since she'd already put her heart on the line, Anna put the rest of herself out there, too. "I don't want a fling."

"Good. Flings are overrated." He kissed her again. "And temporary."

She released the breath she didn't even know she'd been holding. Heath didn't want temporary. Nor a fling. He wanted sex.

That was a solid start since she wanted that, too.

"I'm not done," he said. "Remember, you pick the locket you want." He held up the next one, the gold one, and it also had a single word engraved on it.

Woman.

As in Be My Woman.

Yes, they were so going to that hayloft, and then she was going to the university to start that transfer to Florida.

"Can I wear both the *Lover* and *Woman*?" she asked. Because she wanted both.

"You haven't seen the third one yet."

And she probably couldn't see it before the next kiss crossed her eyes. Along with singeing her eyelashes.

Still, he put the locket in her hand just as her butt landed against the ladder. Anna backed up one step at a time, which wasn't easy to do with Heath kissing her like that. And he kept on kissing her until they made it all the way to the top of the hayloft.

But Anna froze when she saw what was engraved on the tacky cat's head locket.

Love.

"Be My Love," she said, putting the words together. Putting *everything* together.

"The *L* word?" she asked.

Heath nodded. "Sometimes it's the only word that works. What about you? Does the *L* word work for you?"

Anna had to catch her breath just so she could speak. "It works perfectly for me." She kissed him. "Does this mean we're going steady?"

"Oh, yeah," Heath confirmed. "That, and a whole lot more."

REQUEST YOUR FREE BOOKS!
2 FREE NOVELS PLUS 2 FREE GIFTS!

Ⓗ HARLEQUIN®

INTRIGUE

BREATHTAKING ROMANTIC SUSPENSE

HI15

Levi eased into the shadows away from the pulsing neon
bar lights, and he listened. Waiting. It was hard, though,
to pick through the sounds of the crackling lights, the
wind and his own heartbeat drumming in his ears.

But somewhere there was the sound of an engine
running.

Because the driver had the headlights off, it took Levi
a moment to realize the car wasn't approaching from
the street but rather from the back of the bar. No road
there, just a parklike area that the local teenagers used for
making out. It could also be the very route a killer would
likely take.

Before the car eased to a stop, Levi whipped out his
gun and took aim. He froze. And not because of the
weather.

The person stepped out from the car, the watery lights
just enough for him to see her face. Not the Moonlight

Strangler but someone he did recognize. The pale blond hair. The willowy build.

Alexa.

Of all the people that Levi thought he might run into tonight, Alexa Dearborn wasn't anywhere on his radar. Heck, she shouldn't be anywhere near him, this bar or the town of Appaloosa Pass.

Because she had a bounty on her head.

Word on the street was that the hired guns who were after her had orders to shoot to kill.

It'd been five months since Levi had seen her, as the marshals had whisked her away into WITSEC to an unnamed place. A change of name, too. But five months wasn't nearly long enough for the memories to fade.

Don't miss
TROUBLE WITH A BADGE
by USA TODAY *bestselling author Delores Fossen,*
available in April 2016 wherever
Harlequin® Intrigue books and ebooks are sold.

www.Harlequin.com

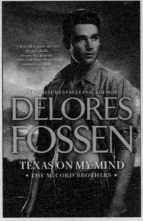

THE WORLD IS BETTER WITH

Romance

1180

Harlequin has everything from contemporary, passionate and heartwarming to suspenseful and inspirational stories.

Whatever your mood,
we have a romance just for you!

Connect with us to find your next great read,
special offers and more.

f /HarlequinBooks

🐦 @HarlequinBooks

www.HarlequinBlog.com

www.Harlequin.com/Newsletters

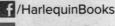

H HARLEQUIN®

A *Romance* FOR EVERY MOOD™

www.Harlequin.com